THE GRAND PUPPET MASTER

EDDIE SHAY

TASMAN TIDE PUBLISHING

The Grand Puppet Master

Copyright © 2024 by Eddie Shay.

All rights reserved.

No part of this book may be reproduced, distributed, or transmitted in any form or by any means, including photocopying, recording, or other electronic or mechanical methods, without the prior written permission of the author, except in the case of brief quotations embodied in critical reviews and certain other noncommercial uses permitted by copyright law.

This book is a work of fiction. Names, characters, businesses, places, events, locales, and incidents are either the products of the author's imagination or used in a fictitious manner. Any resemblance to actual persons, living or dead, or actual events is purely coincidental.

Edited by Jason Letts

Cover design by Terry Todd

ISBN 978-0-473-70470-4 (eBook)

ISBN 978-0-473-70469-8 (Paperback)

ISBN 978-0-473-70471-1 (Kindle)

ISBN 978-0-473-70473-5 (Audiobook)

To Michelle Lee

CONTENTS

1

THE BEAST'S THROAT

A clip from a surveillance camera showed the rush hour bustle in a dim sum restaurant. Waitresses weaved through crowded tables, customers chatting and eating. Even without sound, the noisy, lively atmosphere was evident.

In a secluded corner, a young and elegant woman sat alone at a table for two. A few seconds later, she shocked everyone when she started gnawing on her own hand. Blood splattered everywhere. Some scrambled for the exits, while a few kept their distance and recorded the scene on their phones.

By the time the police arrived, her hands were nothing but skeletal remains.

Nestled in the backseat of a swiftly moving black Uber, Natalia was riveted by the latest viral clip on TikTok.

At first, she thought it was a deepfake, likely generated by AI or some slick special effects. But shock set in when she discovered online that it was an actual event in Hong Kong.

Social media was flooded with speculations, rumours, conspiracy theories, and outright disinformation about the woman. The claims varied wildly: she was battling severe schizophrenia; she was struck with encephalitis, sparking zombie fears; her act was a stark protest against the Hong Kong National Security Law; she was carrying a mysterious virus from a Chinese lab; or she was a pawn in a U.S. scheme to denigrate China.

She replayed the clip, and this time, knowing it was real, she could almost hear the haunting crunch of the woman's biting, even though it was on mute.

Overwhelmed by a mix of terror and nausea, she set her phone down and stared out of the car window. The distant Manhattan Bridge, glowing golden in the twilight, stood majestic against the evening sky. The smooth flow of traffic across it blended motion and stillness, making the bridge seem alive with pulsing energy.

"New York's like Don Juan to all the ladies, enchanting and always after the next thrill," her father used to say.

She couldn't fully agree. To her, some parts of the city were not attractive at all. Tonight, she was heading to one of them: Flushing.

Stepping out of the Uber, she wrestled a heavy suitcase from the trunk. Standing poised in her black twelve-cm high-heeled boots, she paused, feeling almost as though she had stepped into China. It took a bold billboard proclaiming, "We are descendants of dragons and proud to be American citizens," to snap her back to reality.

The November air in New York nipped at her skin, especially late in the evening. Dressed only in a thin lace bra under her brown leather jacket, with a form-fitting leather skirt and lace thong below, she still maintained her professional, seductive composure.

Her appearance quickly caught the eye of two Chinese men squatting curbside, each puffing away on a cigarette.

"Check out that white chick. Quite the looker, huh?"

"How much do you reckon she'd go for a night?"

"I'd say about $1,500?"

She stopped and spun around to face the gossipers. "Add a zero to that," she corrected them in Mandarin, "it's $15,000."

Their faces froze, shock widening their eyes. She smirked and strutted off, her hips swinging with a confidence that seemed to declare she was worth every penny.

Dragging her heavy suitcase through the streets, she finally arrived at an unremarkable bar in southern Flushing. An old sign overhead displayed "Red Star High School" in Chinese characters—a misleading name since the establishment was far from educational.

She took a deep breath and carefully unzipped her jacket to reveal the ornate lace bra beneath. A diamond pendant nestled between her breasts glinted in the faint light, sparkling enticingly. After a quick lipstick touch-up, she walked confidently into the bar.

The soft lighting and gentle music created a mellow vibe. A few patrons dotted the seats, and a bald bartender manned the counter.

She walked up to the bar and announced in a Polish accent, "I'm here for an interview."

"Confirmation?" the bartender asked without looking up.

She flashed him a message on her phone, and he nodded towards the end of the hallway. "Go all the way down and knock."

Navigating the dim corridor felt like descending into a beast's deep throat. The only sound breaking the heavy silence was the steady click of her heels against the floor, echoing in rhythm with her increasingly rapid heartbeat.

At the end of the hallway stood a black iron door. She knocked three times. No answer. As she was about to knock again, a door on her left creaked open, a muffled scream escaping. A sliver of light cut through the darkness, and a raspy voice called out, "Come in."

Summoning her courage, she dragged her suitcase into the shadowy room.

The lighting was dim. At the centre, a dark wooden desk loomed like a coffin. Behind it, shrouded in shadows, a middle-aged man in a crisp black suit sat perfectly still—like a corpse that had climbed out of that very coffin.

He stirred—his eyes, not his body. His sharp, scrutinising gaze swept over her, starting from her boots and leisurely tracing upward—gliding past her legs, over the curve of her skirt, to her slender waist, and finally resting on the hint of her décolletage. When his eyes met hers, a chill shot through her.

She kept her composure.

He glanced at her online application on his phone, checking the details, then asked, "Natalia Nowak?"

She nodded, maintaining a rigid yet poised posture.

"Passport, please," he requested, his English coloured by a Chinese accent.

From her handbag, she handed over a red passport.

He examined it closely.

"Polish. I like Polish girls. Pretty, straightforward, and spicy."

"Thank you."

"And your experience?"

"I did a year as a window girl in Amsterdam then danced in Tokyo. The last two years, I've been in Brooklyn, mostly handling online gigs."

He glanced at her passport. "You've overstayed."

She met his gaze defiantly. "That's why I'm here for a job that offers secure housing."

He leaned back, a smirk playing on his lips. "You're in luck," he drawled. "Around here, my word is law—it's like you're in the Chinese Embassy. The cops? They wouldn't dare show up."

She allowed a small smile. "Sounds promising."

Their eyes locked in a prolonged stare before he commanded, "Take off your clothes."

2

WHITE TIGER AND ABALONE

Natalia's eyebrows shot up. "Excuse me?"

"I need to make sure you fit the bill. This isn't your run-of-the-mill gig," he clarified.

She steeled herself and slowly peeled off her unzipped leather jacket, unveiling the delicate lace bra that hugged her curves tightly. The diamond pendant between her breasts twinkled in the dim light.

He nodded towards her skirt, signalling his next order.

Bracing herself, she smoothly unzipped her tight leather skirt and stepped out of it, leaving only a lacy thong underneath.

His gaze dropped to her towering boots. Getting the hint, she unzipped and removed them.

He took a moment, his eyes sweeping over her figure appreciatively, perhaps letting his thoughts wander a bit too far.

"Now, please turn around for me."

She exhaled deeply and turned, presenting a full view.

"Looks good, but I need to do a more detailed inspection."

"What's that about?"

"Take off your bra and thong."

"No way."

"To make sure you fit the role."

"You've seen enough to make up your mind. And don't try to play me. I know the score."

His smirk widened, clearly amused by her spunk. "Alright, lower your thong a little. I need to check if you're a white tiger."

Her confusion was evident. "White tiger? What's that?"

"Never heard of it?"

She shook her head, puzzled.

"It's Chinese slang for a woman who's completely shaved. It's a standard check here."

She rolled her eyes, letting out a sigh. "Look, I am. There's no need for a show."

His gaze lingered on her lace thong, as if he were trying to see right through it. Eventually, he nodded, satisfied. "Okay, that's all good. Now let me check your abalone type."

"Abalone?"

"Yeah, the Chinese say a woman's private parts kinda resemble an abalone."

Somehow, his face reminded her of an abalone. If she had to pick a fitting nickname for him, "abalone" would be spot on. This amusing thought lightened her mood slightly.

"We need to record your type for our AI app. It matches you with clients—sort of like finding your niche."

She snorted, "Great, now AI's dipping its toes into the adult industry too? What a world." With firm resolve, she added, "The thong stays on."

Abalone stood and approached her. Instinctively, she took a cautious step back.

"Don't worry. I need to check something."

"What?"

"Could you lift your arms? You know, many of my Chinese clients can't stand body odour."

"I don't have that."

"Lift your arms."

When she lifted them, he suddenly grabbed the waistband of her lace thong and yanked upward sharply, stretching the fabric to reveal her intimate contours.

"Fuck off!" She recoiled, jerking her hands away.

With a self-satisfied smirk, he remarked, "There we go. Looks like the gathered-waist style."

She stared at him, bewildered. "What?"

"Gathered-waist style."

"For fuck's sake!"

"All set then. Thanks for your cooperation. Welcome to Red Star High School. Let's head to the dorms so you can drop off your bags, and then we can sort out the paperwork." He moved towards the wall behind the desk and expertly pressed a hidden thumbprint scanner. A concealed door swung open, revealing stairs that spiralled into the depths below.

Hesitating, Natalia felt a wave of foreboding. She couldn't shake the feeling that beneath those stairs, in the veiled shadows, something much more profound and sinister was lurking.

3

THE SLICKED-BACK MAN

As Abalone led Natalia down the staircase to the mysterious space below, the odd name Red Star High School started to make sense to her.

Hidden beneath was a spot-on replica of a 1990s mainland Chinese high school. The layout, shaped like the Chinese character "口," featured everything from classrooms and a cafeteria to restrooms, a bathhouse, a music hall, dorms, a library, research rooms, and offices. Imposing Chinese men in security uniforms, straight out of the era, patrolled the area.

"They run a tight ship here," Abalone explained. "Big school, lots of student, always a few rebels."

Natalia followed Abalone down the dim, lengthy dormitory corridor, eyeing each room they passed. The students, all young Chinese women, were dressed in white tank tops and retro underwear, sporting ponytails or short cuts that screamed '90s mainland China. Each room packed eight to a set of bunk beds, the air thick with the smell of sweat and cheap perfume. Their faces mixed exhaustion, boredom, curiosity, and longing with a sheer grit to endure.

Abalone finally stopped at a dorm tucked at the end of the corridor, nodding that this was Natalia's spot. Standing in the doorway, she peered inside at seven other occupants. One sprawled out asleep, stark naked. The other six, wearing puzzled looks, clearly didn't expect her.

She caught them whispering in Chinese, "What's a white girl doing here?"

After settling down the luggage, Abalone led Natalia through more corridors, past restrooms, showers, a cafeteria, and a library, ending at a principal's office that oozed old-school communist vibes. The walls were plastered with propaganda posters from 1990s mainland China, touting slogans like "Reform and Opening Up," "One Child Policy," and "Hong Kong's Return," alongside portraits of communist icons like Mao Zedong, Deng Xiaoping, and Jiang Zemin. The furniture was stark and functional, a nod to a bygone era of simplicity and austerity.

Abalone pulled a school uniform from a cupboard and handed it to Natalia. "Put this on now," he instructed firmly.

She looked over the uniform—a throwback to late twentieth-century mainland China. It was plain, athletic, and glaringly drab. The included undergarments were basic: a white tank top and plain white panties, like the ones the dorm girls wore.

"Hurry up," he urged.

"I'll change later."

"When I say now, you move. No questions asked. That's the drill here."

"Fine, but I'm keeping my bra and thong on."

She quickly slipped into the school uniform but left a few buttons undone. He noticed, and she shrugged. "It's hot in here."

He pulled out a document from his desk and slid it across to her. "Fill it out now," he commanded.

She glanced at the paper, only to find it blank.

"Are you kidding me?"

As her gaze shifted back to him, she noticed he had subtly moved closer, a spray bottle in hand. He quickly spritzed its contents onto her face.

"Fuck!"

It was too late to dodge. Dizziness overwhelmed her, her vision blurred, her knees buckled, and she leaned against the wall, struggling to stay conscious.

He swiftly left. In a rising panic, she dashed to the door, only to find it locked from the outside.

"Open the fucking door!" she screamed, pounding on it.

"Every new student goes through this," his voice echoed back, eerily calm.

"Let me out!"

The only answer was the fading sound of his footsteps.

She kept trying to force the door, but with each attempt, her strength faded. Her energy sapped, her legs gave way, and her already fuzzy vision dimmed further. A suffocating heat wrapped around her, pushing her discomfort to the brink.

"Damn it!" she cursed, realising the sinister mix in the spray: a sedative laced with an aphrodisiac.

As Abalone's footsteps faded, another set, heavier and distinct, approached.

She felt like a sitting duck.

The sound of a key turning preceded the door creaking open. A squat Asian man, impeccably dressed in a Mao suit, stepped inside. His slicked-back hair gleamed under the light as he fixed her with a leering smirk.

"Red Star High School's really shaking things up, huh? Now we've got foreign exchange students." His Mandarin had the distinct lilt of northern China.

"Keep the fuck away from me!" she snapped back in Mandarin.

His laugh was derisive. "Oh, you speak Mandarin? That's rich!"

He locked the door and began to loosen his clothes.

"I'm gonna fucking kill you," Natalia slurred as the drugs coursed through her, leaving her completely limp and robbing her of the strength to move. She could only watch as the slicked-back man stood in front of her and stripped naked. His disgustingly fat body shook, and his fully erect penis looked particularly daunting.

"I won't hurt you, sweetheart," he reassured her, gently lifting her limp body and setting her flat on the desk.

He began to remove her school uniforms.

As time ticked by, his bulky figure blurred in Natalia's dimming vision. She could painfully feel her consciousness slipping away, dwindling to what seemed like mere seconds.

4

THE CHILDHOOD NIGHTMARE

As the drug's effects intensified, Natalia whispered urgently, "Kiss me."

The slicked-back man dove in to oblige, but it was a setup. She bit down hard on his tongue.

He yelped, flailing to get free, but his struggles only made her clamp down harder. She pressed on, aiming to cut him off mid-sentence, until the drug finally put her lights out.

She appeared in a haze, finding herself on a school bus filled with little kids, aged five and six, climbing a mountain road. The sky was a brilliant blue, scattered with clouds, and the sun blazed overhead. Multicoloured wildflowers burst into life along the roadside, and below stretched a vast sea of blue.

The kids were dead quiet, lost in the stunning views. Suddenly, a whiff of blood caught on the breeze, sneaking through the windows. No one seemed to notice except her.

As the bus wound up the mountain, the smell of blood intensified. She tried to alert everyone, but it was too late. A truck barrelled around the bend and smashed into the bus head-on.

The bus careened off the cliff and fractured against the boulders. She and several kids were thrown clear, tumbling through the air. Time slowed, like a slow-motion sequence from a movie, giving her a final, surreal view of the landscape before she hit the ground.

Lying broken among the wreckage, she watched the clouds overhead, slowly staining red like bleeding ink.

Natalia jolted awake from the nightmare.

She was sprawled on the floor. A few feet away, Abalone was kicked back in a chair, legs crossed, casually puffing on a cigar, with two burly guards standing watch behind him.

Propping herself up, she patted down her clothes, relieved to find everything in place, untouched.

"You're in trouble," Abalone declared.

Despite the fear churning in her stomach, she met his gaze and admitted, "I didn't want to mess up the job like that, but I couldn't help it."

Abalone's eyes narrowed.

"When I was very young, my stepfather—a Chinese businessman with the same slicked-back hair—used to rape me," she said, her voice cracking as old wounds resurfaced. "I swore if I ever saw him again, I'd take him down. I can hold a grudge better than anyone. Honestly, if he'd had any other hairstyle, things might've turned out differently."

The guards behind Abalone exchanged skeptical looks. One leaned in and whispered something to Abalone, who quickly dismissed him with a raised hand before turning back to her. "Are you messing with me?"

She gave him a wry smile. "If I was, I wouldn't have had to carry that fucking nightmare with me all my life."

He stood up, casting a long shadow over her. She braced herself, squeezing her eyes shut.

"Gimme your hand."

Her eyes flew open, and she saw his hand extended towards her. She placed hers in his, and he hoisted her up with a firm grip.

"Go wash up then hit the sack," he instructed.

She hadn't expected to get off this easy. Keeping her guard up, she studied his face for any clue of what might come next but came up empty.

"Take her back to the dorm," he told one of the guards.

"I need to grab some stuff from my place in Brooklyn," she said.

"What stuff?"

"Something important to me."

"I can send someone to get it for you."

"No, I'd rather handle it myself."

His gaze sharpened. "Don't pull any stunts."

"I won't. I love it here but need to grab some personal things. Girl stuff, you know? I'll be back in three hours, max."

He shot her that typical inscrutable look. "Work with me, prove your loyalty, and you'll get more than cash. I could even sort out a green card for you. But betray me, and I promise I'll destroy everyone you care about before I come for you."

His tone was eerily casual, as if issuing threats was part of his daily routine.

"Is that clear?" he pressed.

"Got it." She nodded, sealing their deal.

***

Natalia slipped back into her own clothes, grabbed her luggage, and walked out of Red Star High School. As she hit the dark street, her suspicions grew. It all felt like a trap ready to spring.

She decided it was time to disappear for good.

She walked to the north end of Flushing Meadows-Corona Park, where hidden paths wound along the creek's edge, sheltered by trees and shrubs. Finding a secluded spot, she stripped down to nothing. The moonlight filtering through the branches was the only witness to what came next—with careful fingers, she traced a line from her genitals to her gluteal cleft, found the hidden seam, and began peeling off the full-body skin suit.

The high-tech synthetic skin suit, made of lightweight, breathable polymer, looked and felt like real skin. It covered her from head to toe, topped with a wig to simulate natural hair, with perfect accuracy—even replicating flawless genitals, which Abalone referred to as the "gathered-waist style." It was temperature-regulated with tiny sensors mimicking her natural body heat, so touching or kissing her felt real. The facial part was remarkable, adapting to her contours using heat-sensitive synthetic muscles to perfectly replicate the features of a completely different woman: Natalia Nowak, a character she'd invented. Openings at the eyes, ears, nose, and mouth had ultra-fine mesh, letting her see, hear, and breathe easily. She could even eat and drink without difficulty.

The only way in or out was through the hidden zipper that ran from her genitals to her gluteal cleft. It wasn't easy to put on or take off, but it kept the suit seamless. The suit was also waterproof, perfect for working in wet conditions.

As she shed the suit, she became herself again: Lacey Green, a good-looking young woman with no hair at all, even on her head. She had to stay that way to wear the suit perfectly. She slipped into a casual hoodie, worn jeans, and sneakers then topped it off with a shoulder-length blonde wig, transforming into a regular young woman who could blend into any crowd.

Under the moon's silver glow, Lacey walked to Flushing Creek and tossed her Polish passport, weighed down with a stone, into the water. Watching it sink, a sly grin spread across her face. She turned away, leaving the ripples as the only confidants to her secrets.

5

P.I. OLSEN

Short on cash, Lacey had to catch the 7 train at Flushing–Main Street in the murky pre-dawn hours, the cold night air nipping at her cheeks as she descended into the subway station. The city that never slept murmured through the mostly empty platform, where a drunk guy was trying to fuck a hole in the wall. She couldn't help but feel for him—it must've really hurt. The intermittent rumble of distant trains broke the silence. Boarding the sparse carriage, she settled into a corner seat as the fluorescent lights flickered overhead.

The train whisked her westward, swaying gently through the underground maze. At Times Square–42nd Street, she easily switched to the uptown 1 train, which screeched its arrival. The few passengers were a mix of late-night partiers and early-morning workers, each in their own world.

At the 72nd Street station on the Upper West Side, Lacey emerged into the quiet city above. The streets were empty, and the usual buzz had faded into whispering winds. She pulled her hoodie tighter, her breath visible in the chilly air as she walked the last few blocks to her rental—a classic pre-war Manhattan apartment built in 1912.

She lived in a two-bedroom unit on the second floor, which she called "the grumpy, forgotten veteran." Its chipped, faded walls and well-worn furniture told stories of years past. The windows, clouded with age like weary eyes, had weathered frames that stood firm, silently sharing tales of the past. The creaky floors groaned underfoot, while the radiators hissed and rattled as if grumbling about better days. The plaster ceiling sported stubborn stains like old battle scars, and the light fixtures flickered reluctantly, bathing the place in a dim, nostalgic glow. The air carried a mix of dust and memories, lingering like the scent of a long-lost era.

Living in the "old guy" wasn't cheap—especially for Lacey, who lacked a steady job, family support, or a wealthy boyfriend. She worked in social media, not by chasing trends but by carving out a niche in private investigation. Still, making ends meet was always a struggle.

Throughout her childhood, everyone told her the same thing, and even she believed it: she wasn't talented. That tune changed when she turned ten. That was when her new nanny, Mia Liao, saw something different in her. "You know, Lacey, you've really got something."

"What do I have?" she asked Mia, brimming with curiosity.

Mia smiled. "Right there. Your curiosity."

Lacey had never considered curiosity a talent.

"But isn't everyone curious?" she wondered.

"Yes, but yours is intense. It's special and powerful."

Lacey constantly grilled her about why.

"Don't waste it," she advised.

"How should I use it?" Lacey asked, her curiosity sparked anew.

Without missing a beat, she replied firmly, "Become a detective, like in the books and movies."

Lacey's eyes widened, innocent and eager. "That would be a cool job, wouldn't it?"

"But to be a great detective, the first skill you need is how to disguise yourself," Mia continued.

"Disguise myself as what?"

"Anything. Suppose you want to find out which street dog killed your cat. You've got to blend in, become one of them. You get me?"

"That sounds exciting."

Mia's first gig for Lacey came quickly. She dolled up the little girl with makeup, swapped her blonde hair for a black wig, changed her blue eyes to dark gray with coloured contacts, and applied SFX makeup to her face.

Finally, looking at Lacey, now transformed into a mixed-race girl in the mirror, Mia concluded, "Okay, you're my daughter now."

Mia was on the hunt for a cheap underground apartment, but the tough landlady demanded proof of a legal visa as a strict condition. As an illegal immigrant who had escaped communist China, Mia had nothing to show, which was exactly why Lacey's mother had hired her as a nanny, at rock-bottom wages.

Mia introduced her "mixed-race daughter" to the strict landlady, weaving a tale of woe: her ex, Green, had cheated and kicked her out, messing up her green card process and leaving her without a visa. Lacey's stellar acting, portraying a girl caught between her mother and the legal need to stay with her father, was key to their scheme.

Touched by their story, the landlady approved Mia's application and even offered her reduced rent.

While it wasn't the detective work she'd imagined, little Lacey thrived on the thrill of becoming someone else—a welcome break from her often lonely and dull childhood.

Mia did more than exploit Lacey; she began teaching her the arts of disguise, including makeup and SFX skills, as well as Mandarin, all to boost her ability to transform.

"People judge you by your looks and voice, so make sure you can switch up both," Mia taught.

Mia was more than a nanny to Lacey; she was her mentor and best friend all along.

After graduation, Lacey landed a regular office job, aiming for a bright future. But after two years of tangling with office politics and a sleazy boss, she'd had enough and quit. To make matters worse, her boyfriend cheated on her and maxed out her credit cards.

She broke down when she met up with Mia, now a renowned special effects artist in the film industry and a green card holder.

"Listen, sweetheart, chase your real passion."

"I don't have one."

"Yes, you do. Remember what I told you when you were little? Be a detective."

"Detective in New York? C'mon, get real. I'm not even twenty-five yet, and you need to be to qualify. Plus, three years of playing detective? That's a lot. Then there's the state exam, background checks, sorting out your finances—it's a whole mess!"

Mia rolled her eyes. "All those hoops? Total bullshit."

"I can't throw a punch, and I'm not tech-savvy. I don't have what it takes to be a detective."

"Look, real detectives aren't brawlers like in the movies. And these days, with AI, anyone can get tech smart. If I were you, I'd start a TikTok tomorrow."

"What?" Lacey squinted.

"Seriously, everyone's cashing in! This watch..." Mia flaunted her wrist. "It cost more than that Porsche 911 down the street. Wanna know how I paid for it?"

Mia pulled up her TikTok profile. Branded as "Crazy Mia the VFX Artist," her follower count was off the charts.

"Listen, there aren't many TikTok detectives. You could break new ground. Use what I've taught you, tackle some wild cases, and stream it live. Billions of people are dying for content like that. Kick it off tomorrow. Don't let your talent go to waste!"

Taking her up on it, Lacey turned herself into a TikTok detective, known as P.I. Olsen. Olsen, her rarely used middle name, gave her a bit of anonymity.

Mia had given Lacey three crucial pieces of advice. First, she always flew solo. Partnering up was a waste, because even the best partners fell apart in the end, squandering time, money, and emotions. Second, she never showed her real face on the job. Mia had designed state-of-the-art synthetic skins for film productions and loaned Lacey a collection for a cut of her earnings. These skins were in high demand for Hollywood blockbusters, known for their lifelike detail and versatility. That was where Natalia Nowak and all the other fake personas Lacey adopted had come from. Third, she focused on unique but low-risk cases. The livestreams had to be cozy and mysterious—no risky business.

In the first half of her six-year career, Lacey made good progress. She landed some cool gigs on her TikTok livestream and built a following. Still, it was only a drop in the bucket, and making ends meet was a constant struggle. Over the last three years, she decided to take bigger risks by tackling overseas cases—there were always clients who needed her to look into the disappearance or death of their loved ones abroad.

She handled these cases, earning some cash, but always had to give Mia a cut for her synthetic skins.

Lately, finding overseas cases had gotten tougher. Maybe it was the economic slump cutting down on Americans traveling or something else, but once again she was scraping by.

"Take it easy, Lacey. All this hard work? It's gonna pay off. Keep at it, and the rewards of doing what you love will come," Mia always encouraged her.

Giving up wasn't in Lacey's DNA, but financial pressures backed her into a corner. She found herself mixed up with the Chinese mafia, investigating the communist-themed fetish brothel in Flushing. She decided to stream this risky, dark case on her TikTok— a first for her.

She still had her doubts. Abalone's smooth release smelled like a setup, yet she was convinced Natalia was the real target, not her. She was confident in her mastery of disguises and acting skills.

After a refreshing shower, she popped a stress-relief pill before bed. It wasn't to help her sleep but to keep the recurring nightmare about the school bus accident at bay, which always haunted her during stressful times.

The pill worked like a charm, and she slept straight through to the evening. Waking up famished, she decided to whip up a hefty English breakfast: scrambled eggs, sausages, bacon, black pudding, baked beans, tomatoes, mushrooms, a hash brown, gluten-free toast, and piping hot English tea.

Breakfast was her religion, perfect for any time of day.

While eating, she scrolled through her inbox. Annoyed by ads for kids' toys and clothes, she marked them as spam and deleted them.

After her meal, Lacey slipped into Natalia's skin, transforming into the alluring Polish prostitute once more. At exactly 8 p.m., she launched her TikTok livestream. As expected, her room quickly filled up, mostly with male viewers.

"Hey, everyone, I'm Natalia Nowak. Tonight, I'm taking you to a place that'll blow your mind—beyond anything you've imagined," she said, her voice rich with a thick Polish accent, as she slowly started to unzip her leather jacket.

6

A FRIENDLY REMINDER

Natalia's revealing move aimed not at seduction but to highlight an important prop: the sparkling diamond nestled between her lingerie's cups. She delicately removed the stone, revealing its secret—a hidden miniature camera.

The livestream switched to the camera's perspective, showing the footage to viewers.

When Natalia had approached the bar entrance the previous night, she skilfully unbuttoned her jacket. That was when the diamond camera started rolling. It captured a clear view of the bar's facade and its sign, "Red Star High School," before panning to the grim interior. It recorded a brief exchange with the brash bartender and followed her down the dark corridor. The camera documented the entire sketchy interview with Abalone, delved into the underground world of the communist Chinese school-themed fetish brothel, and caught Pompadour's chilling assault. The recording cut out as Natalia blacked out, leaving her fate hanging by a thread. Lacey did it on purpose.

The first-person video gripped viewers, turning the comment section into a frenzy of emojis, questions, and reactions. Messages flooded in too fast to keep up. Likes flooded the screen nonstop. The excitement went on for hours, keeping Lacey on an adrenaline high.

Late that night in bed, she opened her banking app. The buzz from the gig vanished—the balance served as a sobering wake-up call, barely making a dent in her mounting bills and looming rent.

Her thoughts drifted to Shawn, her father in Hong Kong. She had never asked him for money before. He wasn't rich, but she had run out of options.

She tried calling him, but it went straight to voicemail, typical given his demanding job. She then dropped him a message on Messenger, "Hey, Dad, what's up? Saw the news about that crazy self-harm stuff in Hong Kong – insane, right? Let's catch up tomorrow when you're free."

The next day, she found his reply. "Sorry I missed your call. Work's nuts right now, but all's good. We'll catch up soon."

Feeling it better to discuss money over the phone, she responded, "Sounds good! Take care of yourself, Dad."

Lacey and Shawn shared a rare and deep bond.

Raised in New York by her mother, Lacey only saw her father a few times a year due to his life and work in Hong Kong. As an IT technician with modest earnings, he flew economy class and stayed in budget motels. He never gave Lacey gifts costing more than $200, yet he always knew how to make her feel cherished and blessed. This made him her rock-solid confidant and soulmate.

"Your father's all talk," her mother would often complain. Each time, Lacey would snap back, "At least he talks, which is more than I can say for you!"

She didn't plan to ask Shawn for much, only enough to cover her upcoming rent and bills. She figured that wouldn't be a problem.

The next morning, over her coffee, Lacey turned on her phone and found it buzzing with TikTok notifications. Opening the app, she nearly spilled her drink as the viewer count for her P.I. Olsen stream skyrocketed into the millions. The numbers were staggering, too vast to fully grasp. The comment section for the Communist Chinese school-themed fetish brothel was a vibrant mix of praise, questions, and a flood of fire emojis. Fans and newcomers alike clamoured for more, their excitement palpable. Amid the flurry, mentions from politicians, celebrities, and influencers caught her eye, each adding to the whirlwind of her sudden fame.

"Shocked by the dark truths in NYC's underbelly revealed in this video. Hard to believe this is happening in our great city. #NYCUnderbelly #WakeUpCall"

"I'm outraged by the arrogance in the video! 'Around here, my word is law—it's like you're in the Chinese Embassy. The cops? They wouldn't dare show up.' Seriously? We need accountability now! #JusticeInNYC #NoOneAboveTheLaw"

"My heart goes out to the women in Flushing. Our authorities need to step up and protect their rights. #FlushingTragedy #HumanRights"

Advertisers flocked to P.I. Olsen, eager for partnerships, while media outlets vied for exclusive interviews. Lacey welcomed the ads but turned down the media. She never went public—that was her rule. In her streams, she only portrayed fictional characters like Natalia, using high-tech skin to disguise herself, never revealing her true identity. She also used various VPNs for her P.I. Olsen TikTok account to ensure complete privacy.

Her livestream soon caught the New York Police Department's attention. They acted swiftly, raiding the Red Star High School bar in Flushing. By then, Abalone had vanished, rumoured to have fled to Hong Kong. The "students" were also gone without a trace. A NYPD spokesperson confirmed the investigation was ongoing, emphasising their commitment to solving the case.

The NYPD also reached out to P.I. Olsen on TikTok, seeking details about Natalia. Her response was cryptic, "She's not in the US anymore. No clue where she is or how to contact her now."

Lacey was sure no one knew her true identity—not even the NYPD. Mia was the only one in on the secret.

Mia had watched the livestream, but her call to Lacey wasn't the congratulatory type she expected.

"Remember what I told ya? Go all out, but play it safe. You ain't Supergirl or Wonder Woman!"

"Don't sweat it, Mia. I've got this."

"No, you don't! And messing with the Chinese mafia? You're in over your head!"

"Natalia stirring the pot with them, not me. And I bet they couldn't find her."

"Lacey, listen to me. Cut it out right now."

"What?"

"Lay off the P.I. Olsen thing for a while. Chill out then think about coming back with a new account later."

After years of scraping by, Lacey finally felt fortune smiling upon her. Stop now? Not a chance.

While Lacey tasted success, a chilling message from an ID named I'm Watching You popped up in P.I. Olsen's TikTok inbox, "Betray me, and I promise I'll destroy everyone you care about before I come for you."

She wasn't too worried about herself. Abalone wouldn't dare set foot on U.S. soil since he was on the nation's most wanted list. Her concern was for Shawn, living in Hong Kong where Abalone might have fled.

It seemed unlikely Abalone would target him—he wouldn't even know who Shawn was. Yet the thought gnawed at her, keeping her anxious with worst-case scenarios.

She tried calling Shawn, but the calls went unanswered. She messaged him on Messenger, "Dad, is everything alright?"

The next day, Shawn's response on Messenger left her bewildered. "Lacey, listen. No matter what happens, promise me you won't come to Hong Kong. There are demons here lurking in the shadows. And if they catch you, they'll never let you go. They'll force you to do things you can't even imagine."

It didn't sound like him. Confused, she replied, "Dad, what's going on? Can we chat for a sec?"

A full day passed in silence.

Late one evening, Lacey's phone buzzed with a call from Hong Kong. It wasn't Shawn's number. She didn't have any other connections there. Puzzled, she answered, "Hello?"

There was a brief pause before a voice with a distinct Hong Kong accent replied, "Is this Lacey Green, the daughter of Shawn Green?"

"Yes, who's speaking?"

"Miss Green, do you have a moment?"

"Yes?"

"This is Sergeant Patrick Leung from the West Kowloon Serious Crime Unit in Hong Kong. I regret to inform you that Mr. Green..."

As Sergeant Leung delivered the grim news of Shawn's death, she hoped it was a nightmare and frantically wished to wake up from it.

She failed.

7

ABOUT SHAWN GREEN

Five years ago on a sunny day, Shawn had returned to New York from Hong Kong for a short holiday and took Lacey to Jones Beach. While soaking up the sun, he scooped up a handful of sand and let it scatter in the wind.

"Look at that dust. It drifts aimlessly, never settling. That's what eternity is," he mused.

Sorry, Dad, I don't really get it. It's nonsense, Lacey thought. But what she said was, "Deep stuff, Dad. I dig it."

Shawn, a devout Christian, and Lacey, an atheist, held different beliefs. She chose not to stir up debates, preferring to savour their happy, albeit infrequent, moments together.

Shawn looked at her, eyes earnest. "When I turn to dust, promise me you'll scatter me across the sea near my hometown. I don't want to end up in some dumb urn under a cold gravestone."

She nodded, brushing it off, never imagining his death would come so soon. After all, he was only in his fifties and in good health.

Fate had other plans.

In the cold call, Sergeant Leung broke the news that Shawn had tragically died, having fallen from the rooftop of his Hong Kong apartment two nights ago. The police were leaning towards suicide.

"He wouldn't off himself like that," Lacey countered. Given Shawn's nature—optimistic, cheerful, open-minded, and deeply religious—the idea of him committing suicide didn't make sense.

Sergeant Leung said the Hong Kong police would investigate further and keep her posted then abruptly hung up.

The chilling message replayed in her mind. "Betray me, and I promise I'll destroy everyone you care about before I come for you."

Could this be Abalone's doing? He'd uncovered P.I. Olsen's real identity—a secret even the NYPD hadn't cracked. He found out Shawn was her father, tracked down his Hong Kong address, murdered him, and staged it to look like a suicide.

No way! That's impossible!

She reread her father's final message warning her about Hong Kong and forbidding her from coming. It now felt like something sinister was lurking beneath.

She quickly filled the old bathtub with cold water, dumping in every ice cube she could find. In the brisk New York autumn, she stripped and slid into the freezing bath. The shock of the cold water hit her like a reset button, instantly sharpening her focus and clarifying her next moves.

First, she contacted the U.S. Consulate General in Hong Kong for help. They put her in touch with Jerry Jagger from American Citizen Services, who would be her primary contact.

Next, she called Sergeant Patrick Leung. Ostensibly to bid her father a final farewell, her real intent was to thoroughly examine Shawn's remains for any overlooked clues. Sergeant Leung agreed to preserve the body for an additional week.

Turning down the fancy hotel offered by Shawn's employer, GrandTech Group, she planned to stay at Shawn's apartment once she arrived in Hong Kong. She needed to search the place where he died for any clues or leads.

Lastly, Lacey treated Mia to lunch at her favourite bagel diner.

As Mia bit into her everything bagel with scallion cream cheese, Lacey leaned in. "I need two girls. Young, hot, Chinese. By tomorrow."

Mia's eyes narrowed. "You tangling with the Chinese mafia again?"

"No, I'm done with that. It's for an investigation in Hong Kong. I need to blend in."

"Hong Kong?"

"Yeah."

"You know it's dangerous there now, right? The CCP screwed it up."

"I know, but it's a simple gig, nothing risky."

Mia narrowed her eyes. "Sorry, honey, I'm not putting you in danger."

"I've got an offer from a French lingerie brand. They loved my last gig and will sponsor me a hundred grand for the next one. I can give you sixty percent of that," Lacey improvised.

Mia had been griping about AI taking over a lot of her VFX gigs, leaving her strapped for cash.

Lacey's pitch hit the mark.

Mia stopped eating and eyed Lacey carefully.

"It's quick money, you know." Lacey shrugged.

"Seventy percent," Mia said. "You still owe me for the damage to Natalia."

"What damage?"

"Some scratches."

"Come on, Mia, I... Alright, seventy percent. Deal?"

Money first, friendship second, sex third—that was Mia's motto. The next day, Lacey picked up the "two Chinese girls," hidden in a high-tech suitcase that scrambled customs scans to look like ordinary clothes.

As Lacey finished packing for Hong Kong, her phone buzzed. The screen lit up with "The Colossal Twat."

"Shit!" she muttered.

The timing couldn't have been worse.

8

THE COLOSSAL TWAT

Lacey picked up the phone and snapped, "What?"

"Blimey, it's been nonstop yakking on this dog and bone!" The Colossal Twat chided, her tone dripping with sarcasm, complete with a forced posh London accent that teetered on the edge of cliché and old-fashioned.

"I'm swamped, so make it quick."

"Caught that TikTok? The scandalous one about Flushing's brothels with that communist twist?"

The gig really went viral, even catching the attention of The Colossal Twat, who never watched TikTok.

"I don't do TikTok," Lacey retorted.

"It's a cracking story! I'm thinking of snagging the rights for a film."

"And how's that my concern?"

"Thought you might fancy a stab at this one. It's a winner, Lacey. We could be raking it in before I even yell 'action.'"

"If that's all, I've got to run."

"Let me lay out the plan—"

"Shawn's gone," Lacey blurted out.

"Shawn? Which Shawn?" The confusion was genuine.

With clenched teeth, Lacey thought about the series of Shawns from The Colossal Twat's turbulent past.

"The one who knocked you up with me, alright?" Trembling with anger, she abruptly hung up the phone.

Lacey was supposed to call her "Mom" but hardly ever did. If Shawn was her anchor, then her mom was the storm, always threatening to throw her off course.

Michelle Leigh Weaver was a film industry all on her own: investor, producer, director, screenwriter, lead actress, and editor. Her life, a blend of filmmaking and hedonism, sidelined everything else, including Lacey's upbringing, which fell to a series of ever-changing nannies. This cast Michelle in the unwavering role of a thoroughly neglectful mother. Echoing the turmoil of her personal life, her professional endeavours fell short of success. Over two decades, she produced seven indie films, all featuring her own nude scenes. She declared each one a masterpiece, but the reality was starkly different: every film flopped, never scoring above ten percent on Rotten Tomatoes or higher than a four on IMDb.

In middle school, a bully displayed a montage of Michelle's nude scenes in class, taunting Lacey by calling her "a porn star's bastard." Lacey's gut reaction was to knock out his front teeth with a chair, an action that swiftly earned her a severe reprimand from the school.

Lacey had always been puzzled by Michelle's ability to secure funding despite numerous flops, until she grasped the grim realities of the industry's "casting couch."

Even in her forties, Michelle retained a magnetic allure. Taller and more voluptuous than Lacey, her striking looks and rumoured prowess were well-known. Her real skill was in managing men. With a variety of benefactors—a sugar daddy, a sugar brother, and even a sugar son—she handled these relationships with ease, regardless of their age, race, status, or temperament.

***

The next day, Michelle called Lacey. "What's your plan?"

"Off to Hong Kong for the funeral."

"You haven't been back to Hong Kong since you were a toddler. Everything's going to be unfamiliar, and it's pretty risky to go it alone. I'll come with you."

"That's none of your business," Lacey shot back, then hung up. She didn't need company, especially not Michelle's.

Michelle always had a plan up her sleeve. She contacted Shawn's employer, GrandTech Group, and convinced them she was Shawn's ex-wife and co-parent, securing an invitation to the funeral. As a result, Lacey found herself stuck traveling with her.

GrandTech Group generously provided first-class tickets for their trip to Hong Kong. Lacey was relieved to find their cabin free of children, which she always tried to avoid.

As the plane cut through the clouds, Michelle leaned towards Lacey and whispered, "Having a bit of trouble with the *Cleopatra* remake funds."

"Why don't you ask your sugar son for some help?"

Ignoring Lacey's pointed remark, Michelle sighed deeply. "The recent hike in interest rates has really tightened things up. Considering the original *Cleopatra* nearly bankrupted 20th Century Fox, drumming up funds for this remake has been a nightmare."

"Get to the point."

"Would you consider fronting some initial funding, enough to help me rally more support?"

Lacey took a deliberate sip of water, letting the silence stretch as she waited for Michelle's next move.

"Honestly, half a mil should cover it."

Lacey nearly choked on her water.

"Or maybe 200k?"

"I've barely got $700 to my name."

Michelle's laughter filled the cabin. "That's about to change, darling. You're sitting on a gold mine."

Lacey looked puzzled. "What do you mean?"

Leaning in, Michelle's voice dripped with excitement. "As Shawn Green's sole heir, everything he had is now yours. He wasn't rich, but there might be a life insurance policy with you as the beneficiary..."

Lacey's expression hardened.

What a relentless, gold-digging bitch!

"You've been waiting for this, haven't you?" Lacey's voice trembled with barely contained anger.

Michelle paused then admitted, "Yes, but listen, this *Cleopatra* script—I'm on draft thirty-eight—it's revolutionary. Everyone says so! Trust me, I'll pay you back tenfold!"

"For fuck's sake!" Lacey burst out. "Shawn's gone, his death's a mystery, and you're after his money?"

Her outburst drew attention. She forced herself to calm down, not wanting to make a scene in first class. Despite her efforts, she couldn't hold back the tears.

Michelle quickly put on a sympathetic face, offering a tissue and cooing, "Oh, darling."

Lacey jerked away. "Leave me alone!"

The two women sat in tense silence, the air thick with things left unsaid.

Finally, Michelle spoke in a soft, measured tone, "Lacey, you've got to see it...for him, this might've been some sort of escape."

The weight of Michelle's words hung in the air, hinting at an unsettling truth about Shawn's fate, a reality Lacey wasn't ready to confront but couldn't completely dismiss.

9

CELESTIAL MANOR

"Shawn was battling his own demons," said Michelle.

Lacey snapped, "The Hong Kong police are speculating. Nothing's been confirmed yet!"

On the eve of their departure from New York to Hong Kong, Sergeant Leung called Lacey with an update on Shawn's case, revealing a hidden struggle. Shawn had started treatment for diagnosed depression five years ago, but his mental health had inevitably declined. Lacey couldn't accept it. She believed she knew her father's mind better than anyone and was confident in his mental resilience. Moreover, she questioned whether Shawn's therapy sessions necessarily suggested a tendency towards suicide.

"Actually, that incident," Michelle began, hesitating before lowering her voice, "it really took a toll on Shawn, didn't it?"

"Don't go there!" Lacey howled sharply, her eyes flashing with anger. "That had nothing to do with Shawn's death!"

Michelle fell silent, getting the message.

Lacey grabbed a blanket and wrapped herself in it, seeking a moment of peace.

The "incident" Michelle referred to touched on a part of Lacey's past that she fiercely protected, a shadow she never allowed to surface. She forbade any discussion of it, even with herself.

The plane touched down smoothly at Hong Kong International Airport after a gruelling fifteen-hour flight. Greeting them on behalf of GrandTech Group was a strikingly handsome man. Towering over six feet, he boasted broad shoulders and lean legs, his meticulously tailored suit subtly highlighting his well-defined muscles, radiating effortless elegance. His deep, introspective eyes sparkled with a captivating intensity.

With a refined British accent, he introduced himself, "Pleasure to meet you, Ms. Green and Ms. Weaver. I'm Hugo."

Michelle leaned in, whispering to Lacey, "Quite the heart-stealer, isn't he?"

"Shut up!" Lacey wished she could mute her mother's constant chatter.

"Ms. Yip's been tied up in meetings all day," Hugo informed them, his voice smooth and courteous. "But she's eager to see you as soon as you're settled."

Lacey, well-prepared, knew that Ms. Yip was Shawn's boss, the CEO of GrandTech Group.

As Hugo guided them through the bustling crowd towards the parking lot, a pair of dark, penetrating eyes seemed to follow Lacey from the shadows. Every time she turned to look, they disappeared, only to reappear as she continued walking, playing what felt like a game of hide and seek.

Wondering if she was being paranoid, Lacey tried to distract herself. Yet those haunting eyes kept reappearing in her peripheral vision. Pretending not to notice, she suddenly spun around towards them, and they vanished once more.

"Fuck!" she blurted out.

"What's wrong, darling?" Michelle asked, turning towards her.

Hugo stopped and looked at her, visibly confused.

"Sorry..." She flushed with embarrassment. "Never mind, let's keep going."

She recalled what Abalone had said. "Betray me, and I promise I'll destroy everyone you care about before I come for you." Those sinister words echoed in her mind, sending chills down her spine, quickening her heartbeat, and making her palms sweat.

"Come on, get a grip," she muttered to herself.

They eventually reached their ride, a golden Rolls-Royce Phantom parked in the VIP lot. Sitting in the rear seats, which were more comfortable than the finest first-class airplane accommodation, Lacey and Michelle felt like they were sinking into a plush sofa. Between the seats, an elegant aquarium with a red and a blue fish added a touch of opulence. Above them, an LCD screen displayed a captivating starry sky. The sound system's Nordic melodies enveloped them, each note resonating deeply.

Within the luxurious limo, Lacey and Michelle wove through the heart of Hong Kong's Central district, surrounded by towering skyscrapers. They passed a group of young protesters, silently barricading themselves. Each one wore a tagged number and had their names clearly displayed, holding placards that read, "Fight for Hong Kong — Reclaim our Freedom!" Under the watchful gaze of a few police officers, the scene was eerily quiet.

"I don't get it. Why would they encircle themselves with barriers?" Michelle asked.

Hugo explained, "It's a government regulation here in Hong Kong. Protests are limited to one hundred people. They set up their own barricades, and everyone must wear an ID tag. No outsiders can join, and it's off-limits for the media. Violating these rules can lead to serious National Security Law consequences."

Lacey observed the protesters, noting the tension beneath their composed exteriors. The situation struck her as strangely solemn.

As the sun dipped, painting the sky in brilliant sunset hues, the Rolls-Royce pulled up to a skyscraper luxury apartment marked "Celestial Manor." Entering the underground parking, Lacey found it reminiscent of an exclusive club, showcasing an array of extremely rare and luxurious sports cars, grand RVs, and classic vintage models.

"Did Shawn live here?" Michelle asked, her curiosity evident.

"Yes, Dr. Green lived here," Hugo replied, causing Lacey to wonder about the use of "Dr." for Shawn.

A technician with such a title?

"Wow, really?" Michelle seemed more intrigued by something else. "How much was the rent?"

"I'm not sure about the rent. Dr. Green owned his place."

Lacey and Michelle exchanged a look of sheer surprise.

"And what do these apartments go for?" Michelle pressed.

"They start at around fifty million Hong Kong dollars. The higher up, the pricier. Penthouse, I reckon, is about one hundred and fifty million, give or take."

"And Shawn's?"

"The penthouse."

Michelle's eyes widened, her disbelief and awe momentarily silencing her usual quips.

Lacey quickly did the math. That was roughly nineteen million US dollars.

"Right, we've arrived. Dr. Green's parking bay is around the corner," Hugo announced as the Rolls-Royce came to a gentle stop.

Stepping out of the car, they were greeted by the VIP parking spot. There sat a breathtaking sky-blue Aston Martin DB12, a limited-edition marvel.

Hugo pulled a car key from his bag and handed it to Lacey. "This belonged to Dr. Green."

As Lacey took the key to the exclusive DB12, a subtle tremor ran through her fingers. She heard Michelle whisper in her ear, "Things are getting interesting, aren't they?"

10

THE SHADOW

As Lacey, Michelle, and Hugo rose in the panoramic elevator, the setting sun draped Victoria Harbour, the distant hills, and the towering skyline in a warm glow—an absolute feast for the eyes.

Reaching the eighty-eighth floor, they stepped out into a corridor of translucent glass, bathed in twilight's crimson. It felt like walking on air in paradise.

The penthouse was a sight to behold: a sprawling five-hundred square meters of pure luxury. From the plush velvet sofa and the ornately carved dining table to the minutiae like the hand-painted teacups and the glittering crystal vase, every inch screamed opulence. A grand floor-to-ceiling window dominated the living room, framing the deep reds and purples of the twilight sky like a royal tapestry.

"Fucking hell," Michelle murmured, echoing Lacey's disbelief.

This didn't add up. Shawn was just an IT guy. How could he afford this? And where were the family photos? It wasn't like him not to have personal touches around.

"Stocked the fridge for you—milk, bread, cheese, and veggies. Got some fresh fruit on the coffee table, and there are a couple of top-shelf reds in the cabinet," Hugo explained, playing the perfect host.

Michelle gave him a warm smile. "Wow, that's really thoughtful, Hugo."

"Ah, it's nothing," he replied with a modest shrug.

Lacey, glancing towards the staircase, piped up with a question. "That goes up to the rooftop?"

"Yeah, it does." Hugo nodded, a hint of caution in his voice. "It can get pretty chilly up there at night."

Lacey had a feeling Hugo knew more about Shawn than he was letting on.

"Ms. Yip will swing by sometime this week to talk about Dr. Green's memorial and a few other things," he said as he handed Lacey a mobile phone, smiling warmly. "Here's a phone with a local SIM. Need any-thing? Give me a ring."

After Hugo left, Michelle plopped down on the plush sofa, her eyes sparkling with excitement as she turned to Lacey.

Lacey knew what was coming. She wasn't in the mood, but Michelle didn't need an invitation to speak her mind.

"I mentioned a hefty sum coming your way, right? This penthouse alone is worth a fortune. Look around—artwork, antiques, top-notch furnishings. And don't forget the Aston fucking Martin! Who knows what other fancy digs he had? Shawn was a master at hiding his goodies."

Lacey was at a loss for words.

"Not one photo of us anywhere, like we never even existed!" Michelle fumed. "Shawn really screwed us over, didn't he?"

"Hey, how about a shower? It's starting to smell funky in here," Lacey quipped, making her way to the spiral staircase.

As she climbed the stairs, the air thickened with a rich floral scent, hinting at a botanical wonderland above. Stepping onto the rooftop, she was blown away. She saw a vast garden under a sprawling glass dome—a true Eden. It was bursting with colourful flowers, exotic plants, and a meandering stream filled with vibrant fish. An absolute paradise, a hidden gem tucked away above the cityscape. She couldn't fathom the time and money it must have taken to create and maintain this lofty oasis.

The cold Hugo had warned about hit hard. The biting chill of high altitude swept through the dome's ventilation gaps. Near the edge, a low railing marked the terrace. Faint chalk lines, likely drawn by the police, hinted at where Shawn might have jumped.

With a heavy heart, Lacey edged closer, her resolve to document the scene battling with a pounding heart and shaky legs. The city stretched out below, a distant world. She tried to steady her phone for a clear shot, but the dim light and her trembling hands made the images blur.

"Come on," she muttered, trying to pull herself together.

As she steadied herself for another photo, a noise stopped her cold: footsteps echoing from deep within the garden.

"Michelle? Is that you?" she called out, peering into the dim moonlight. The sight that met her eyes made her blood run cold—the same haunting eyes she had seen at the airport, now glaring at her from the shadows.

As she grabbed a glass vase nearby, the eyes vanished into the lush greenery. Then she caught a glimpse of a fleeting silhouette darting towards the rooftop's exit, quickly scrambling down into the penthouse.

"Stop!" she yelled, launching herself into chase.

Upon returning to the penthouse, Lacey swapped the vase for a kitchen knife and methodically searched each room—the bedrooms, bathrooms, and study. She found no one. Approaching the third bathroom, she noticed its door slightly ajar, with a soft glow spilling out. The only sound was the faint hum of a fan. Gripping the knife tighter, she crept forward and with a swift, decisive kick flung the door open.

Twin screams of shock pierced the air, the voices of two women clashing in a jarring duet of surprise. Heart pounding, Lacey stood frozen at the threshold, the knife gleaming menacingly in her hand. Her eyes widened as they fixated on Michelle, shamelessly draped across the cool, polished surface of the marble washbasin, her legs spread open in a butterfly position, engaging in self-pleasure.

"What the fuck are you doing?" the two exclaimed at the same time.

As Lacey turned to leave, frustrated, she heard Michelle mutter, "You did that on purpose."

Lacey spun around, her eyes sharp. "Excuse me, what was that?"

Michelle replied coolly, her voice dripping with sarcasm, "Oh, I reckon you heard me fine. Putting on an act, are we?"

"Look, I didn't come in here to watch you...whatever that was! I saw someone enter the room, and I..."

"Oh, come on! You used to do the same thing back in middle school—with pillows, your hand, even a beer bottle, remember? I knew all about it but kept quiet out of respect for your privacy."

"When the hell did I ever use a beer bottle?" Lacey's voice rose in frustration.

Their conversation was suddenly interrupted by the loud slamming of the apartment's front door.

"Jesus Christ!" Michelle gasped.

Without hesitation, Lacey whipped around and darted towards the living room, gripping the knife tightly.

"Be careful!" Michelle called after her, hurrying to keep up.

As Lacey reached the living room, her eyes locked on the closed front door, the echo of its slam still hanging in the air. She flung the door open, only to be met by the expansive, empty corridor. Right at her feet was a lone white envelope.

She opened the envelope and found a card inside. In elegant, handwritten script, it read, "Please dial 91915352."

"What's this?" Michelle asked, peering over Lacey's shoulder.

Lacey took the phone Hugo gave her and dialled the number. After two rings, she heard a click, signalling a connection.

"Hello?" Lacey called into the void.

A deep, unmistakably familiar voice answered after a brief pause. "Lacey, it's me…"

Frozen in place, Lacey and Michelle felt a chill run down their spines.

The voice was undeniably her father's.

11

—— • ——

BREAKING NEWS

"**D**ad!" Lacey gasped.

"Oh my God!" Michelle added, her eyes wide.

As the message played, it hit them that this wasn't Shawn speaking live. A recording played. "Lacey, listen. No matter what happens, promise me you won't come to Hong Kong. There are demons here lurking in the shadows. And if they catch you, they'll never let you go. They'll force you to do things you can't even imagine."

Suddenly, the line went dead, leaving them reeling in shock.

"I was expecting some juicy gossip or a nice fat inheritance, not...this nonsense," Michelle grumbled.

Lacey tried redialing, only to be met by an automated message stating the number was out of service.

"Listen," Michelle said, leaning in, "I've got a lot on my mind. Fancy a chat?"

"Not now." Lacey was already overwhelmed and unpredictable Michelle could complicate things further.

"So what's the plan? Call the cops? Or maybe Hugo?" Michelle mused.

"Going to bed."

Lacey didn't go to bed, too stressed from the day's events and having forgotten her relief pill, which meant she was more likely to revisit that dreaded school bus nightmare once she fell asleep.

She unpacked and hid the high-tech suitcase with "the two Chinese girls" under the luxurious bed.

Standing by the floor-to-ceiling windows, she gazed at the stunning cityscape below, her mind racing with memories, theories, and gut feelings.

With everything that had unfolded since her arrival in Hong Kong, she was sure there was more to dig up than she had first thought. But first things first, she needed to visit Shawn's body, hoping to uncover some clues.

She spent the night wide awake.

At dawn, Lacey's phone buzzed.

"Hello?"

"Good morning, Miss Green. Sorry for the early call, but have you seen the breaking news?" Hugo said urgently.

"No, what's happening?"

He sighed deeply. "It's complicated. I seriously suggest you both stay in today."

"I was supposed to visit Shawn's body."

"That might be tricky."

"They're planning to cremate him tomorrow," she said.

"Hold tight for now, okay? I'll sort it out. Stand by for my call," Hugo said, sounding tense.

Confused, Lacey set the phone down and stared out the large windows. The early morning light cast a peaceful glow over the city, but her unease persisted.

She wandered into the living room and turned on the TV. The images flashing across the screen sent a jolt through her. Urgent headlines scrolled by, while Shawn's voice, hauntingly familiar, echoed in her ears.

Her dad had warned her not to come to Hong Kong, and she was starting to see why.

12

THE SATAN VIRUS

Overnight, Hong Kong was rocked by a staggering 2,135 cases of severe self-harm, pushing the government to declare a state of emergency and urge everyone to stay put unless absolutely necessary.

Lacey's deep dive online unearthed a slew of viral videos that eerily confirmed Shawn's earlier warnings.

In one clip, chaos erupted in a subway car. A businessman in glasses suddenly started convulsing. As the camera closed in, it captured the horrifying scene of him biting his hands, blood splattering, while other passengers panicked and scattered.

The next clip, filmed on a cell phone, showed a taxi stalled in the middle of the street, causing a traffic jam. The middle-aged driver was gnawing on his fingers as if they were a guilty pleasure.

In another, a gym scene showed women screaming and dashing out of the showers. The camera advanced to reveal a woman under the spray, ferociously chewing on her own severed leg.

"Jesus!" Lacey gasped, shocked to her core.

"This is nuts!" Michelle blurted out, catching Lacey off guard.

"Look at this! This guy's chomping on his toes—bet he wishes he skipped those yoga classes," Michelle chuckled, weirdly entertained by the gruesome sight.

Lacey dove headfirst into the web, scouring for any leads on the unfolding chaos. A post from a health expert at the Hong Kong Centre for Health Protection grabbed her attention, pointing to a "severe and transmissible atypical neuro-virus" as the culprit. The online crowd quickly slapped it with the nickname "Satan," a nod to the initials of its lengthy description.

The internet soon buzzed with wild speculation about the so-called "Hong Kong Satan Virus." Some chalked it up to demonic forces wreaking havoc. Others floated the idea that it was a U.S. bio-weapon aimed at throwing Hong Kong into disarray, while a few whispered about it being a bone-chilling next step in COVID-19's evolution.

Michelle leaned in, whispering, "Shawn's recording really struck a nerve, didn't it? Feel like chatting? Maybe share some theories?"

Lacking patience for the person she considered a colossal twat, Lacey retreated to the study, quickly turned the lock behind her, and dialled Sergeant Leung.

"Hong Kong is currently under a state of emergency, so we strongly advise everyone to stay indoors. Unfortunately, this means visiting your father's body at the hospital isn't possible right now," Sergeant Leung explained.

Lacey's response was firm. "I need to see him. It's non-negotiable."

"Miss Green, I've already outlined our policy."

"This feels like a violation of our human rights, doesn't it?"

"We take human rights seriously in Hong Kong, but the current crisis requires some tough calls."

"Tell me one thing. Can I see my dad before they cremate him?"

"I've given you the situation, Miss Green."

"Fine, I'll contact the U.S. Consulate. They'll hear about this."

"Do whatever you think is best."

Lacey dialled Jerry Jagger, her contact at the U.S. Consulate General in Hong Kong.

"Miss Green," Jerry began, his voice filled with regret, "I'll touch base with the police and the hospital, but I can't promise anything."

"They're planning to cremate him tomorrow. Isn't there some angle you can work? Maybe a loophole?"

Jerry sighed deeply. "It's chaotic right now, especially with the US-China tensions. But I'll try to pull some strings."

"They can't go ahead without my consent, Jerry!"

"I'm on it," Jerry reassured her. "I'll pull out all the stops."

After hanging up, Lacey felt her resolve harden. She wouldn't wait for red tape or permissions. She was determined to get to the hospital, no matter what.

As Lacey was about to leave, her phone buzzed. It was a call from the "Celestial Manor" property department.

"Dear resident, due to government directives, Celestial Manor is now under lockdown," the voice on the other end calmly informed her.

"What? Locked down?"

"Yes. All residents must stay inside. If you need anything essential, let us know, and we'll get it delivered to you," the voice continued.

"I need to leave, like now!"

"I'm really sorry, but all exits are sealed. No one can leave."

"When can we get out?"

"We can't provide an exact timeframe. But we'll keep you updated." The line went dead.

"I can't believe this!" Lacey exclaimed, her frustration evident.

Michelle knocked gently on the study door.

"What now?" Lacey snapped.

"I was thinking, maybe we could have a chat, you know? A real heart-to-heart?"

"Not fucking now!"

***

After a day filled with anxiety and confinement in the penthouse, Lacey's hopes crumbled the next morning.

A joint press conference by the Hong Kong government and the Centre for Health Protection reported a spike in extreme self-harm incidents citywide, linked to a mysterious new virus called the "Hong Kong Encephalitis Virus," or "HKEV." The primary symptoms included severe self-harm, especially limb-biting. The centre admitted there was no cure yet but promised to find one. Contrary to expectations, the government excluded foreign experts from the US, UK, Japan, and even the World Health Organisation, permitting only mainland Chinese specialists. Furthermore, martial law was enforced, mandating acid tests for all city residents.

Lacey tried reaching Hugo and Jerry, but both phones were off.

"For God's sake!" she burst out, overwhelmed with frustration.

"Sweetheart, take a breather. How about we grab some breakfast? It might help you unwind," Michelle suggested.

That wasn't a bad idea.

Using the provisions Hugo had left, Lacey whipped up a hearty English fry-up.

Midway through the meal, Michelle paused and stared at her left hand oddly. "Weird, why do I suddenly feel like biting my hand?"

Lacey, seeing it as a distasteful joke, replied sarcastically, "Maybe add some salt and pepper?"

Michelle didn't hesitate. She bit into her hand, drawing blood that splattered the pristine tablecloth and sprayed Lacey's face.

13

—— ◆ ——

A LITTLE ACTING

Lacey sprang into action, grabbing Michelle, wrestling her hand from her mouth. Then she spotted it—a squished blood bag in Michelle's palm.

"What the fuck are you doing?" Lacey shoved Michelle back.

"The wonders of cinematic craft!" Michelle waved the blood bag with a smirk. "Ketchup, a pinch of salt, a dash of water—my little concoction. Convincing, isn't it?"

Lacey's face contorted in disgust as she wiped off the sticky faux blood. "This isn't fucking funny!"

"Lighten up, darling," Michelle chided, her eyes sparkling with mischief. "It's a bit of fun."

Rushing to clean up, Lacey realised she had to figure out a way to ditch The Colossal Twat.

An hour later, the property department called with unsettling news. Quarantine officers were combing the building, conducting acid tests on all residents, starting from the top. Living in the penthouse, Lacey and Michelle were up first.

Michelle sidled up to Lacey, her expression dead serious. "You think we should, you know, tidy up a bit down there?"

"What?"

"I've heard stories about those COVID days in China, with rectal swabs and everything."

"Can you stop fucking around?"

"Just putting it out there," Michelle quipped, a sly grin on her lips as she sauntered off to the bathroom.

Minutes later, the doorbell rang. Outside stood three figures dressed head-to-toe in white protective gear, looking like something straight out of a sci-fi movie, reminiscent of "Baymax." After checking their passports, one of the figures swabbed Lacey and Michelle's noses. The test was uncomfortable but not the horror Michelle had braced for.

"Can we clear out if this comes back negative?" Lacey asked.

"We have to wait for further instructions," the agent replied.

"And how long until we know?"

"Between twelve to twenty-four hours."

Lacey felt the walls closing in. With only five hours until Shawn's cremation, every exit of the Celestial Manor was tightly guarded. Her frantic calls to Hugo and Jerry Jagger fell on deaf ears. She was trapped.

A bold idea struck her.

Lacey sidled up to Michelle, who was engrossed in her phone. "I'm thinking of backing your *Cleopatra* project," she hinted.

Michelle's head snapped up. "Seriously?"

Lacey nodded.

Michelle brightened. "Brilliant! I'll get my lawyer on it. Looks like you're about to cash in big. What's your investment?"

"Starting at half a mil," Lacey redirected smoothly.

Michelle raised an eyebrow. "A bit on the low side, but it works."

"I've got one condition."

Michelle leaned in, curious. "Yeah?"

"Acting," Lacey said bluntly.

Michelle chuckled. "Pick your part, sweetheart. I'm Cleo though—no debates there."

Lacey shook her head, undeterred.

Seeing Michelle's confusion, Lacey laid out her plan. "Fake a heart attack. I'll call 999—that's the emergency number here. They'll take you to the only nearby hospital, where Shawn's body is. I'll come along. Once we're inside, cause a scene while I sneak away to see Shawn. Nail it, and the half million is yours. Deal?"

Michelle's smile turned sly. "Interesting."

As Lacey got ready, Michelle held up a hand. "Hold on."

Their eyes locked. Lacey braced herself. "How much more?"

Quick on the draw, Michelle replied with a spreading grin, "Given the jackpot you're eyeing from Shawn..." She paused for effect. "A million, and you'll witness an Oscar-worthy act. Not a penny less."

A mix of disbelief and resignation etched Lacey's face as she muttered, "Damn, deal!"

Lacey had no plans to pay and was just stringing Michelle along.

As Lacey was about to call the ambulance, the doorbell rang.

Opening the door, Lacey faced an intimidating sight: police officers in full protective gear, transforming the usually peaceful corridor into a scene straight out of a pandemic thriller.

An officer stepped forward, flashed his badge, and announced that both Lacey and Michelle had tested positive for the dreaded Hong Kong Encephalitis Virus, according to their latest nucleic acid tests.

14

—·—

DEMON

"Please pack your essential items and accompany us to the designated isolation facility," the officer stated bluntly.

Lacey took a deep breath and replied with firm clarity, "We're American citizens. We have the right to refuse this."

"And I'm also British—got dual citizenship," Michelle added, seizing every opportunity to flaunt her dual identity.

Unmoved, the officer repeated, "As I said, according to the Hong Kong government's quarantine policy, please pack your essentials..."

Cutting him off, Lacey slammed the door shut. Her hands trembled as she scrambled to dial Jerry Jagger.

Meanwhile, Michelle looked at her hands, confused. "What the hell?"

"Hi, Lacey," Jerry's voice crackled through.

"Help! We're in trouble!" Lacey gasped.

Suddenly, a loud crash reverberated as the door gave way to a battering ram. Officers poured in, quickly overpowering both women and restraining their wrists.

"What the fuck is going on here?" Lacey yelled.

"Do you have a warrant? You can't arrest us like this!" Michelle snapped, struggling in vain against their grip.

Jerry's worried voice came from the dropped phone. "Lacey! What's happening?"

Before another word, an officer grabbed the phone and cut the connection.

Another officer approached Michelle, wielding a syringe filled with a sinister-looking liquid. He quickly injected her in the neck, and she lost consciousness.

"Fuck you!" Lacey's cry filled the room. But before she could react, a sharp prick on her neck dimmed her senses. The world faded to black as the drug took hold.

***

Lacey found herself on the school bus again.

The bus navigated the bustling city centre, surrounded by towering buildings and swamped with traffic. Inside, the same group of kids sat in utter silence, a stark contrast to the chaos outside.

At an intersection, the bus stopped, and a man in a suit, clutching a briefcase, got on. When she saw his face, she gasped, "Dad!"

Shawn seemed not to hear. He took a seat near the front, the only adult among the children, sticking out like a sore thumb.

She tried to stand, but it was as if she were glued to her seat.

The bus plunged into a tunnel.

She smelled blood. She screamed, trying to alert Shawn and the other children, but it seemed no one could hear her. She remained stuck in her seat.

As the bus shot out of the tunnel, blinding sunlight bleached everything outside the windows to a glaring white.

A container truck loomed ahead, colliding with them in a deafening roar.

The bus tipped over and spun, tossing Lacey, Shawn, and the kids around the cabin. It felt like her insides were being ripped apart.

Eventually, the bus smashed against a roadside barrier and burst into flames.

Lacey watched as fierce flames devoured Shawn and the children and finally closed in around her.

Burning, excruciating pain engulfed her as her body slowly turned to ash.

Lacey jolted awake.

She heard laboured breathing and hacking coughs mingled with deep snores and the occasional farts. The air was thick with a blend of body odours. She couldn't open her eyes, which felt as heavy as lead. Her body was numb, detached.

Seconds later, a commanding force snapped her eyes open, revealing a ceiling dotted with glaring lights that cast a harsh, clinical glow.

The force didn't let up. It yanked her upright, her head swivelling with unnerving precision, revealing her surroundings—an expansive warehouse. Stark white walls enclosed the vast space. Rows of pristine white hospital beds lined up, each holding a figure dressed in a white gown, like hers, creating a seamless, uninterrupted scene. It eerily mirrored the massive isolation centres in China she remembered from news clips during the height of the COVID-19 pandemic.

She began to question whether she was truly awake.

"Attention all personnel, it's time for sanitation. Formation 1, please line up for procedures," an authoritative voice commanded, reverberating through the vast space.

Patients in Formation 1 slowly got up from their beds, moving in unison towards the makeshift bathrooms at the far end of the large cabin. Their movements were precise and synchronised, creating a quiet, almost spectral display.

In a coordinated fashion, one formation after another began their movements, each group seamlessly falling into a single rhythm, their silent, eerie dance unfolding without a supervisor in sight—no staff, no guards, only the hollow echo of their orderly footsteps.

As it was Formation 7's turn, Lacey found herself rising automatically, her movements syncing perfectly with the others as they headed towards the bathrooms. It felt like an unseen force controlled her every move. She could do nothing but watch as her body acted against her will.

Her bladder was bursting, yet what awaited her in the bathroom was a scene from a nightmare.

The air was thick with a foul stench from an overflowing toilet. The floor, a sickening mix of unidentified muck and fluids, assaulted all her senses.

Despite wanting to retreat, her body moved on its own.

Reluctantly, she sat on the filthy toilet. As she relieved herself, a disgusting splash hit her butt. Standing up, she approached the sink—a vision of neglect, coated in mold and grime. She had no choice but to wash herself there.

As the last groups of patients wrapped up their morning rituals, the announcement echoed again: "Breakfast is now served. Please be seated on your beds and await your meal."

Simultaneously, sixteen automatic doors in the sterile walls slid open. Like actors in a well-rehearsed play, sixteen electric food carts rolled in, weaving through the rows of beds to serve breakfast.

Lacey received a steaming bowl of instant noodles topped with two slices of luncheon meat and a perfect soft-boiled egg, accompanied by a typical Chinese milk tea. She would never have chosen noodles for breakfast, yet there she was, eating mechanically, driven by the unseen force.

While she ate, the man across from her suddenly shoved his meal aside and began gnawing on his own hand.

Each bite was a battle. His muscles tensed as his teeth struggled to tear through the tough sinew. This wasn't eating; it was a savage, primal struggle—a fight between raw hunger and indomitable will. The gruesome sound of teeth grinding against bone filled the air. His eyes, wide and wild, revealed a disturbing primal urge, pushing him beyond control.

She watched, horrified, as the gruesome scene unfolded inches away. An eerie echo of the pain resonated within her, as if the gnawing and tearing were happening to her own flesh. Yet under the unseen force's relentless grip, she found herself eating mechanically. Her actions, and those of others, were eerily subdued.

A team clad in white burst in, their uniforms reminiscent of the fictional character "Baymax." With swift precision, they restrained the man mid-self-harm and whisked him away.

Lacey came to a chilling realisation. Everything happening was terrifyingly real. Everyone, herself included, was being treated as if infected with HKEV. It felt as though an unseen force was controlling her actions and likely those of others, leaving only their minds free. It seemed the "demon" Shawn had warned her about actually existed.

Horrified, confused, and feeling helpless, she then heard the intercom system blare again. This time, the announcement was specifically for her: "Formation 7, Patient 732, Lacey Green, you are requested in the visitation room. A visitor awaits."

15

THE TORTURE

The visitation room felt more like a prison cell, separated by a sealed glass pane and equipped only with an intercom.

The sharply dressed visitor behind the glass oozed sophistication. His face, marked by genuine concern, lit up at the sight of Lacey. As he spoke, she recognised him, even though they had never met. "Lacey, I'm Jerry Jagger. We were cut off earlier, and I've been trying to track you down."

Lacey's heart raced—a glimmer of hope in her grim situation. Yet her expression remained eerily blank, as if the demon had paralysed her muscles.

"Thanks for coming, Jerry. So you know, they're treating us pretty well here," she said. As the words left her mouth, a horrible chill ran down her spine—they weren't her own. The demon was not only controlling her every move but also dictating her speech.

Jerry shot her a sharp look, conveying his skepticism. "Lacey," he began cautiously, "we're really worried about you. We've got a plan to get you both out safe."

She desperately wanted to yell, "I'm trapped here, can't control my body, and can't even control what I'm saying! I can't take this anymore! You've got to help me get out!"

But the demon had other plans.

"We all love it here. It feels safe," she said simply.

Jerry paused, searching her eyes for the truth. Lowering his voice, he said, "Keeping every U.S. citizen safe is our top priority. We've got what it takes. Level with me."

She spoke quickly, "My mom and I aren't planning to leave until we're confirmed negative for the virus."

Recognising the resolve in her eyes, Jerry sighed in resignation. "Okay, I'm really hoping for a quick recovery for both of you. I'll speak with your mother next."

"Good luck with that," she said coldly then turned and quickly left the room.

Hopeless, helpless, and terrified, Lacey watched herself act and speak, nothing more than a puppet of the demon's will.

As Lacey walked the pristine corridors, she spotted Michelle approaching in a sterile white gown like her own. They hadn't seen each other since quarantine began, making her think they had been kept in separate areas.

"How's it going, darling?" Michelle asked, her voice unmistakably hers, yet there was something about her tone that didn't sit right.

"Fine, you?" Lacey answered, feeling herself fade away.

"Not too bad, actually."

She was now convinced that Michelle was also under the demon's control and that her meeting with Jerry would be sabotaged as well.

That afternoon, the familiar announcement rang through the cabin, "Time for nucleic acid testing. Everyone, please stay at your assigned beds."

The cabin's sixteen automatic doors opened simultaneously, revealing electric trolleys equipped with automated arms. They moved smoothly from bed to bed, deftly managing cotton swabs, inserting them into patients' nostrils with precision, and securely sealing the swabs in sterile pouches.

Six hours later, the same voice called out to Lacey. "Formation 7, Patient 732, Lacey Green, please proceed to the examination department."

The unseen force guided her to the examination department, where a doctor in full protective gear awaited.

"Your nucleic acid test is still positive," the doctor informed her. "The vaccine takes time to work. You might not see any changes for a week. Any side effects today?"

She wanted to blurt out, "Vaccine? What are you talking about? When did I even get one?" Instead, she was compelled to respond, "So far, so good."

The doctor checked his watch and nodded. "Great, it's been twenty-four hours already. That probably means your body is accepting it fine."

Twenty-four hours? They jabbed me with that after the cops knocked me out?

Lacey's mind raced with unanswered questions but could only mutter, "Thanks." She left the room.

She clung to the hope that this was all a nightmare, one she'd wake up from any minute.

Reality hit harder. For two weeks, the demon kept her locked in that cabin, controlling her every move, every word. She didn't know what she might do or say next, turning into a stranger to herself. It was like the demon left her mind free on purpose, not to be kind, but to make her suffer more.

Then the doctor delivered good news, "Both you and your mother have tested negative. You're free to go." But she felt no relief, the grip remaining as tight as ever.

On the day of her release, the demon led her to the changing room, where she robotically changed back into her own clothes. Soon, she was mechanically filling out a standard questionnaire about her quarantine experience—freedom, rights, medical care quality, satisfaction. Her hand was guided to mark positive responses down the list.

Upon exiting the cabin, a breathtaking sight unfolded before her. A vast expanse peppered with enormous structures, each resembling a giant stadium, formed a daunting panorama of isolation units.

When she met Michelle at the exit of another large cabin, their greeting was overly warm and uncharacteristic. The embrace and conversation felt unnervingly distant and artificial. It was clear that Michelle too was still under the demon's control.

The golden Rolls-Royce slid to a stop next to them. Hugo stepped out, looking sharp and effortlessly cool. With a warm smile, he greeted them, "Great to see you both looking so good."

During the drive back to Celestial Manor, Hugo explained how he had avoided the HKEV by getting the VitalGuard Vaccine before the outbreak.

"It's foolproof for preventing infection if you haven't been exposed yet, and it gives a seventy percent chance of recovery if you're already infected. Looks like you two are were lucky."

Shawn's employer, GrandTech Group, had developed the VitalGuard Vaccine. Initially reserved for essential government staff, police, healthcare workers, high-risk individuals, and GrandTech employees, supplies were limited. However, upon learning that Lacey and Michelle were infected, Yip made an exception to ensure they each received a dose.

Cruising through downtown, Lacey spotted familiar street protesters who had encircled themselves with barricades, each marked with a number and name. Their signs declared, "Reject Isolation Cabins — Protect Hong Kong Human Rights."

A young protester caught her eye. She wanted to share a supportive glance, but her expression twisted into disdain instead. The hurt that flashed across his face was unmistakable and painful.

***

Everything in the penthouse was in tip-top shape and felt like home. Hugo probably had a hand in this.

"Ms. Yip's arranged a welcome banquet for you. I'll pick you up at 5 tomorrow," he said, waving goodbye.

The demon seemed to have a plan. It drove Michelle to the kitchen to make dinner and rooted Lacey to the sofa, her eyes glued to the evening news.

The broadcast provided updates on the HKEV outbreak before switching to highlights from GrandTech Group's latest press conference, where they unveiled the promising VitalGuard Vaccine.

CEO Yip appeared on screen, the epitome of youth and elegance. Her sophisticated demeanour stood out.

She delivered a passionate speech at the conference, "The board of directors at GrandTech Group has unanimously decided that our VitalGuard Vaccine will be freely distributed to all Hong Kong residents as soon as it's ready for mass release. This isn't about profit; it's about our city's well-being. We're committed to freeing every citizen from the clutches of HKEV and speeding up Hong Kong's recovery. As a company born and bred in Hong Kong, our fate is tied to this city. Our future plans are bold, aimed at pioneering technological advances that will further lift Hong Kong. We stand united in forging a brighter, more prosperous future!"

As Lacey watched, a seed of doubt sprouted in her mind. She had received the vaccine yet couldn't control her own body or words. Something didn't add up.

Suddenly, the sharp *bang* of a heavy door echoed from the rooftop. Driven by the demon, Lacey leapt from the sofa, her eyes shooting towards the spiralling staircase leading up.

The door's clamour persisted, echoing a disturbing *bang, bang, bang* rhythm.

Michelle burst from the kitchen into the living room, her gaze fixed on Lacey. It felt like two demons were silently communicating. Standing her ground, Michelle watched as the demon forced Lacey to ascend the stairs to the rooftop.

The sky garden, bathed in moonlight, had a ghostly glow. Ethereal flowers and plants cast mesmerising shadows. Under the demon's control, Lacey meticulously searched the area.

Out of nowhere, a cold touch of metal pressed against the back of her head. Instinctively, she knew it was a gun.

As the demon scrambled to react, the sharp click of the trigger shattered the silence. She felt a searing pain, like a star bursting in her skull, plunging her consciousness into a void of darkness.

16

AN OVERDUE DEBT

"Lacey! Can you hear me? Wake up!"

Jolted by Michelle's shout, Lacey snapped her eyes open. Soft, ambient light cast a glow on the stark white ceiling above. She quickly assessed her situation, strapped to a chilly metal bed, a stiff collar around her neck. Beside her, Michelle was also bound and immobilised on an identical bed.

"Where the fuck are we?" Lacey blurted out, her voice shattering the silence. She realised the demon's control had somehow slipped away.

"I have no idea!" Michelle yelled.

"Is that really you talking?" Lacey asked.

"Hell yes, it's me. Finally saying what I want!"

"You were under that thing's spell too?"

"Absolutely! Everyone in that cabin was, I think. I actually have some clues about it—"

"Let's talk about that later," Lacey interrupted. "We need to get out of here now. How much can you move?"

"Only my fingers. We can't break free, Lacey. We're stuck here."

Suddenly, they both heard footsteps approaching from outside the door.

"Shit." Lacey had a bad feeling.

Both held their breath, tense with anticipation. The footsteps halted nearby, followed by the sound of a door creaking open.

"Don't worry, darling," Michelle whispered. "I know how to handle this."

The footsteps approached then stopped just out of sight. "I'm sorting something out here," someone declared.

His voice, a deep baritone with a typical posh accent, filled the room, crisp and clear.

"Ah, you're from the UK? Me too! I used to live in Mayfair, London. How about you?" Michelle attempted to forge a connection, something she'd always been good at.

"We haven't got all day, I'm afraid. Let's focus on the matter at hand," Baritone replied, his calm unsettling.

"What matter?" Michelle's tone was relaxed. "Anyway, let's talk about it!"

Lacey kept quiet, realising the situation was more complicated than she had first thought.

"A simple one," Baritone said, fiddling with some metal objects. "An old debt to settle."

"What?" Michelle asked, confused. "Who are you? Do I owe you?"

"Nah, you're good," Baritone replied bluntly.

Michelle turned to Lacey. "Do you owe someone?"

"Shut up," Lacey whispered back.

"Quiet, ladies," Baritone commanded.

The sound of metallic clinks intensified, echoing ominously, hinting at a sinister collection of various tools.

17

SHAWN'S SECRET

"Look, you don't have to do this," Lacey said, her voice calm but edged with fear. "There's a fat chunk of change in my account. Let me go, and it's all yours."

Mia always told her, "You know what the most lethal weapon is? Money. It can solve everything, screw everyone over. When you've got nothing else, use it. If you don't have it, bluff."

But this didn't seem to sway Baritone as he replied, "Nah, it's not about the money." Without a pause, he blindfolded Lacey and silenced her with tape. Michelle received the same treatment.

"I have no intention of harming you," Baritone stated with the cold comfort of a predator to its prey before the end. "After I settle this one with Shawn, we'll be even."

That startled Lacey. *Is this about Dad?*

"By midnight, you'll be in a black Toyota Alphard about twenty minutes from the Hong Kong airport. You'll find car keys, passports, wallets, and two phones in the front console. Those phones have your flight details to New York, leaving at 2 a.m. Don't mess this up like last time," Baritone instructed, his voice unsettlingly calm.

The last time?

Memories of her time in Hong Kong flashed through Lacey's mind.

Is he the one who left the envelope with the number for Shawn's final warning?

As the familiar touch of cold metal pressed against the top of Lacey's head, she fell into darkness once again.

***

"Are you alright, darling?" Michelle's voice pulled Lacey back.

Blinking awake, she mumbled, "Where are we?"

"Maybe, like he said, about twenty minutes from the airport?"

As Lacey regained her bearings, she noticed they were in a black Toyota Alphard, eerily silent and isolated. Free to move, she quickly rummaged through the console compartment and found car keys, passports, wallets, and two phones.

She turned on one of the phones, navigated to the email app, and found the booking confirmation for two one-way tickets to New York, departing at 2 a.m. The tickets were stored in the digital wallet, ready to scan at the airport.

"Looks like that young chap wasn't lying. Let's head to the airport," Michelle said, sliding into the driver's seat and setting the GPS for Hong Kong International.

"How'd you know he's young? Did you see his face?"

"Not at all. But when he blindfolded me, his fingers brushed mine. They felt youthful. Trust me, I'm rather good at guessing ages from a touch. Fancy a brief explanation?"

Lacey said sharply, "Not now."

"Right, let's get out of here first. Perhaps later I can tell you about the art of telling men's ages by their hands. You'll find it fascinating, I assure you. It's quite the skill to have, especially in your dating life, darling."

"Can you shut up?"

"I'm shutting up now." But during the drive to the airport, Michelle's chatter was incessant. "I do wonder what sort of connection that chap might have had with Shawn, who wasn't gay. Of that I was quite sure..." Her confidence faltered. "Who knows, maybe he was bisexual?"

Lacey barely listened, already planning her next move.

Upon reaching the airport, they checked in and lined up for customs. Then she said, "I need to pee. You go ahead."

"Okay, hurry," Michelle replied, moving forward in line.

Instead of heading to the restroom, Lacey made a beeline for the parking lot.

Her time in Hong Kong had only deepened the mystery of Shawn's death. Determined to uncover the truth, she knew she first needed to shake off her excess baggage.

As Lacey started the car, the passenger door swung open, and the excess baggage climbed in.

Frustration mounting, Lacey shouted, "Why did you come back?"

"Why did you?" Michelle replied calmly.

"Get back and board the plane!"

"I will if you will."

"For fuck's sake, can you leave me alone?"

"I can't, darling. You're my only daughter, my only family. I have to protect you."

"Bullshit! You're staying for Shawn's inheritance, aren't you? Admit it!"

"Exactly! For Shawn and our priceless inheritance," Michelle said, her eyes sparkling with a mix of mischief and sincerity.

"Get real! You don't have a real claim on his inheritance."

"But Shawn fathered you," Michelle countered, her tone still cheerful.

"You divorced him! You're not entitled to anything now."

"True. But I've secured the most priceless inheritance. And that's you, darling."

Lacey burst out laughing. "That's the most ridiculous thing I've ever heard!"

"I can protect you. I understand more than you think," Michelle insisted earnestly.

"Okay, I'm getting out."

Lacey thrust the door open and strode into the night.

Michelle called after her, "Everything we've been through, it all comes back to Shawn's secret!" Her words echoed behind Lacey's swiftly retreating form.

Unfazed, Lacey blended into the shadows, determined, until Michelle's voice pierced the silence again. "We have chat logs, loads of them! I bet you're dying to take a peek!"

Lacey stopped in her tracks.

"Fuck!" she muttered.

18

THE FERRIS WHEEL

A muscular man forcefully pushed a naked woman from behind, driving her towards the office's towering floor-to-ceiling window.

He pressed her bare body against the cool, smooth glass, and started raping her from behind.

She surrendered completely, bathed in the night's twinkling city lights.

Amid helpless howls and uncontrollable moans, she slowly turned her head to gaze into the ominous darkness behind her.

"Cut!" The director's frustration echoed across the set. "I don't want to see your damn face! Got it?"

Defiant, she faced him and the crew in her state of undress, her tone calm but firm, "Who am I?"

"What?" the director snapped, rising from his chair.

A tense silence fell, the crew taken aback by the young actress's audacity in challenging the director.

With a steady tone, she said, "I'm the 'baby-faced' secretary, the first victim of the villain, right? Showing a bit of her face, her innocence, would really deepen the tragedy, wouldn't it? It's more than sex appeal."

This marked Michelle's first speaking role in a feature film, an American erotic thriller set against the backdrop of British-era Hong Kong. She was determined to leave a lasting impression.

As the director was about to erupt, the producer stepped in, whispering something that immediately calmed him down.

"Fine, let's try something new: the Ferris wheel outside. Look at it, and we'll capture your baby face in the reflection," the director conceded.

Michelle ended up gazing intensely at that beautiful Ferris wheel for a gruelling seven hours.

Her hard work paid off: $5,000 cash, her name in the credits, and a lavish week at a top-tier Hong Kong hotel with a daily spending allowance.

Eager to make the most of her week, she started at the Central Ferris wheel—the very spot that had given her the first opportunity to shine in mainstream cinema.

As she stepped into what she thought was her cabin, she found a young man already there.

"Sorry, wrong cabin," she said, turning to leave.

Before she could exit, he spoke up with a distinct British accent. "You from the UK?"

She paused and met his gaze. "Coventry. You?"

"Auckland, New Zealand."

"Beautiful city," she said, deciding to stay. "Michelle Weaver. And you?"

"Shawn," he said, shifting aside to make room for her.

"Shawn what?"

"Shawn Green."

During the ride, she learned he was born in Birmingham but moved to New Zealand at five. He grew up in Auckland, studied in San Francisco, and now worked in Hong Kong. He found out she was a British actress in New York, though still a nobody, dreaming of winning an Oscar someday.

That night, Michelle found sleep elusive. Every time she closed her eyes, she saw Shawn—unexplainably attractive and stubbornly present in her thoughts. The next evening, she felt an irresistible pull back to the Central Ferris wheel, hoping against hope to see him there again.

And, as if by fate, there he was, as though waiting for her.

Without a word, they sat together, united by an unspoken pact.

As their cabin hit the top of the wheel, they embraced. His kiss was deep, his hands exploring tenderly. Caught up in the moment, she whispered, "What's next?"

"Another spin," he murmured, his voice gentle yet exciting.

Enveloped by the night and swayed by the rhythmic motion of the Ferris wheel, they gave in to their passion.

"You two were in that cabin?" Lacey sounded utterly incredulous.

"It was really late, only the two of us," Michelle responded with a hint of innocence.

"Jesus, I can't believe it..."

Michelle vividly remembered how, with each descent of the Ferris wheel, they'd adjust their clothes, chat casually, and tell the staff they wanted another round. At the apex, they gave in to their desires and made love. Before reaching the ground, they composed themselves, resumed their conversation, and asked for another ride.

"Honestly, it was the most thrilling one-night stand I've ever had," Michelle reminisced, her eyes sparkling with the memory.

"Can we move on?" Lacey interjected, visibly uncomfortable.

"It's where your story truly began."

"What?"

Once back in New York, Michelle realised she was two weeks late. A pregnancy test confirmed her suspicion—she was expecting. Shawn was the only man she'd been with recently. Everything traced back to that night on the Ferris wheel.

Without panicking, she calmly called him to inform him of her decision to have an abortion.

Two days later, the doorbell rang early in the morning, briefly lifting her spirits—maybe it was Shawn. But when she opened the door, she found her landlady, a middle-aged Chinese woman with limited English and a kind demeanour, reminding her of the overdue rent. She had one week to pay up or face eviction.

After Michelle paid the rent and bills, she only had $89.40 left. With winter coming, even buying a warm jacket was out of the question.

As she frantically applied to numerous casting calls online, a sudden knock at the door jolted her.

Expecting her landlord, she braced herself and blurted out, "I sent the rent over to you!"

Her words hung in the air as she opened the door.

Before her stood a disheveled Shawn, a hefty travel bag slung over his shoulder.

"Sorry I didn't show up sooner," he admitted, regret flickering in his eyes.

Silent and steadfast, she didn't budge to welcome him inside.

He set his bag down, took a deep breath, then knelt on one knee. He carefully pulled a modest diamond ring from his pocket, offering it to her.

"Michelle, I love you. Will you marry me?" His gaze lingered on hers, seeking an answer.

She couldn't help but laugh.

"0.3 carats?"

"0.5," he corrected.

With a smirk and a thoughtful look at the ring, she suggested, "How about this? I sell it and get the cash. If you're cool with that, come on in. If not, there's the door."

That night, they had sex seven times.

After the last and most intense round, he settled down, exhausted, and whispered, "Think about keeping the baby, yeah?"

"Look, the whole mom thing isn't me. I'm gonna win that Oscar and make a killing. Honestly, Hong Kong's not my scene."

"Keep doing what you're doing here. I'll cover both of you—rent, everything."

"Really?"

"I've run the numbers. We can swing it," he said confidently.

"How much do you make?" she probed.

"Not much. A little side hustle I'm cooking up—could hit big though."

"Drug running?" she quipped, eyebrows raised.

He chuckled lightly. "Even riskier. Bigger payoff."

19

THE GRAND PUPPET MASTER

Shawn showed Michelle a clip where he controlled a small white mouse through typed commands.

"Type command: Eat." The mouse immediately started nibbling on its food.

"Type command: Stop." It stopped eating instantly.

"Type command: Squeak." Right on cue, it squeaked.

"Type command: Louder." The squeaks intensified.

"Type command: Run east for two meters then walk west for one meter." It executed the complex directions flawlessly.

"Type command: Tap the wall with your head, but don't knock yourself out." It gently tapped the wall, careful not to harm itself.

"Type command: Now, knock yourself out." It slammed head-first into the wall and instantly lost consciousness.

It wasn't a high-tech toy; it was a real, live mouse. Shawn had embedded a tiny chip in its brain, called a puppet chip. Barely the size of a grain of rice, this gadget was a souped-up version of the ID microchips used in pets. It worked like a remote puppeteer, responding to Shawn's wireless commands to manipulate the mouse's movements and sounds.

Shawn's ambitions went far beyond animal experiments. He aimed to use this technology on humans—those with severe mental disorders, the violent, or potential threats. His goal was to create a powerful art-ificial general intelligence to keep them in check. He called it the Grand Puppet Master, or GPM for short.

GPM was designed to manage vast amounts of data and control neural interfaces with precision. Built on advanced neural networks and powered by quantum computing, GPM's decentralised architecture would let it manipulate millions of puppet chips without any latency issues. It could manage thousands of patients implanted with puppet chips simultaneously, orchestrating their actions and speech to make them behave like typical, everyday people.

"It's not only about keeping those mental health patients in check. It could also cut down on gun incidents and terror attacks, you know?" Shawn said to Michelle, his eyes lighting up. "If this thing takes off, I'll be rolling in dough."

"Blimey, that's wild!" Michelle replied, her eyes wide.

"But snagging someone for the trials is the tough part."

She chuckled, "Hey, I'm game if the money's good."

"It's risky. I'm not dragging anyone I care about into this." He turned serious and sighed. "It might be a pipe dream."

"Why not pitch it to the big shots? Maybe you won't hit the jackpot, but you'd still rake in a tidy sum."

"I can't sell it. It's like my baby, you know? If I can't pull it off myself, I'd rather bury it." He fixed her with a meaningful look. "Do me a solid and keep this under wraps, yeah?"

Michelle had kept Shawn's secret under wraps, a detail she hadn't spilled to anyone, not even to Lacey until now. It wasn't out of loyalty. She couldn't care less about tech stuff. In fact, she'd completely forgotten about it until their ordeal in quarantine jogged her memory.

"I swear, it's the spitting image of Shawn's GPM thing," Michelle said flatly.

Lacey eyed her skeptically, as if trying to suss out if she was being spun a yarn.

"I'm not pulling your leg. Think about it. What if Shawn actually pulled it off? Explains his fancy penthouse and the Aston Martin, doesn't it? And now, what if the Hong Kong government's using it to handle those HKEV cases? It'd be a clever way to cut staffing costs and take some pressure off healthcare, right?"

Lacey had to admit The Colossal Twat might actually be onto something this time.

"And he's got every reason for it. The Greens have always battled with depression. Didn't your gran suffer from it?" Michelle pressed.

"What? What the hell are you on about?"

"Shawn never let on to you, did he? Bloody hell! He's been keeping heaps from you!"

Shawn had always told Lacey his grandmother died of cancer when he was young. But Michelle let the cat out of the bag. At eight, Shawn discovered his mother lifeless in the bathroom, succumbing to her long battle with severe depression. That trauma rocked him to his core, driving him to study data science and artificial intelligence in San Francisco. He had concluded that traditional psychology wasn't enough for mental illness. He believed that only rigorous science could tackle mental health issues. That was why he conceived "The Grand Puppet Master."

"That's all he told me, I swear," Michelle said.

Lacey stayed silent.

Michelle locked eyes with Lacey, took a deep breath, and said, "We know why he became depressed five years ago, right?"

"No," Lacey said, getting uneasy and irritated.

"We should've had this talk sooner. We can't ignore that it happened."

"I mean it. Don't go there," Lacey warned, her voice trembling yet firm, knowing exactly where Michelle was heading.

"Look, darling, you can't ignore the elephant in the room. Shawn took his own life, and we all know the reason."

"Don't..."

"It's all about Oliver," Michelle continued, her tone even but resolute.

The name hit Lacey like a bolt from the blue, shattering her defences and exposing the secrets she'd buried deep within.

20

OLIVER

Lacey celebrated her seventeenth birthday alone, munching on left-over pizza and washing it down with two cold beers.

As she picked at the stale crust, her phone buzzed. "The Colossal Twat" flashed on the screen.

This was no birthday greeting but a reminder from Michelle that she'd be back from Tokyo tomorrow. "Slip the keys under the flowerpot by the front door before you head out," she instructed then added, almost as an afterthought, "I'm three months late. Explains the nausea, doesn't it?"

At first, Lacey thought the baby might belong to another man. After all, Shawn and Michelle had been separated for ages, even if they were still technically married. Plus, Michelle's flings weren't exactly top secret. But then, during a late-night chat, Shawn dropped a bombshell. He had made a quick trip to see Michelle on set in Tokyo, and that was when Oliver James Green — the name he'd already picked for Lacey's unborn brother — was conceived.

The thought of a new sibling brought Lacey a mix of excitement and a possible cure for her loneliness. Yet, it also triggered some anxiety. Who would look after the little one?

"I'm not signing on to be his babysitter!" Lacey declared to Michelle, who waved her off,

"Whatever, darling."

But the minute Lacey first set eyes on Oliver—the adorable, delicate little boy—she couldn't help but be drawn into babysitting him.

Oliver had Shawn's brains and Michelle's good looks, but what really struck Lacey was his natural empathy.

She remembered a time when he saw her crying and asked with that innocent look, "Why are you crying?"

"Someone betrayed me," she had told him, thinking the words were too complex for a three-year-old to understand.

"Hey, don't be sad. I'm here for you forever. And we could get married if you like!" Oliver offered then gave her a wide, goofy grin that made her burst out laughing.

Oliver wasn't all talk.

During a stroll near their home, they ran into a menacing dog. Before Lacey could blink, the four-year-old bravely stepped in front of her, brandishing a stick and letting out what he thought was a fierce roar. Amazingly, the dog paused, turned tail, and walked away.

What else but pure love could drive a four-year-old to defend someone so fearlessly?

On New York's coldest winter night, a cherished memory played out. As Lacey tucked Oliver into bed, she mentioned offhandedly, "You know what would be perfect right now? A hot water bottle." The next morning, she woke up to find a warm little body snuggled against her.

"Who's there?" she teased.

"A hot water bottle," his voice muffled beneath the blankets.

That moment was pure warmth and love.

She once thought he'd always be by her side, forever.

But fate always had its twists for her, like something out of a thriller.

When Oliver turned five, Michelle started divorce proceedings against Shawn. Given the shallowness of their marriage, it was expected. Yet Lacey struggled to accept Michelle's demand for Shawn to get custody of Oliver.

"I can't look after him. It's better this way," Michelle stated firmly.

"He's only five! You can't ship him off to Hong Kong. He doesn't even speak a word of Chinese!" Lacey argued, her voice edged with desperation.

"Kids pick up new languages fast. He'll probably end up speaking Chinese better than you."

"Shawn's barely getting by! Are you sure he can take care of Oliver?"

"Can you?"

Lacey was speechless. She had kicked off her TikTok career and was nowhere near making ends meet. To scrape by, she took on low-paying, high-risk PI gigs. She didn't have the time or money to spare for Oliver's care.

Before sending Oliver off to Hong Kong, Lacey took him for one last visit to Central Park. They always made a point to grab cotton candy from their favourite Mexican vendor and play a game they dubbed "Candy Race."

They sat on a bench, facing each other, with the huge cotton candy between them.

"Ready?" asked Lacey.

"Come on!" Oliver sounded super excited.

They started eating the cotton candy from opposite ends as fast as they could. By the time they were done, their faces were comically smeared with sugar. Watching the innocent, happy Oliver, Lacey had to use all her strength to hold back her tears.

At the airport, in their bittersweet goodbye, Lacey tried to soften the blow by spinning a tale about aliens vacationing in Hong Kong, promising him an adventure to meet these otherworldly beings. Oliver, ever the fan of alien stories, was buzzing with excitement about the trip. This turned their farewell into a moment of excitement rather than sadness.

"Once I finish up here, I'll fly to Hong Kong to be with you, okay?" she reassured him.

"You promise?" he asked.

"Cross my heart," she whispered, her voice shaking as she fought back tears.

Six months later, Lacey had wrapped up a chilling serial murder case, marking a grim milestone in her career. With her long-awaited trip to Hong Kong around the corner, an abrupt news alert on her phone broke the silence: a catastrophic traffic accident in Hong Kong, where a truck had slammed into a school bus, flipping it and setting it ablaze. Three children were reported dead, nineteen others injured.

Tragedies like this had become all too common, and initially she only gave it a brief thought. But then a call from Shawn pierced the ordinary, delivering heart-wrenching news. Oliver had been on that bus, one of the young lives tragically cut short.

After Oliver's death, Lacey plummeted into the darkest period of her life.

Wracked with guilt, she tortured herself with thoughts that if she hadn't let him go to Hong Kong that things might have been different. The next six months blurred into a continuous stream of sorrow, punctuated only by therapy sessions as she struggled to claw her way out of the darkness.

Eventually, she found a way to cope. She turned a blind eye, keeping her distance from children and anything related to them. Surprisingly, this strategy worked quite well for her.

However, one problem lingered: the nightmare about the school bus. It lurked in the back of her mind, rearing its ugly head during periods of intense stress, anxiety, or shock to haunt her dreams. Despite consulting numerous psychologists and trying various therapies, no relief came. Her only comfort was in stress relief pills.

***

"Shawn's been dealing with depression since that incident five years ago," Michelle broke Lacey's silence, dropping another bombshell. "I've got chat logs to prove it."

Lacey had always figured Shawn and Michelle barely spoke, but the extensive chat logs from the past decade painted a different picture.

"He didn't want you to know about it. Feared it might burden you," Michelle explained, scrolling through their chats to a point five years back.

Shawn: "Got the confirmation – it's depression. The doc's set up a treatment plan."

Michelle: "Best to stick with the doc's plan, right?"

Shawn: "Promise you won't tell Lacey about this."

Michelle: "No worries, we hardly ever chat."

Shawn: "I'm sure I'll beat this."

Michelle: "Definitely, you'll be fine."

Lacey was shocked, realising Shawn had kept more from her than she'd ever imagined.

As she pored over the chat logs, she caught Michelle's gaze. Their eyes locked, and a silent understanding passed between them.

She sensed Michelle had more to spill.

"Go on," she pressed.

"Darling, I think it's high time you knew the whole story," Michelle began, pausing as she gathered her thoughts. "Truth is, I'm the one to blame. The divorce, sending Oliver to Hong Kong, it was all part of a deal."

A deal?

21

CASE CLOSED

Twenty-five years ago, Shawn started at GrandTec Group as a junior technician. That year, he attended the company's annual gala, a lavish event on a luxury cruise ship where employees were encouraged to bring their families. Michelle came along, bringing two-year-old Lacey with her.

The gala buzzed with excitement. Yip, the young CEO of GrandTec Group, came over to Shawn's table. With a friendly smile, she warmly greeted Michelle, who had traveled from New York, and the toddler Lacey. The young Asian tycoon's blend of youthful elegance and commanding presence made a lasting impression on Michelle.

Their next meeting took place twenty-two years later in New York when Yip unexpectedly called Michelle, inviting her for afternoon tea at the Mark Hotel's presidential suite to discuss something important. Michelle was eager to meet Yip and never missed a chance to rub shoulders with the wealthy.

In her presidential suite, Yip openly admitted to a two-year affair with Shawn. Michelle was floored—how had her average Joe husband, neither rich nor a ladies' man, snagged such a high-profile figure?

Far from apologetic, the billionaire stated calmly to Michelle, "I've got a proposition for you."

"I'm all ears," Michelle responded, sensing money in the conversation.

Without hesitation, Yip laid out her terms. "You'll start the divorce proceedings within two months. I'm offering a thirty-percent down payment as compensation, with the balance to be paid five days after the divorce is finalised."

Michelle was ready to haggle, but Yip named her price. "Five million dollars."

The figure stunned Michelle, yet she was quick to push for more.

"You know, I'm in filmmaking, always juggling projects. Time's literally money for me, and a divorce... Well, it's too much of a hassle."

Yip snapped, "Let's cut to the chase. How much do you want?"

Without missing a beat, Michelle countered, "Fifteen million dollars."

"Done," Yip agreed, not missing a beat.

Michelle realised she'd aimed too low.

Yip continued, "Fifteen million hits your account in three days. Finalise the divorce within two months, and the remaining thirty-five million is yours."

Michelle was visibly shaken. It was only a deposit? She instantly regretted not asking for more.

Yip had one more condition. "Oliver's custody needs to go to Shawn. He's missed too much of his daughter's life and won't let that happen with Oliver. He's adamant about bringing him to Hong Kong, believing it's for the best." She fixed Michelle with a steady gaze. "And from what I gather, Oliver could benefit from a change in care."

***

"You sold Oliver!" Lacey burst out, her eyes a mix of fury and disbelief.

"That's not how it was. Neither of us could give Oliver what he truly needed. Yip promised to handle his education and give him a better life. It looked like a win-win for everyone. I've been meaning to tell you but never found the right moment."

Tears streamed down Lacey's cheeks, overwhelmed by a storm of helplessness, anger, and sorrow. Michelle had a point—they couldn't give Oliver what he needed. Sending him to Hong Kong to live with Shawn and his wealthy partner wasn't a compromise; it was a shot at a better future for him. Besides, every phone call with Oliver showed he was happy living there.

"Listen, none of this was your fault or Shawn's. If anyone's to blame, it's me," Michelle said, her voice heavy with guilt.

This was the first time Lacey had ever heard Michelle admit something so directly.

"Shawn really loved Oliver. He never got over not being able to protect him. That's what triggered his depression. He was in therapy for five years, but he kept sinking deeper."

Michelle scrolled through more chats for Lacey to see.

Shawn: "Every day pulls me deeper into despair. Feels like hope is a mirage now."

Shawn: "Haven't slept a wink in over one hundred hours. Every time I close my eyes, I see Oliver."

Shawn: "Lacey haunts me the most. She loves and trusts me, and I've let her down."

On the eve of Shawn's death, his final message to Michelle was telling.

Shawn: "I've made up my mind. It's my only shot to set things right. Keep Lacey out of Hong Kong—this place is too dangerous."

Michelle cleared her throat. "I'm pretty sure he was behind it, you know. He was adamant we should stay away from Hong Kong and definitely knew something was off. Like they tried covering up Covid in Wuhan, right? Bet it's the same story here."

Lacey struggled to argue against Michelle's reasoning.

She remembered the video from that Hong Kong dim sum joint—a woman biting herself, a dead giveaway of the HKEV outbreak. It was like the early Covid-19 cover-ups in China, with Hong Kong's government following the same playbook, sweeping things under the rug instead of protecting public health. The fact that GrandTec Group rolled out the VitalGuard vaccine so quickly made it clear they had a heads-up about the virus. Shawn's persistent advice to steer clear of Hong Kong made sense. He knew what was coming.

The puzzle pieces were finally falling into place.

"You should've shown me these chats earlier," Lacey said.

"I didn't want to bring it up. I know it took a lot for you to get past that nightmare. I didn't want to drag it all back up."

Lacey shot Michelle a look that was a mix of anger, contempt, sadness, helplessness, and despair.

For the first time, Michelle allowed tears to stream down her face in front of Lacey. "I know I'm to blame. I've been a terrible mum, a neglectful wife. Thought success and money would fix everything, make life great. But it's all been a facade. Like Joyce Meyer says, 'You can't wait for life to be perfect to enjoy it.' When that fifty million from Yip hit my account, ambition blinded me. Dropped my indie projects for *Cleopatra*, blew money on rights, effects, design. Didn't see the costs piling up. Before I knew it, the money was gone, and I was left with a half-baked script and some 3D models. No one would touch such a gamble... And in the mess, I lost Oliver, lost Shawn. I ruined everything."

A wave of pity washed over Lacey. This was her mother, her only family, after all.

"I didn't come here for Shawn's inheritance—I didn't even know about it. I came for you. Shawn warned me about the dangers. I couldn't stop you, so I had to keep you safe. I've nearly lost everything, Lacey. I can't stand the thought of losing you too."

Lacey believed Michelle was telling the truth.

"Wherever you end up, whatever path you take, I won't get in the way. But let me be there with you," Michelle pleaded.

After a moment of silence, Lacey said, "Let's go."

"Go where?"

"Boarding gate. Back to New York. Case closed then." She really meant it now.

Michelle's eyes sparkled. "Really? Are you serious?"

"I don't joke around at times like this."

A smile spread across Michelle's tear-stained face. "Right, no time to waste. Let's catch that flight!"

As they got ready to leave, Lacey's phone rang.

"Don't pick it up," Michelle suggested.

Lacey paused then decided to answer. It might be something critical.

Baritone's voice came through, sharp, "Why the hell did you go back to the car park?"

"We're about to head back to the gate... Wait, how do you know where we are?"

"Start the car—now!"

"What's going on?"

"They're after you. Run, now!"

The line went dead. Lacey and Michelle exchanged a quick, alarmed look. Almost immediately, two black SUVs barrelled into the lot, their headlights slicing through the dark. As their windows rolled down, a hail of bullets flew.

With a quick move, Michelle shoved Lacey down into the seat, covering her. Glass exploded around them as bullets peppered the car.

Seizing a brief pause, Lacey leapt into action. She fired up the engine and floored it. As the gunfire picked up again, she gunned the black Alphard towards the exit, pushing it to its limits.

22

MOM

Fighting for survival, Lacey turned the tame black Toyota Alphard into a raging beast, tearing through the airport roundabouts and onto the highway. Yet she made a critical error—she veered into oncoming traffic, causing vehicles to scatter.

"Fuck!" she screamed, gripping the steering wheel tightly as she zigzagged between oncoming cars. Headlights flashed past, casting ghostly shadows inside the Alphard. A massive container truck, taken by surprise, swerved to dodge her. It tipped over with a gut-wrenching groan, its metal body grinding against the asphalt. Sparks flew, igniting a trail of fuel that exploded into a towering inferno.

Flames lit up the night, forming a wall of fire that engulfed the highway and stopped the pursuing SUVs in their tracks.

Seizing the moment, Lacey slammed on the accelerator. The engine roared as she sped away from the blazing turmoil, her heart pounding with adrenaline.

"Navigate!" Lacey shouted at Michelle.

"Where to?"

"Nearest police station!"

Michelle froze, unable to respond.

With no time to waste, Lacey took an exit off the highway. The path ahead plunged into darkness, devoid of streetlights, but she didn't let up, pushing the car as fast as it would go.

"Dial 999!" Lacey barked, urgency slicing through her voice.

Silence.

"What's wrong with you?" Frustration tinged Lacey's tone as she pounded on the steering wheel. "Phone. Now!"

Still no answer.

Realising she couldn't rely on her useless mother, Lacey frantically rifled through the console and grabbed her phone. Then something ahead made her heart sink.

"Shit! No, no, no!"

Ahead, a vast expanse of water loomed, the road ending abruptly at an unfinished bridge.

She slammed on the brakes. Propelled by momentum, the car skidded forward, halting with a shudder at the edge of the abyss.

Terrified, she contemplated reversing, while Michelle slumped over the console.

"Hey!"

Trying to lift Michelle, she felt an unexpected weight. The dim moonlight exposed blood on her back.

"Oh God, no!"

With all her might, Lacey hoisted Michelle, revealing multiple gunshot wounds. Blood oozed from the injuries in her chest and back, her body chilling rapidly. Under the moon's glow, her face took on a ghostly pallor, stark against the night around them.

A flashback hit Lacey. As gunshots rang out, Michelle had shoved her down into the seat, covering her.

"No, no!" she screamed, pulling Michelle close, attempting to ward off the cold with her own warmth.

"Stay with me!" she pleaded, gently slapping Michelle's cheek to keep her alert.

"Mom!" The word burst from her after years of disuse, laden with desperation.

Michelle's eyelids fluttered weakly, a faint sign of life. She seemed too weak to speak.

"You're with me," Lacey whispered, her voice trembling. "Stay awake, Mom. I'm right here."

As she scrambled to administer first aid, Michelle weakly grasped her hand.

"You know my email, right? My iCloud password is your birthday."

She hadn't expected Michelle to remember her birthday.

"Let's get to the hospital!" Lacey's eyes widened with fear as she saw the blood keep flowing.

"You'll find bank details in my iCloud... I've saved money for you every birthday. It's not a fortune, but it's yours..."

Lacey fought to stem the bleeding, to no avail.

Tears mixed with blood on Michelle's face as she tenderly touched Lacey's cheek, leaving a kiss she couldn't recall ever receiving before.

"Don't waste time, darling. I'm not going to make it. Go back to New York, marry, have kids... Be a better mother than I was."

"You're gonna make it! We'll go back together!" Lacey's efforts to stop the blood seemed futile.

"Stop messing with this. Life's your own script, isn't it? So why make it a thriller? Go for comedy, romance, even porn...whatever makes you happy."

Michelle coughed, blood spilling from her lips.

"No, no, no…" Lacey sobbed.

Michelle gave out a weak smile, her eyes filled with love and regret as her grip loosened, her hand slipping lifelessly from Lacey's grasp. Her face went slack, her final breath escaping in a whisper that hung in the air, lost to the night.

Refusing to give up, Lacey began CPR. Her hands, trembling but resolute, pumped Michelle's chest, each compression fuelled by a cocktail of hope and desperation.

"Come on, Mom, stay with me!" she pleaded between compressions. The night air echoed with the rhythm of her efforts. "Don't you quit on me now!"

Each push was a prayer, each breath she gave Michelle a plea for life. But Michelle's responses grew fainter, her body unyielding under the pale moonlight.

"Please, Mom…come back!" Tears streamed down Lacey's cheeks as she fought against the inevitable.

"I'm not fucking ready to let you go!" she yelled desperately, her efforts intensifying. The silence only grew thicker, heavier, swallowing every shard of her crumbling hope.

Michelle didn't come back. The cold crept into Lacey's bones as she clung to Michelle, trying to warm a heart that had stopped beating. A gust of wind blew through the shattered car window, sweeping her cries into the night. She held her mom tightly, her heart shattering.

She had lost her only family. Now she was utterly alone.

Suddenly, blinding headlights cut through the darkness, accompanied by the ominous growl of engines. Glancing back, Lacey saw the black SUVs closing in.

A fierce thirst for vengeance ignited within her.

She feigned death, lying still atop Michelle's motionless body, waiting for the attackers to draw near, determined to take at least one of them down with her.

As footsteps neared, her heart pounded so loudly she feared it might give her away. Out of nowhere, gunshots shattered the quiet. None hit her black Alphard. Confusion and fear swelled inside her, yet she dared not move.

A tense silence followed.

Unable to stand the suspense, she cautiously lifted her head and saw the SUVs parked silently, their headlights still cutting through the darkness. No one was in sight.

Bewildered, she gingerly opened the car door and stepped into the eerie stillness outside. The scene before her was both shocking and terrifying. Men in black suits were scattered across the ground, their bodies riddled with bullets, resembling honeycombs.

As she felt the cold, familiar touch of metal against the back of her head, darkness swiftly engulfed her world once again.

23

⸺ ◦ ⸺

CASE OPENED

As Lacey regained consciousness, a wave of vertigo hit her. She couldn't see anything. A thick cloth was tied over her eyes. Her hands were tightly bound behind her back, and her ankles were tied up, preventing her from sitting up. She felt a gentle sway and smelled saltwater and despair, with a sharp tang of timber.

A ship's hold?

"Is anyone there? Help!"

She shuffled back and forth, searching for a wall or anything to hoist herself up.

"Don't bother. It won't help you," a familiar voice pierced the quiet.

Baritone!

"What do you want from me?" Lacey asked.

"That's my line," Baritone said, resignation in his voice. "If you'd followed my lead, your mum wouldn't have ended up that way."

His accusation struck a chord, embedding a painful truth. She couldn't deny her part in Michelle's demise.

"Now, tell me. Why are you still in Hong Kong? What's your endgame?" he demanded.

"Who are you?" she snapped back.

"Answer my question."

"I was ready to leave, but now...I've changed my mind."

"And?"

"Who's after us, and who killed my mother?"

After a tense silence, he replied, "What will you do if you find out?"

"I'll make whoever did that pay!"

He paused. She thought he might reveal more, but he finally said, "The less you know, the safer you are."

He silenced her with tape.

"This cargo ship is headed for Osaka Port in Japan, leaving in four hours. I need to sedate you so you'll wake up in about five hours, well on your way at sea. Captain Tony Lee will look after you. Once in Osaka, you can make your way back to New York."

She tried to speak, but only muffled sounds came out.

"Farewell, Lacey."

A cool numbness spread across her neck, quickly swallowing her into darkness.

***

She found herself back on the school bus, now hurtling across a bridge over a churning sea, its waves thrashing violently, as if stirred by demons.

Ahead, past the silent kids, a couple sat side by side.

She recognised them just by seeing their backs.

"Mom! Dad!" Tears welled up uncontrollably.

They didn't turn around.

The bus somehow sped up, its engine roaring, barreling towards an oncoming semi-truck as if on a mission. The impact sent it tumbling, flames igniting instantly, then erupting into an explosion. As she flew through the air, she caught a glimpse of Shawn and Michelle, blood-ied, plummeting into the turbulent waters below, swallowed by monstrous waves.

She crashed onto the bridge. In her final moments, she saw a reflection in the metal guardrails: a shattered, blood-drenched boy—Oliver.

As the haunting echo of the cargo ship's horn reverberated through the dimly lit hold, the effects of the anaesthetic began to wane. Lacey emerged from her recurring nightmare, unbound yet still trapped within the dark, cavernous hold of what seemed to be a bulk carrier. She rose and groped through the darkness, finally finding a rusty hatch on top. She pushed it open, momentarily blinded by sunlight. She climbed up to the deck of a large cargo ship. The vast sea's waves were both menacing and mesmerising. The distant silhouette of the port suggested they hadn't strayed far from shore.

As Baritone had told her, the ship was supposed to leave the port an hour before she woke up. But it now seemed to have only just departed, suggesting either a delay or the anaesthetic wearing off sooner than expected. Regardless, she still had a chance to go back.

It wasn't time for her to leave Hong Kong. Shawn's case was closed, but Michelle's was only beginning.

She scoured the deck until she stumbled upon a group of sailors chatting in Cantonese.

"Can someone please take me to Captain Tony Lee?" she asked in Mandarin.

They ignored her. Mia had only taught her Mandarin, not Cantonese. She tried again in English. "I need to see Captain Tony Lee!"

An older sailor stepped forward, quieting the group with a few words in Cantonese. He then gave her a quick once-over and gestured for her to follow.

She followed the seaman through the ship's labyrinthine corridors, finally stopping in front of an ajar office door deep within the vessel. The seaman knocked.

"Yeah?" came a neutral voice.

The seaman pushed the door open, revealing a commanding, lean figure seated behind a wooden desk, indulging in a plate of chicken feet. Their savoury aroma wafted through the dimly lit room.

"Do you know her, Tony?" asked the seaman.

Tony's gaze met Lacey's, and in that brief exchange she realised that Tony, despite the masculine name, was a woman.

"Come in," Tony said, before turning to the seaman. "You can leave now."

The seaman nodded and left. Lacey stepped in and without hesitation got straight to the point. "Let's turn back to the port."

Tony responded with a nonchalant smirk. She picked up a chicken foot and savoured it before replying, "I only got paid for a one-way trip."

"How much do you want?"

"Ten grand, in US dollars, cash only."

"You've got to be kidding!"

"Otherwise, feel free to stay on board until we hit Osaka."

Lacey leaned forward, scrutinising Tony. "Who's behind this? I need a name."

Tony met her gaze, her expression unreadable. "Eleven grand to drop the name, cash only."

"Come on, I need to get back to Hong Kong!"

"Cash or get out."

Returning to the deck, Lacey braced against the sharp sea breeze. The harbour's silhouette faded into the distance, a metaphor for the elusive truth she chased. She couldn't let herself give in. When she had nothing left, no one to care about, she lost her fear.

Securing and inflating a life jacket, she approached the railing. Below, the sea's roar mingled with the ship's engines in a tumultuous symphony.

Taking a deep breath, she fixed her gaze on the vast sea ahead. Then, with a determined leap, she plunged into the churning waters, embracing the ocean's formidable power.

24

SAFE HOUSE

Lacey was caught in the grasp of a whirlpool created by the ship's hull cutting through the currents.

In that fraught moment, Mia's theory flashed into her mind, "When you're up against something way stronger than you, that's when you pull out the Tai Chi moves. You know the trick? It's all about borrowing. You take your enemy's strength and turn it right back against them."

To borrow power from the vortex meant to blend with it. Lacey steadied her breath, streamlined her posture, and kept her head above water, aligning herself with its flow to reduce resistance. She became one with the water, tricking it into believing she was part of its fluid dynamics. Then, seizing a brief opportunity, she broke free with a swift move—escaping its clutches.

Looking back towards the port, now a blur in the distance, she realised it was a long way to swim. Knowing the cold waters would be lethal if she lingered, she clenched her teeth, summoned every bit of willpower, and pushed towards the harbour.

As she swam, her body temperature dropped, and each breath became a struggle, yet her determination pushed her forward. Her life had crumbled around her, and turning back was no longer an option. She had to uncover who was behind Michelle's death, no matter the cost.

Pushing her limits, she continued and reached the harbour's edge, exhausted, her vision blurring, and the icy sea biting deep into her bones. She didn't relent until she touched the shore, hauled herself onto solid ground, and collapsed onto the wet pavement, shaking from cold and fatigue.

A voice cut through, "Are you okay?"

She barely lifted her eyes to find a security guard, uniform on, squatting next to her, concern etched on his face.

"Can you...call my friend? Thanks." Her voice shook, barely holding together.

"Sure," the guard said, taking out his phone. "What's the number?"

After she gave Jerry's number, hope sparked a bit.

Jerry picked up fast. The guard put the phone by her ear.

"Hello? Who's this?" Jerry's voice came through.

"It's me..."

"Lacey? Are you alright?"

"I'm in trouble. Can you come get me?"

"Where are you?"

Exhaustion overtook her before she could answer, pulling her into unconsciousness.

***

As Lacey's senses returned, her first view was the deserted city streets through the windshield of an SUV. She realised she was riding shotgun in a moving car. She turned to the driver, finding Jerry Jagger steering the Range Rover.

"Thank God you're up," Jerry said, shooting a worried look her way. "Feeling okay?"

"Starving…" Lacey mumbled, a wave of relief hitting her. Being with someone from the U.S. Consulate felt like a safety net.

"I've got a sandwich in my bag—was gonna be my lunch, but take it."

"Where is it?"

"Right by your feet."

She grabbed the briefcase, found the sandwich inside, and devoured it without a second thought. The mere act of eating, feeling the carbs mix with her saliva, hit the spot like nothing else.

Finishing it, she perked up a bit.

"Thanks, Jerry, that was delicious."

He shot her a kind smile. "When things calm down, I'll take you out for some top-notch dim sum. Sound good?"

"Jerry, are we going to the consulate?"

"Nope, a safe house."

"Safe house?"

"It's where we keep folks out of trouble, standard stuff for Americans caught up in a mess like this."

"Sounds like a plan."

As her strength trickled back, she felt better, Jerry's badge of office giving her solid ground.

"My mom died," she managed to say with as much calm as she could muster, "and I'm sure someone's behind it."

He gave a small, odd chuckle. "Death's part of life, right?"

Her gaze fixed on him, disbelief clear in her eyes.

"Ever heard of GPM?" He looked at her with a sly twinkle.

"You know about it too?"

He suddenly braked the Range Rover, swiftly steering it towards a secluded gate leading into an underground lot. As they approached, the gate swung open, then sealed shut behind them.

"What is this, Jerry?" she demanded.

The lot was dim, lit sporadically by the car's beams and some sensors, giving everything a ghostly aura.

"This is the safe house," he announced, easing the car to a halt.

"How do you know about GPM?" She felt uneasy.

He turned to face her, his grin becoming wider and more unsettling. A shiver of dread swept over her.

"You know, Lacey, GPM can turn anyone into its puppet—even me."

She burst from the car, sprinting away at breakneck speed.

He stepped out, not bothering to pursue, merely glancing at his watch before calling out, "Six seconds left, thanks to that sandwich!"

As she fled, regret gnawed at her, cursing herself for eating that damned sandwich.

"Only three seconds left!" His voice echoed after her.

Her legs buckled, dissolving beneath her. Collapsing, she made a futile attempt to rise, only to succumb to darkness creeping into her consciousness.

25

MEAT WALL MAZE

"This is unbelievable!" Lacey overheard a man with an American accent say, his voice filled with wonder. "It's acting like it's following every GPM command to the letter!"

"Why can't GPM catch this?" a woman asked, her voice strikingly familiar to Lacey.

"Because the data it's sending back is flawless," he explained. "It's got GPM convinced she's still at Celestial Manor."

Lacey slowly blinked her eyes open to find herself lying flat on a bed with a man and a woman towering over her.

The man, tall and slim with a shiny bald head and glasses, wore a white lab coat, screaming scientist or researcher.

The woman appeared elegant and authoritative. Her makeup was flawless, and she wore a chic, expensive black suit. Her short hair was styled to perfection, radiating intelligence and power.

Yip!

What baffled Lacey was Yip's apparent agelessness. She was supposed to be nearing fifty yet looked like she was in her twenties.

As Lacey tried to sit up, she realised she was strapped down. "What's going on? Where am I?" she blurted out.

"Step outside for a sec, would you?" Yip said to the man, who didn't waste any time leaving. Locking eyes with Lacey, she asked, "How's it going, Lacey?"

"Not great," Lacey replied, keeping her tone steady. She knew she was at a disadvantage, so playing tough wasn't an option. "Tired of lying here. Can I sit up?"

"Sure," Yip said, "as long as you're straight with me."

"I'm pretty straightforward."

"How did you manage it?"

"Manage what?"

Yip looked at Lacey, paused for a moment, then said, "Let me show you."

She picked up a pair of tweezers from the tray beside her, holding a tiny, blood-stained microchip close to Lacey's face.

"What did you do to it?" Yip asked.

Seeing the chip—about one millimetre in diameter and five millimetres long—Lacey recalled everything Michelle had revealed to her. She assumed it was the puppet chip. Unsure of Yip's intentions, she decided to play dumb and bide her time.

"I don't know what you're talking about."

"You know exactly what I mean. This was Michelle's. You have one too. Stop beating around the bush, or I'll remove it the hard way."

Lacey was utterly shocked.

"Wait, you said what?"

"I had to crack open her skull to get this out. Don't worry, no pain—it's a corpse."

Lacey was shaken to her core, her eyes locked on Yip as a horrible truth became clear. "Did you... Who killed my mom?"

Yip remained disturbingly calm. "Everyone has their time. I sped hers up."

Fury ignited within Lacey.

"You fucking bitch! You murdered her!" she shouted, overcome with the urge to strike her. Yet no matter how much she struggled, the restraints held tight.

"Help me solve this, or end up like your mom," Yip said, her voice icy.

Lacey screamed and thrashed, completely losing control.

"Okay, let's talk when you've calmed down," Yip said then walked away.

Though grief, shame, anger, confusion, and helplessness overwhelmed Lacey all at once, she forced herself to pull it together. The situation was far more complicated than she had ever imagined, but at least she knew who her enemy was now.

As Lacey tried to think of a way out, the lights abruptly went out. Gunshots rang out outside, followed by an ear-splitting alarm. Moments later, the sound of the door being forced open reached her ears, and the silhouette of a towering man appeared before her, his face shrouded in darkness.

He pressed a strip of duct tape over her mouth and whispered, "Be quiet. Follow my lead."

Baritone again!

Outside, the chaos of gunshots, shouts, and various noises continued, echoing like a battlefield.

Baritone freed her limbs in an impressive four seconds, and before she could even think of standing, he hoisted her over his shoulder like a sack of potatoes. His shoulders and back felt like a solid wall, grounding her amidst the chaos.

He manoeuvred through the darkness, deftly dodging gunfire, shouts, footsteps, and explosions with her on his shoulder. Bullets zipped past her ears and buttocks, grazing her skin. She wasn't even sure if she'd been hit.

In the midst of the pandemonium, he suddenly stopped then hurled her into what seemed like a vehicle's compartment, slamming the door shut before she could get a good look at him.

The car roared to life and sped off, screeching as it tore away from the chaos. Lacey scrambled to her feet, finding herself in a sealed compartment. The rapid acceleration drowned out the fading gunfire and shouts, tossing her around like a rag doll. The car shot forward, slammed the brakes, reversed, zigzagged, and even pulled off slick drifts. At one point, it teetered on two wheels, nearly flipping. Inside, she felt like a pinball, bouncing in every direction. All she could do was curl up and protect her head with her arms.

After what seemed like forever, the chaos finally wound down. The roar from outside tapered off into silence. A cold draft sneaked in through the cracks in the door, sending shivers down her spine. When the car eased to a soft stop and the engine's growl faded, she heard the driver's door open and shut.

"Hey! Let me out!" Lacey yelled, yanking futilely at the locked back door of the compartment.

Footsteps faded to an eerie hush. As the temperature dropped, a bone-chilling cold seeped in, making her wonder if she'd been stashed in a morgue.

Moments later, the footsteps came back, closer this time, until they stopped right outside the rear door. The sound of a key turning in the lock preceded the door swinging open. A coat flew at her, briefly blocking her view. By the time she grabbed it, the figure outside had disappeared into thin air.

Wrapped in the coat, Lacey found a small degree of comfort in its meager warmth despite the grime. She jumped down from the compartment, immediately struck by the scene: a sprawling cold storage room, dimly lit and packed with rows of frozen beef carcasses, whole and halved, hanging in the chilled air. They formed a daunting labyrinth of meat walls.

Even with the coat, the cold was biting. Worse yet, she was barefoot, and every step on the icy concrete was like walking on knives—a sharp, excruciating pain.

She hopped from foot to foot, trying to keep warm, her eyes scanning the meat maze. No exit in sight, a tall figure looming in the distance.

"Wait up!" she called out, chasing after the figure.

He ignored her completely, powering through the maze of meat walls with long, swift strides that left her trailing. Soon enough, she lost him. Wandering through the labyrinth, her frustration mounted until she stumbled upon a door, slightly ajar.

Pushing it open, she stepped into a small, cozy room bathed in soft, dim light. It was decked out with a long wooden table and benches, plush sofas, a heater, and notably a makeshift coffee bar in one corner. As she took it all in, the silence was pierced by a woman's voice.

"You need some shoes."

Startled, Lacey spun around to find a woman in a grimy cotton coat and snow boots, holding an extra pair. Her face was obscured by a thick wool hat pulled low.

She tossed the boots to Lacey, who quickly shoved her freezing feet into them.

"Black coffee here. Need sugar?" the woman asked, already stationed behind the coffee bar.

"Yes, please, with sugar!" Lacey replied, deviating from her usual black coffee due to her need for a quick sugar hit.

As she prepared the drink, the woman introduced herself, "Call me Yvonne, Lacey."

"You know my name?"

"We all do."

"We?"

"No sugar for me, thanks!" a new male voice chimed in.

Lacey turned to see the guy, tall and slim with a shiny bald head and glasses. She remembered him—he had once worn a white lab coat and discussed her puppet chip with Yip while she was strapped down in the lab. Now, he was in a grimy cotton coat like Yvonne's, trudging over to the long table and sitting down with a MacBook Pro.

"Chris Taylor, from L.A.," he said, introducing himself.

Before she could respond, another figure barged in—a broad, muscular man with a face marked by scars and a fresh cut on his forehead. He headed straight for the sugar, grabbed a handful of cubes, and began munching them, muttering, "I don't see why we had to save that bitch. Nearly got killed out there!"

He didn't look at her, but Lacey felt certain she was the bitch he mentioned.

Yvonne slid the freshly made coffee across the table, casually saying to Lacey, "Help yourself."

"Damn bitch," the stocky man muttered under his breath.

Yvonne smiled at Lacey. "Don't worry about him. Politeness was missing in his DNA. We call him Sandbag. He looks like one, doesn't he?"

Cradling the steaming cup, Lacey edged towards the table and took a sip, letting the warmth seep through her. "Can someone fill me in on what's happening?"

"That bitch was practically begging to get herself killed, and here we are, busting our asses to save her," Sandbag grumbled, shoving more sugar cubes into his mouth.

At that, Lacey knew for sure she was the bitch.

"That's only part of the story," Yvonne interjected, preparing another cup of coffee.

"What's the whole story then?" Lacey pressed.

"He'll clue you in," Chris said, not looking up from his MacBook Pro.

"Who?" Lacey felt utterly confused.

"No sugar, thanks," Baritone's deep voice suddenly came from behind her.

She spun around, her jaw dropping in shock.

Lacey had always had a hunch that Baritone might actually be Shawn. His strong British accent could easily disguise the baritone's voice, and since she'd never seen Shawn's body, the doubt gnawed at her. The way Baritone always protected her and Michelle fuelled her suspicions. But the second Baritone tossed her over his shoulder, she knew he wasn't Shawn, who wasn't a hulking figure with muscles to spare.

Still, she had never expected him to turn out to be...

"Hugo?" she gasped in disbelief.

Hugo walked to the far end of the long table and settled into a chair, keeping his distance from Lacey. The once impeccable-looking secretary now had the air of a warrior back from battle, his face, neck, hands, and clothes smeared with blood. He didn't seem hurt. The blood was probably someone else's.

The room fell silent.

Hugo raised his hand to silence Lacey before she could speak. "Time's tight, so here's the plan. I talk, you listen, then we hash it out. Sound good?"

His expression was icy, a stark contrast to what she knew about him before.

"Alright," she nodded, seeing no other option.

26

—◆—

THE PUPPET PROJECT

"**M**ental health issues are a ticking time bomb."

Twenty-five years ago, Shawn Green stood before a packed house at the 6th Global AI Venture Capital Conference in Hong Kong, ready to pitch his big idea.

He had recently ditched his nine-to-five IT programming gig to chase his dream as a solo developer of artificial general intelligence.

"Think about it. Self-harm, suicide, domestic violence, sexual abuse, mass shootings, any crime you can name, economic crashes, dictatorships, even the threat of another world war—all of it could be tied back to untreated mental health issues."

He was decked out in a rented suit. His own was trashed, thanks to a vengeful rat that had left twenty-seven holes in it after its family was wiped out by his landlord right before Shawn moved into his tiny basement flat in Hong Kong's North District.

"But do all these psychological treatments, old or new, really make a difference? I'd say no. If they were the magic bullet, we wouldn't still be drowning in crises."

With a deliberate cough and a pause for effect, Shawn continued, "Imagine if we tackled these issues head-on. We'd turn the world into a paradise. And here's the kicker. I think I've found the answer."

After carefully setting the stage, he unveiled what he believed was a game-changer.

"Ladies and gentlemen, let me introduce you to GPM—an AGI that's set to change the game in mental health care. Using advanced 'puppet chips' implanted in patients' brains, GPM helps regulate physical actions while keeping personal thoughts and consciousness intact. It's a fresh take on healing, working from the outside in.

"Normally, psychological therapies dig into the mind, trying to change behaviour by tackling mental issues. But GPM flips the script. It controls physical actions first—what you say, how you move—creating a stable environment where the mind can heal itself. This approach provides a structure for recovery, letting the mind mend in a more organic way.

"The benefits for society are huge. GPM reduces the need for large mental health facilities and a lot of staff, allowing us to use those resources for other important health initiatives. This tech not only cuts costs but also makes mental health care more efficient and sustainable, helping integrate it better into our overall health system.

"GPM can also curb violent behaviour, reducing all kinds of violence. It's more than a tech breakthrough; it's a potential turning point in human history. We're tackling global challenges not on the surface but at their behavioural roots. I invite you to join me on this groundbreaking journey to reshape mental health care, promote global peace, and push the boundaries of human evolution. Thank you."

He expected a moment of awed silence followed by a storm of applause. After a pregnant pause, a judge's offhand comment, caught by a hot mic, broke the silence. "Sounds like this guy's got his own demons to fight."

Despite attempts to keep straight faces, the crowd couldn't hold back. Laughter erupted, turning Shawn's heartfelt pitch into the day's biggest joke.

During the conference break, Shawn splashed cold water on his face in the restroom, the chill a welcome relief against his flushed skin. Looking up, he met the gaze of a man in the mirror.

"Dad?" he gasped.

"Remember what I told you, Shawn. Keep at it," his father's image advised before fading from the mirror.

Shawn took a deep breath, locking eyes with his own reflection. "You've got this," he muttered. "They don't see it yet, but you do. Don't let them shake you."

The click of high heels from behind interrupted his pep talk. Puzzled—he was in the men's restroom, after all—he saw a sophisticated, elegantly dressed Asian woman in the mirror.

"I waited outside, but you didn't come out," she said, extending her card.

He accepted the card, recognising Ming Yip, CEO of GrandTech Group—a powerhouse on the Hong Kong Stock Exchange.

"I love your idea. Call me when you're free," she said.

Yip left with a warm smile.

"That night, he called her, and it changed his life," Hugo concluded, having shared Shawn's story—one that her father had never told Lacey.

"Think about it. What if Shawn actually pulled it off? Explains his fancy penthouse and the Aston Martin, doesn't it?" As her mother's words echoed in her ears, Lacey started piecing everything together.

"So that's why you call him Dr. Green. He wasn't really an IT tech. It was a..."

"A cover," Hugo confirmed. "Yip funded Shawn's GPM project but demanded total secrecy to avoid leaks and manage human trial risks. Shawn agreed but needed a title to stay under the radar."

Lacey narrowed her eyes. "So who are you guys, really?"

"Shawn's AI R&D team."

Yip had spent a fortune to poach top-tier talent from Silicon Valley. He brought in Chris Taylor, one of the best data scientists in the U.S., and Yvonne, a top neural network specialist from L.A., along with about two hundred other machine learning engineers, data scientists, neural network specialists, software engineers, cybersecurity experts, robotics engineers, and HCI specialists. Everyone was paid triple their previous salaries. That was why they were eager to move to Hong Kong and work on this project.

The team worked closely with Shawn as their leader for nearly two decades. Six years ago, they finally developed the first operational version of GPM, known as the GPM Prototype. This was a significant milestone. Despite being an early iteration, the prototype could regulate the actions, words, and muscle movements of up to three hundred individuals simultaneously. Everyone believed they had made human history and would achieve financial freedom for the rest of their lives.

Yip rewarded the team handsomely and threw a lavish party. Given the project's secretive nature, the celebration was held at one of her mansions in the Mid-Levels, one of Hong Kong's most exclusive neighbourhoods. She had transformed the mansion into a seaside palace, styled after the Qing dynasty's "Palace of Gathering Excellence," the opulent quarters of Empress Dowager Cixi in the Forbidden City.

The party was a visual feast. Everyone enjoyed fine wines from around the world, a lavish spread of traditional Chinese dishes, waitresses dressed as Qing dynasty maids, and dancers performing courtly routines.

As the evening wore on, the fine wines, exquisite food, and lively conversations had everyone in high spirits. Yip took the stage, commanding attention as she grabbed the microphone.

"Empress Dowager Cixi has always been my inspiration. I've tried to emulate her strength and cunning," she began, her gaze locking on Shawn. "Twenty years ago, I was in the crowd when you pitched your bold vision. My heart raced," she confessed, eyes still fixed on him. "I wondered if I could surpass Cixi—not only in ruling Hong Kong or China but the entire world."

Laughter rippled through the room. The boss knew how to work a crowd.

"For twenty years, I've dreamed of this day, and here it is. Shawn, you've handed this planet a new ruler."

Laughter still echoed when the doors burst open. Heavily armed men in black suits stormed in, their movements swift and methodical. The festive ambiance shattered as masked intruders barked commands, herding everyone to the centre with rifle barrels. Panic surged through the crowd like a jolt of electricity.

A sharp cry rang out as the first resister tried to run—cut short by a precise headshot. Blood splattered the pristine marble floor, and a collective gasp of horror swept through the room. Fear thickened the air, replacing the earlier joviality with sheer terror.

The team huddled together, eyes wide with disbelief and dread. Some clutched friends, others stood frozen, too shocked to move. The men in black moved like phantoms, blindfolding captives with rough, practiced motions. The fabric was tight and suffocating, plunging each person into darkness.

Before anyone could fully comprehend, needles pierced their skin. The cold, metallic scent of the anaesthetic mixed with the lingering aroma of fine wine and exotic dishes. One by one, bodies went limp, sinking to the floor as consciousness slipped away.

Amid the chaos, Yip remained seated, casually resuming her meal. Next to her, Shawn's expression was unreadable, but the betrayal was clear. The brutal efficiency of the ambush left no doubt. Shawn had sold out the team that supported him for over two decades.

"Maybe Yip turned Dad into a puppet first?" Lacey suggested, trying to sound like she was analysing rather than excusing her father.

"GPM keeps a detailed log of all its puppets. Shawn's not on it. He was never controlled," Hugo explained.

Everyone looked at Lacey, deadly quiet.

"Shawn and Yip had an affair, starting from the early days of their partnership. It wasn't a secret to any of us," Hugo said calmly. "They must've planned to screw us over from the very beginning."

"But why would they do this?"

"Using GPM to control the top team was a game-changer for them. It's efficient, cost-effective, and central to Yip's master plan, The Puppet Project."

Hugo then revealed something that sent chills down Lacey's spine.

Channeling Mao Zedong's dictum that "political power grows from the barrel of a gun," Yip set up a covert militia called "Red." Composed of former special ops from mainland China, she turned them into her personal marionettes with puppet chips.

She had Red gather a bunch of random people and rigged them with puppet chips, creating the Patient Zero for HKEV—the young woman in the dim sum joint, frantically gnawing at her hands. She shelled out big money to make sure this eerie scene went viral on TikTok, setting the stage for a pandemic.

Next, she had Red covertly install puppet chips in every Hong Kong government and police official, seizing total control over the city's reins. Meanwhile, she engineered a wave of self-harm among her puppets to mimic a pandemic, pushing the puppet government to declare an emergency.

As the city sank into severe lockdowns and mandatory nucleic acid tests, she rigged the tests to always return positive. This manoeuvre validated the puppet government's push for mass quarantine camps, where puppet cops corralled people. Upon entry, each person was implanted with a puppet chip, turning them into Yip's puppets. Simultaneously, GrandTec Group rolled out the "VitalGuard Vaccine," marketed as the ultimate protection against HKEV. The puppet government swiftly mandated it, ostensibly to halt the virus. In truth, the vaccine was a front for mass implantation of puppet chips—the quickest way to spread the technology.

Once every resident was under Yip's thumb, HKEV would miraculously vanish. Celebrated as Hong Kong's saviour, her ties to the Chinese Communist Party's central committee and surging popularity would easily secure her the Chief Executive spot, a role she'd eyed for ages.

The playbook would repeat in mainland China. Yip aimed to be the first woman to claim the top posts of General Secretary of the Chinese Communist Party, Chairperson of the People's Republic of China, and Chair of the Military Commission, dominating the entire country.

Taiwan was next in line. The long-sought unification by the CCP would be achieved on her watch in peace, not a war.

With Greater China under her control, she planned to spread the Puppet Project to Japan, Korea, Europe, Oceania, and finally the United States—the last holdout against China's influence. Once that was done, a few simple commands would let her dominate the globe effortlessly.

"Yip's ambition knew no bounds, a chasm so deep even she couldn't see the bottom. And Shawn was her rock, doing everything he could to support her," Hugo finally said.

Given what Lacey had seen and experienced, she felt powerless to argue.

Hugo continued, detailing how the Puppet Project had been sailing smoothly until two hitches threw Yip for a loop. First, Shawn took his own life. No surprise there. Since his son's tragic accident five years ago, he'd been spiralling. But the timing couldn't have been worse for Yip. Second, two puppets—Michelle and Lacey—slipped under the radar. Their brain chips tricked GPM into thinking they were still in Shawn's penthouse, even though they'd already escaped. If Yip's puppets at customs hadn't caught them at the airport, they'd be in New York by now. It was a glitch that baffled everyone, GPM included.

Yip didn't kill Lacey because she was Shawn's daughter. She suspected Lacey might know something about the glitch and worried there were other rogue puppets like her out there. And she was right. Hugo, Chris, Yvonne, and Sandbag had been free from GPM's control for a while but pretended to be puppets. That was how they managed to get Lacey out of Yip's place.

Lacey took a moment to process everything before asking Hugo, "Was it you who left that number for me on our first night here?"

He nodded.

"Why?"

"To keep you and Michelle out of this mess."

"But I'm the daughter of your enemy."

"You're not to blame. We can't stand back and watch more innocents turn into Yip's puppets. If Jerry Jagger hadn't rushed to the quarantine cabin to get you out, he wouldn't have become one of them."

"Damn," Lacey muttered, the weight of Hugo's revelations hitting her. Poor Jerry had been doing his job, trying to help her. He must be terrified, feeling like he was in hell right now.

"Listen, it's not too late. We can help you get out of here," Hugo said.

"Are you guys leaving too?"

"We've still got unfinished business here."

"With Yip?"

He agreed silently.

"Count me in," she declared, her eyes locked with his.

Lacey was wary of these guys, but joining forces with them was her best bet for now. She knew who had killed her mother, and walking away wasn't an option.

Hugo's eyes narrowed, a flicker of mistrust crossing his face.

"Come on, man. I don't want anything in return other than to make sure the one who took my mom's life pays for it! You all want some payback too, right?"

"But you're white," he said.

"Wait, what?" She looked around the room. No one met her gaze. "Sorry, I don't get it."

"The only way to shut down all the puppet chips and set everyone free is to destroy GPM's core. It's in the top chamber of GrandTec Tower. Yip's the only one who can access it because of the high-tech AI security system. We'll have to kidnap her and force her to take us there."

"Alright, so what's the problem with me being white?"

The room fell silent for a moment before Hugo began to explain.

Yip usually had tight security around the clock, making her a tough nut to crack. But the day after tomorrow, there'd be a rare window. Minister Gu, a high-ranking Central Committee official, was coming to Hong Kong to check on the pandemic response. He was close to Yip, and they always met up when he was in town. Yip understood the committee officials well, so she kept a low profile when meeting him. This meant minimal security around her. And that was Hugo's only shot at getting to her.

Gu was around fifty. Every time he visited Hong Kong, he traveled in his luxury van, escorted by two other cars. He never stayed overnight. Once his business wrapped up, he'd head back to a hotel in Shenzhen. He didn't trust any hotel in Hong Kong since some other CCP officials were bugged while staying overnight in the city, leading to serious consequences. Gu was a sex addict, and that was probably the only reason he loved Hong Kong—it was easier and safer to get a call girl here than in mainland China, where he had too many rivals watching him. Gu would be accompanied by government officials during the day, but his evenings were his own. That was when he'd have some backseat action since he didn't stay in hotels.

Hugo had hacked Gu's personal phone and snagged his schedule for that night. Gu had arranged to meet a call girl named Lily in his van in Sha Tau Kok at 8 p.m. sharp, right after dinner. He had never met her in person, only seen her profile on his phone. Forty minutes later, he would meet with Yip in Central, inviting her for a van cruise, drinks, and a chat. So it looked like he planned to have a wild backseat session with Lily on the way to Central, drop her off, and then pick up Yip for drinks before heading back to Shenzhen.

Hugo had bribed Lily to help him kidnap Gu, hiding in his van when it picked up Yip. But Lily went missing yesterday, so he needed another Chinese girl to disguise as Lily but hadn't found one yet.

"Ah, I got it," Lacey said with a sly grin. "I've got someone perfect for you."

Everyone gawked at her, clearly unconvinced.

She cleared her throat and finished her coffee. "There's a black suitcase under Shawn's bed in his penthouse. Get it for me, and you'll have another Lily."

27

BAIT AND SWITCH

The streetlights bathed the colourful yet aging facades of Sha Tau Kok Estate's public housing, casting an eerie, surreal play of light and shadow. The area was typically deserted, but on this pandemic night, the stillness was even more foreboding. The only sound was the crash of waves against the shore, hinting at the hidden conspiracies lurking in the city's shadows.

A woman in a grey coat stood alone by the waterfront. Her black hair fluttered in the sea breeze, and her pale bare feet glowed under the moonlight, adding to her enigmatic allure.

A convoy of three black cars appeared in the distance. Leading and trailing were two Chinese-made SUVs, sandwiching a completely black Toyota Vellfire in the middle. The emblems on the Vellfire had been removed, as if the owner didn't want anyone to know its make, though most people could recognise it without the logo. The convoy eased up beside the woman, and the Vellfire's electric door slid open. Without hesitation, she walked up to the door. The dim lighting obscured the faces inside, but she could vaguely see a pair of small eyes scanning her from head to toe.

"Lily?" Minister Gu's voice sounded like a mix between a human and a braying donkey.

She brushed her long hair out of her face, the sea breeze tugging at the strands. Her delicate, strikingly beautiful Chinese features came into view. She nodded gracefully. "Yeah, that's me."

"Mm," Gu grunted approvingly as he looked her over. "You're wearing a lot."

"I don't think so," she explained, slightly opening her coat. Underneath, she wore nothing, her porcelain-like, shapely body glowing in the moonlight.

A plump, middle-aged hand, like a pig's trotter, reached out from the car. She had apparently passed the inspection.

With a seductive smile, she placed her slender hand confidently in his. He pulled her into the car, the door slid shut, and the three-car convoy eased into motion, heading towards the city.

The interior of the Vellfire had been transformed into a mini VIP suite, complete with a wide, plush loveseat, a crystal glass coffee table, a mini fridge, a small bar, a wine cabinet, and mood lighting that created an intimate ambiance. She had to admit, the vibe was perfect—if only the looping soundtrack of tacky Chinese folk music wasn't so grating.

Gu was fat and planted squarely in the middle of the loveseat, leaving no room for her. He wore a Mao suit, collar open, with his shoes off, exposing a pair of grotesque feet covered in fungal toenails. With a jab of his big toe, he pointed to the wooden floor in front of the couch, apparently suggesting she sit there.

She complied and sat down, but he shook his head.

"Kneel," he commanded, lighting a cigarette.

She shifted from sitting to kneeling.

"Lose it."

Without hesitation, she slipped off her coat, kneeling naked before him. Her full, firm breasts gently quivered with the car's movement.

He took a greedy drag from his cigarette and slowly exhaled. She finally got a good look at his bloated, round face and slicked-back hair, reminding her of the slicked-back man in Flushing.

Is Slicked-Back the go-to hairstyle for communist governors?

Puffing on his cigarette, he eyed her up and down. "I'm figuring out how we'll fuck."

"Why not lie flat on your tummy, like a baby?" she cooed. "I can work out all those knots for you."

His face lit up with a wide, eager grin. "Sounds good."

He quickly stripped and hit the floor. Lily hopped onto his back—wide as a barn—and got to work on his shoulders. He moaned in delight, clueless as Lily's hand stealthily dipped into her coat to snatch a slim syringe.

"Right there, you got it," he murmured appreciatively.

"Ready for a real thrill?"

"Yeah?"

As quick as lightning, she jammed the needle into his neck.

"Hey, what the—" A chilling sensation spread from the injection site. His eyes rolled back, and he collapsed, knocked out cold.

Lily shrugged on her coat and stepped over the hefty body sprawled on the floor. She moved towards the privacy partition, her eyes scanning for controls. Spotting an electronic button, she pulled another slim syringe from her pocket and pressed it.

The partition slid open silently. Without waiting for the driver to react, she jabbed the syringe into his neck, knocking him out cold. Swiftly, she grabbed the wheel, shoved the unconscious man aside, and took control. Her movements were so smooth that the trailing bodyguard vehicles didn't suspect a thing.

Lily drove for five minutes before spotting the Red House Restaurant at an alley entrance. Bracing herself, she swerved sharply and gunned the engine, speeding into the alley. The trailing bodyguards realised too late. They screeched to a halt and gave chase, but the black Toyota Vellfire had already vanished.

The alley was a maze of forks that baffled the bodyguards. After a frantic search, they found the Vellfire at a junction, rocking violently. As they approached, a window rolled down, and the sound of a woman's moans spilled out. A hand, clearly belonging to Gu, emerged, waving them off with a tired "shoo." The bodyguards paused, exchanging awkward glances.

Clearly, the boss was enjoying some backseat antics and wanted no interruptions.

Getting the message, the bodyguards retreated to their cars, eyes on the Vellfire as it continued to shake wildly.

Unbeknownst to them, as soon as Lily darted into the chaotic alley, she headed straight for a prearranged spot. Hugo, Chris, Yvonne, and Sandbag were waiting there in an exact replica of Gu's Vellfire, down to the tiniest scratches. They executed a classic bait-and-switch. Lily jumped out and hopped into the decoy while Yvonne and Sandbag slipped into the real black Vellfire. The decoy then sped off in another direction.

Sandbag drove the replica to a junction and started rocking the car vigorously with Yvonne, mimicking a steamy rendezvous. As the bodyguard vehicles caught up, Yvonne expertly faked the sounds of a woman in the throes of passion, her moans loud and convincing. As the body-guards drew closer, Yvonne manoeuvred the unconscious man's hand to wave dismissively from the window. The dim interior and convincing performance were enough to fool them into thinking the boss was having a private moment.

Meanwhile, Hugo, Lily, and Chris were already speeding towards Central in the decoy Vellfire. Chris was behind the wheel, while Lily and Hugo sat in the back. Hugo silently fitted a silencer onto his pistol, stealing glances at Lily now and then.

"Does it look convincing?" she asked.

He nodded.

"Turn around. I need to change," she said. "I want Yip to see the real me."

He raised an eyebrow. "Is that necessary?"

"Absolutely."

As Hugo turned his back, Lacey started peeling off the skin suit, the task gruelling and leaving her drenched in sweat.

"All set, thanks," she said, finally changing back into her own clothes and wig.

He turned around, meeting her confident, triumphant smile.

The bustling days were long gone. Amidst the pandemic, Central had become a ghost town. The decoy Vellfire pulled up in front of St. John's Cathedral, next to Yip's black Rolls-Royce Cullinan.

As usual, Yip kept a low profile when meeting mainland officials. She had only one person with her: her driver, who also doubled as her bodyguard.

Yip walked to the decoy, her bodyguard close behind. As they approached, the car door slid open slowly, revealing the dark barrel of a silenced pistol.

Bang!

The bodyguard's head jerked back. A bullet dropped him instantly as Hugo pulled Yip into the vehicle. The doors slammed shut, and the decoy disappeared into the night.

"Hugo?" Yip gasped in shock at the sight of her captor.

Lacey stepped forward and delivered a backhand punch to Yip's face. Her years as a private detective had taught her that a backhand could pack a surprising wallop for the untrained.

Yip hit the ground hard, blood trickling from her nose and mouth.

"There's more to come, bitch!" Lacey warned, her voice cold and steady. She reined in her urge to strike again, knowing she had a score to settle.

Hugo pressed the gun to Yip's head. "Clear all your security and take us to the top chamber."

Spitting out a bloodied tooth, Yip met Hugo's gaze then glanced at Lacey and smirked. "You're barking up the wrong tree."

Hugo tapped her forehead with the gun barrel. "Mess with me, and you'll regret it."

Yip's phone suddenly rang. She looked at Hugo and said, "Pick it up, she's the one you want. Ask her."

Her?

Hugo kept the gun on Yip while signalling for Lacey to dig out the phone. Lacey pulled it from Yip's pocket and saw that the incoming FaceTime call was from "Yip."

Yip calling Yip?

Lacey showed Hugo the screen, his brow knitting together.

"Answer it," Yip pressed.

Hugo frowned, taking the phone with his free hand and answering the call. Another Yip appeared on the screen as the FaceTime connected.

"Mess with me, and you'll regret it," the Yip in the video said, grinning broadly.

Hugo and Lacey stared in disbelief at face on the screen. Realisation hit Hugo. As he locked eyes with the Yip in front of him, she grinned.

"Hugo, honestly, I never thought you'd double-cross me. But it's too late for regrets now. And Lacey, I'm genuinely happy for you—you'll see your parents again soon," Yip said nonchalantly, reclining in a luxurious, bubble-filled bathtub.

Without a word, Hugo ended the call and shot the fake in front of him in the head.

"Fuck me!" Lacey shouted.

"Body double," Hugo muttered, his eyes then snapping to meet Chris's in the rearview mirror.

"Step on it, now!"

No sooner had he spoken than gunfire erupted. Bullets whizzed by, and one hit Chris. His head snapped back, splattering blood and brain matter on the windshield.

28

DIE HARD

Hugo dove into the driver's seat like a madman, ripping the wheel from Chris's lifeless grip.

"Get down!" he yelled.

Lacey hit the floor as bullets shattered the windows, whizzing past her. Some tore through the car, inches from her head. The car swerved, and Yip's double, half her head gone, rolled next to her. No time to think—she hugged it tight as a shield.

"Toss me the gun!" Hugo shouted.

She spotted the pistol under the back seat. Crawling over the swaying car, she grabbed it and tossed it forward. The car jerked hard. The gun hit the back of the front seat and flew out the window.

"Fantastic!" she cursed.

With a loud bang, another car slammed into the back of the Vellfire. Hugo jerked the steering wheel, sending the Vellfire into a sharp spin. Lacey flipped, almost flying out of the car.

"You still with me?" Hugo shouted as the Vellfire straightened out.

"Guess so!" she yelled back.

The gunfire ceased. Peeking out the window, she saw they were now on the main road through Central. Behind them, several black SUVs had crashed and were burning. She quickly pieced it together—Hugo's wild driving had made their pursuers crash into each other.

"What now?" she shouted over the wind whipping through the bullet-riddled car.

"Stay alive!" he answered bluntly.

With a loud crash, the Vellfire took a brutal hit on the left side. Hugo reacted instantly, keeping the car steady. Lacey glanced left and saw a black Range Rover tailing them closely. Hugo floored it, pushing the Vellfire to its limit. The Range Rover, with more horsepower, quickly closed in. As it rammed them again, Hugo slammed the brakes and spun the car into a 360-degree drift.

Caught off guard, the Range Rover missed, veered off the road, crashed into a storefront, and exploded in flames.

Under Hugo's masterful control, the Vellfire barely slowed down and kept moving forward.

In the distance, a line of police cars blocked the road, lights flashing and officers armed and ready. Yip had clearly used GPM to mobilise her puppet cops.

Hugo slammed on the brakes and turned down another street without hesitation. But they were still surrounded. Yip could command as many puppets as she wanted. Taxis, private cars, and trucks came at the black Vellfire like kamikaze drivers, but Hugo's expert driving dodged them all.

Things took a turn for the worse. A Chinese-made military SUV, known as a "tank," appeared, its driver relentless and nearly forcing Hugo to stop several times. Desperate, Hugo drove straight into a nearby mall.

The black Vellfire crashed into a pillar inside the mall. Hugo and Lacey scrambled out, and she noticed a large bloodstain on his abdomen, blood dripping down his leg.

"You're hurt?"

Hugo took off his jacket, tore off a sleeve, and tied it around his waist to stop the bleeding.

Behind them, the tank tried to follow but got stuck in the mall's narrow passage. Hugo led Lacey to a hidden corner, watching as a giant figure climbed out of the tank and headed towards their Vellfire.

"Shit, I left Lily there!" Lacey gasped.

Hugo grabbed her before she could go back. "That's Rhino, one of Yip's most dangerous killers."

"It's not mine! I have to return it!" Lacey insisted.

If she lost or damaged the skin, she'd be in serious debt. Mia wouldn't let it go.

"Forget about it."

"What? Fuck!"

"Shut up!" Hugo hissed. He watched Rhino approaching the Vellfire and pulled out a remote from his pocket. "Run!"

As Hugo grabbed Lacey and rushed to the exit, he pressed the button on the remote. The Vellfire exploded as Rhino was inspecting it. The massive blast propelled them towards the exit.

"Great! I'm fucking broke now!" Lacey exclaimed as Lily went up in flames.

They navigated through the streets until they reached a block packed with protesters. Mostly young people held signs reading "No Quarantine Camps" and "Protect Hong Kong Freedom." This was clearly an organised, premeditated protest. More demonstrators poured in from all directions.

Hugo and Lacey pushed through the crowd, holding hands tightly to avoid getting separated. After a struggle, they finally reached an alley and slipped into the narrow passage.

They wound through the dark, twisting alleys. Hugo's pace slowed until he finally collapsed.

"Jesus! Are you okay?" Lacey rushed to him, seeing blood pouring from his abdomen.

He breathed heavily as he rummaged through his pocket, pulling out a blood-stained business card and handing it to her.

"That truck's heading to Shenzhen tonight, loaded with beef. The driver's my guy. Show him this card. He'll get you across the border."

"What about you?"

"Don't waste time! Fly back to New York before she gets you!"

Lacey left Hugo and sprinted to the alley's entrance, blending with the crowd of protesters. She tried to hurry, but her legs felt like lead.

Her mind was a whirlwind. Abruptly, she stopped and cursed, "Fuck!"

With a determined spin, she dashed back to the alley.

He had saved her too many times to count. Though she still doubted his reasons, she couldn't leave him. The debt weighed heavily on her—she hated owing anyone.

He was unconscious, curled up in the corner. Summoning all her strength, she hoisted him onto her back and emerged from the alley, merging into the crowd.

The main road throbbed with the protesters' passion, their chants echoing loudly together.

"Reject the quarantine camp, restore our freedom!"

"We want Santa Claus, not Satan's isolation!"

"Oppose the lockdown. Liberate Hong Kong!"

As Lacey moved with the crowd, she spotted a pharmacy nearby and hurried inside. It was deserted but well-stocked with medicine. In a secluded corner, she carefully laid Hugo down and started tending to his injuries, quickly unbuttoning his shirt.

"Damn it!" she whispered fiercely, eyeing the wound with the bullet lodged inside, blood seeping out steadily.

She came up with a crazy idea and quickly grabbed alcohol, gauze, cotton swabs, and other essentials from the shelf. Booting up the reception computer, she connected to Wi-Fi and found a professional bullet extraction video. Watching it intently three times, she then sterilised the tweezers with alcohol, her hands trembling.

"Sorry, man. I might mess this up, but it's your only shot."

The chaos outside contrasted sharply with the pharmacy's tense silence.

She inhaled deeply, bracing herself as she leaned over him and began the surgery.

The intense pain roused him to semi-consciousness.

Examining the wound closely, she found the bullet. It was stubborn, buried deep, and greedily absorbing blood. Beads of sweat formed on her forehead as she tried again and again. Finally, she got it out, the bullet slick with blood. She swiftly placed gauze over the wound, pressing firmly to stem the bleeding, then secured it with tape, fashioning a makeshift bandage.

Before she could savour a moment of relief, a hushed voice shattered the silence behind her. "I think I found them."

She whirled around to face a cop, his eyes locked on hers, walkie-talkie in hand.

A voice from the device commanded, "Take them out. Grab the body."

The cop confirmed without hesitation, "Copy."

In that instant, she realised he was a puppet.

He moved closer, his vantage point offering a clear shot at Lacey and Hugo. He lifted his pistol, aiming directly at her forehead.

"Shit..." she muttered, never imagining her end would come like this.

29

' THE RIOT

Lacey shut her eyes as the cop pulled the trigger.

A dull thud echoed in her ears. She was still alive. She hesitated before slowly opening her eyes—the cop was sprawled on the ground, knocked out cold. Standing between her and the fallen officer was a young man in a black hoodie and sweatpants, holding a baseball bat.

"You okay?" asked the young man.

"Yeah…" She managed a nod, her whole body trembling.

"You all international students? Here for the protest?"

"Yeah!"

His eyes lit up with appreciation and relief.

"Thanks for having our backs! But we gotta go, fast. Cops are coming in hard!"

Lacey hoisted Hugo onto her back and stepped out of the pharmacy into a street that had turned into a war zone.

The air crackled with tension as riot police advanced, their visors down and shields up. They fired off tear gas canisters, sending plumes of choking smoke into the air, while rubber bullets zipped through the haze, thudding into makeshift barriers. In retaliation, protesters, faces masked against the gas, hurled stones and glass bottles.

Amid the chaos, a police car became the protesters' makeshift podium. They tipped it over with a ground-shaking thud, its alarms blaring in protest. Atop the overturned vehicle, a young man emerged as a figure of resistance, brandishing the British Hong Kong flag. His voice, hoarse yet unwavering, cut through the tumult as he led the crowd with cries of "Liberate Hong Kong! Freedom forever!" The roaring crowd swelled around him, a united front in the face of escalating aggression.

As riot police reinforcements arrived, armed officers leaped from their vehicles, firing tranquilliser darts at the protesters. Many were hit and fell, plunging the scene into chaos.

More protesters resisted violently, turning the entire Sheung Wan area into a smoke-filled battlefield.

Lacey, with Hugo on her back, finally escaped the inferno. They slipped into a narrow alley and found an abandoned convenience store.

Inside, she gently laid him on the floor and pulled down the shop's metal shutter, creating a makeshift safe house.

She grabbed some snacks from the shelf and quickly ate to regain her strength. Then she turned to Hugo. He was virtually still, but his faint breathing showed he was still alive. Exhausted, she leaned against the wall near him.

"Need to keep talking or I'll crash like Sleeping Beauty. Gotta stay sharp. You never know what's coming next." She sighed deeply. "Damn, I miss my mom, my Ollie. I've got no one left." She paused, glancing at the unconscious man. "But really, who are you? Why do you keep saving m e?"

"Do you know Nara?" Hugo responded faintly.

She nearly jumped. "What the hell? You're awake?"

Hugo's eyes slowly opened, fixing on her with a frail yet intense look. "It's a place in Japan."

She stayed quiet, sensing he was about to reveal more from the depth of his enigmatic gaze.

30

THE DEER OF NARA

Masaki Misaki grew up in Nara, Japan. With his pale complexion, distinct nose, deep-set eyes, and tall frame, he stood out among the local kids. He had never known his father, adding to the mystery of his unique features.

"Your dad was an amazing pilot, but he died in a plane crash," his mother, Nami Misaki, told him.

"What was his name? Was he Japanese?" Masaki asked.

"That's not important. What matters is he was good-looking and loving."

"Got a picture of him?"

"Nah, he didn't leave any."

Seeing her son's look of disappointment, Nami gave him a comforting hug.

"Do you want to see him?"

He nodded then hesitated. "Wait... Is he, like, a ghost now?"

Nami gave a mysterious smile. "You'll find out."

On a radiant, sunny day, Nami brought Masaki to Nara Park. She pointed to the elegant sika deer roaming through the foliage and said, "When people full of love pass away, they turn into these beautiful deer, living free and peaceful lives."

Masaki looked at Nami then at the deer. He blinked and asked, "Can I find him here?"

"Let's see how it goes. Here's a hint. He has blue eyes," she replied.

As the sun dipped, casting the park in a golden glow, Masaki spotted a stag he was certain was his father. Majestic with impressive antlers, it lounged under a tree, its eyes a remarkable shade of blue.

Nami validated her son's belief. They bought deer crackers and offered them to "Dad." Watching the stag eat contentedly, Masaki imagined his father's happiness. The deer, remarkably polite, nodded its thanks. When Masaki reached out, the stag leaned in, welcoming his touch. Its tranquil blue eyes met his with a warmth that felt like a hug.

"Dad, I'll come see you a lot," he promised.

From that day forward, Masaki made regular visits to Nara Park to see his dad. He didn't always see him, but when he did, he would feed him crackers, chat with him, and gently pat his head. He never felt the absence of a father. As his mother said, "Your dad didn't leave us. He's just with us in a different form."

Masaki never faced questions or racism about his mixed background—half white, half Japanese—until he turned eleven.

One evening, as he pedalled his red bicycle home, he was confronted by a notorious troublemaker. Known among local kids as Spiky Hair, he was easily identified by his distinctive spikes dyed in vibrant yellows and greens.

"Time to pay up, don't you think?" Spiky Hair challenged.

"People don't pay tolls around here," Masaki said firmly.

Spiky Hair pulled him off his bike and shoved him to the ground.

"Bet your mom never told you she was a call girl in the States, huh?" he sneered. "Got knocked up by some random white guy. Take a good look in the mirror, and you'll see the real story!"

Despite his efforts to stay strong, Masaki couldn't hold back his tears when he got home and saw Nami. He shared with her what happened.

As she carefully wiped his swollen eyes with a damp towel, she said, "Never blame that boy, Masaki."

Confused, he looked at his mom.

"Pray for him. Pray he gets better. That's all you can do, right? Remember what I told you? Be kind, always. One day, you'll get what you deserve."

He chose to trust her, but he still had one more question.

"So Dad was really an amazing pilot, not some random white guy, right?"

"Why don't you ask him yourself?"

The next morning, Masaki woke up early and headed to Nara Park. Near a quaint bridge, he found his father—the serene, majestic stag. While feeding him crackers, he earnestly asked, "You were an amazing pilot and pretty handsome too, right? Not some random white guy?"

The stag gave a solemn nod while enjoying the crackers, a gesture Masaki took as confirmation. He felt an immense sense of relief.

A year later, as Masaki was riding home, he got a flat tire. Staring at the limp tire, unsure of what to do next, he heard a voice from behind.

"Need a hand?"

Turning around, he was surprised to see Spiky Hair, though the nickname no longer fit. The once wild hair was now cut into a neat, student-style trim. Clad in a school uniform with a backpack over his shoulder, he appeared taller and carried himself with a newfound politeness.

"Looks like there's a nail in your tire," Spiky Hair noted, kneeling to take a closer look. Glancing up at Masaki, he added, "No worries, I've got this."

Under the soft glow of twilight in Nara, Spiky Hair fetched a basin of water, located the tire's puncture, sealed it with a patch, and reinflated the tire.

"Thank you." Masaki said.

"It's nothing," Spiky Hair replied humbly.

As Masaki watched Spiky Hair walk away, he finally understood what Nami had told him.

Masaki felt like the happiest kid in the world, a sensation that lasted until a year later, when Nami was diagnosed with advanced liver cancer.

Even from her hospital bed, amidst excruciating pain, she radiated dignity, tenderly drying her son's tears. "I'm gonna be with Dad soon. You've gotta be happy for me," she whispered with gentle strength.

"Can I find you in Nara Park too?" he asked.

"You'll see." She blinked at him, giving him a gentle smile.

Honouring her promise, shortly after her passing, Masaki ventured to Nara Park on a tranquil afternoon. Beside his dad, a snow-white deer stood, as if plucked from the pages of a fairy tale.

"Mom!" he called out.

She nodded, approaching him. Embracing her, tears flowed uncontrollably.

There she was, alongside dad, her truth untarnished.

From then on, Masaki visited Nara Park often, bringing crackers for his deer parents, chatting with them, and sometimes just sitting in their company for hours.

He never felt like an orphan. Convinced of a peaceful life ahead in Nara, he believed that one day, he too would join his parents, transforming into another deer amidst the park's tranquility.

But destiny had other plans.

At fourteen, Masaki was called into a solemn meeting by the orphanage director. There, he discovered an extraordinary exception was being made to their policy on non-Japanese adoptions, all because of the remarkable identity of someone interested in adopting him.

"She's one of the biggest tech entrepreneurs in the world. Her business spans the globe, and she's involved in charity work in ninety-six countries. She even made the cover of Time magazine last year. With her looking out for you, your future's limitless," the director, his gray hair a testament to his years, excitedly told him.

Masaki, surprisingly calm, had one question. "Does this mean I have to leave Nara?"

"Nara will always be your home, no matter where you go," his soon-to-be adoptive mother reassured him.

Right from their first meeting, Masaki felt a connection with her. Dressed elegantly, she carried herself with a calm grace. Her Japanese, though not her first language, was impeccable. Her manner and expressions were filled with kindness and warmth, reminding him of Nami. Talking to her and meeting her gaze brought a sense of comfort and safety.

"I'd rather be your best friend than your mom," she said with a warm smile. "Call me Ming."

He soon learned her full name was Ming Yip, and she was one of the richest people in Asia. Yip quickly assumed the role of his guardian, whisking him away to her opulent mansion in the Mid-Levels of Hong Kong. Upon arrival, he was welcomed by a personal butler, five Filipino maids, and four formidable bodyguards. Almost overnight, the half-white Japanese orphan was catapulted into the life of a tycoon's son, amidst the wealth and luxury of Hong Kong's elite.

Despite the luxury that now enveloped him, he couldn't shake a sense of alienation. The lavish lifestyle felt strangely unsettling.

Soon after his arrival, Yip had him undergo a thorough medical check-up and genetic tests.

A week later, while having breakfast in the sun-drenched dining room of the magnificent mansion, he received a jolt.

"Looks like you're up for surgery tomorrow," she said casually.

Shocked, he asked, "Am I sick or something?"

"You're perfectly healthy," she reassured him.

"So why the surgery?"

"It's all about embracing a big humanitarian dream. You've got to be a bit of a pioneer for that."

He was clearly baffled, not quite catching her drift.

"You came into this world through a sperm donor, and you've inherited some exceptional genes. This makes you an ideal candidate for something truly extraordinary."

His confusion deepened. "Hold up, how can I be a test-tube baby? I've got parents!"

"True, you have parents. Your mom picked some top-notch sperm from a bank, and voilà, here you are," she explained plainly.

Taken aback, he responded, "No way, that's not possible. My dad was an amazing pilot!"

She shrugged. "He might have been. But donor details are always kept secret. Either way, you come from some elite lineage."

"That's not possible!" His distress was palpable as he pushed his food around. "I need to talk to her."

"Talk to whom?"

"My mom."

Yip looked taken aback. "You're not serious, are you?"

"She's not gone. She's...differently present," he said with conviction, puzzling her even more. "When people full of love pass away, they turn into those beautiful deer in Nara Park, living free and peaceful lives. That's what happened to my mom and dad!"

She paused then chuckled softly, her eyes warm. "Quite the tale, isn't it?"

His frustration boiled over, and he slammed his utensils down. "My mom's never lied to me!"

Yip, a bit surprised but still smiling, said, "Stick with what makes you happy. But rest up, you've got a big day tomorrow."

"I'm heading back to Nara now!"

"I've donated enough to keep that orphanage running for centuries. They're not backing out of our deal," she replied, unfazed.

"I don't give a shit about that!"

He tried to leave but was instantly tackled by his bodyguard. His struggles were useless. She continued her breakfast. A guard injected him with a sedative, and Masaki's world went dark.

Time had lost all meaning when he felt a gentle kiss on his cheek. He blinked awake and saw his mother's face, the white deer with flawless fur.

"Mom!"

He was in Nara Park, the midsummer sun warming his skin. His parents, both deer, stood beside him, their presence comforting.

But when he tried to hug his mother, his arms grasped nothing but air. The deer, like a ghostly hologram, was there but untouchable. The same happened with his father. Confusion washed over him as his surroundings twisted, and suddenly he was falling into an endless void.

31

HUGO

Masaki couldn't open his eyes, which felt like they were glued shut. His mouth wouldn't budge either, like his lips were sewn together with iron wire. He was numb, unaware of his own body. His mind floated, detached, in a sea of solitude. He wondered if he was dead but felt no fear. He imagined turning into one of the peaceful deer from Nara Park, joining his parents forever.

Out of nowhere, a gruff voice barked, "Wake up."

An unseen force pried his eyes open. Blinding white light stabbed at them like a thousand needles. He wanted to scream but couldn't, his lips numb. Slowly, the pain and temporary blindness faded, and he found himself staring at an endless, glaring white ceiling.

"Stand up." The deep voice persisted, compelling him. The unseen force gently lifted him to his feet, like invisible hands guiding him upright.

"Check your clothes then turn around slowly and take in your surroundings," the voice directed.

Compelled by the force, Masaki looked down. He was in a plain white patient's uniform, his feet bare. Slowly, he turned in a circle, taking in his surroundings. He was in a glass chamber at the heart of a sprawling research lab, surrounded by computers and strange instruments. Researchers, men and women, were busy at their stations. Some glanced his way, their faces showing a mix of anxiety and anticipation.

"Pleased to meet you. I'm Shawn Green," announced the man outside the glass chamber as the unseen force stopped Masaki's rotation. Wearing glasses and a suit, he had a small microphone clipped to his collar. His voice resonated within the chamber through a speaker.

"From now on, you're Hugo," Shawn said.

Masaki tried to yell, "I'm not Hugo! I'm Masaki Misaki! I want to go home! Please, let me go home!"

But what happened next was truly unsettling. The unseen force didn't only control his movements. It also seized his voice, forcing him to say, "I like this new name, thank you."

"Hugo, will you follow my orders without question?" Shawn asked.

"Yes, I will," Masaki answered, the unseen force commanding his words. He'd never faced anything like this before.

Shawn pressed his right hand against the glass chamber. "Come here," he said, "and match your palm to mine."

As the unseen force pushed Masaki towards Shawn, something inside him fought back, slowing him down. Shawn noticed, and his brow furrowed with concern.

Finally, Masaki stood directly in front of Shawn, separated only by the glass wall. Overcoming his resistance, he slowly lifted his left hand, pressing his palm against the glass to align with Shawn's.

Outside the chamber, over two hundred scientists erupted in applause, some even cheering, yet Shawn's face showed unease. His keen eyes detected a subtle dissonance in Masaki's gaze.

"You are still Hugo, aren't you?" Shawn asked.

"I am... I am..." Masaki's reply wavered as he struggled for control. A deep, buzzing noise echoed in his mind, followed by a wave of warmth as his circulation kicked in. "I am Masaki Misaki! Let me out! I want to go home!" He hammered on the glass.

A wave of agony slammed into him. His head felt like it was teeming with worms. The pain was so intense that he dropped, curling up on the floor in sheer torment.

The research lab fell into stunned silence.

Shawn, watching Masaki's tortured movements, looked disappointed.

Masaki felt the unseen force inside his brain returning, ready to take over his body. He wouldn't let it. Staggering to his feet, he took a few steps back and hurled himself at the glass wall.

Bang!

His head smashed into the glass. An explosive sensation reverberated through his skull. The world twisted, shattered, and spiralled into a dark vortex that swallowed him whole.

"I wish I'd died and woken up in Nara Park with my mom and dad," Hugo laughed, turning to Lacey. "Stupid, right?"

Lacey looked into his eyes, a captivating mix of Caucasian and East Asian heritage. Somehow, she believed his story, even though he was still a stranger.

"Humans cling to hope, even if it's a lie. They want 'forever,' but nothing lasts," he continued. "That's why AI will probably take over. They don't hope, and they don't care about 'forever.' They keep learning and changing everything." He paused, wincing from the pain in his wound.

"I'm gonna grab some painkillers."

She stood up, but he stopped her. "No need. I've had so much pain over the past two decades that I'm almost immune to it."

They exchanged a look, and he added, "I'm not kidding. Sit down, and I'll tell you about your family's secret."

"My family?" she asked, puzzled.

"Yeah, the Greens. Bet Shawn never told you about that, did he?"

She sat back down.

"That's what Shawn told me when I woke up in that lab. I was strapped to a metal bed with my head wrapped in bandages. Shawn said I'd hurt myself badly but wasn't in any danger. And then he said..."

"We gotta talk, Hugo."

Hugo didn't reply, closing his eyes.

"I'm gonna tell you something I've never told anyone, not even my family. I once vowed to take it to the grave. But I need to tell you now, because it's the only way to convince you why we have to make this project happen, no matter what."

32

GISELLE

George Green was born into a prestigious family of doctors in Birmingham, England. He followed his passion for psychology and quickly established himself in the field. By his early thirties, he had opened his own therapy clinic in Birmingham. Leveraging his family's extensive network, he attracted high-society clients. His growing reputation eventually led to an invitation to provide therapy for the royal family, significantly boosting his career.

One of George's clients, Edward Sinclair, hailed from a wealthy real estate family. Despite his seemingly perfect life, he plunged into a deep depression. His success had been handed to him on a silver platter, not earned through his own grit. This left him feeling alone and empty, haunted by the hollowness of his existence.

George, always on the cutting edge, knew Edward needed a comprehensive treatment plan. Back then, options were limited, but some emerging therapies showed promise.

Imipramine, a new tricyclic antidepressant, had been making waves with good results. George believed its impact on neurotransmitter activity could lift Edward's spirits faster than older treatments.

Alongside the medication, George used cognitive behavioural therapy (CBT) to tackle negative thought patterns. This dual approach aimed to hit both the biochemical and psychological roots of Edward's depression.

Over the next few weeks, George carefully monitored Edward's progress. The imipramine began to take effect, gradually improving Edward's mood. Their therapy sessions were intense but productive, with George guiding Edward through the process of challenging and reframing his negative thoughts. Edward responded well to the combination of medication and therapy, showing steady signs of improvement.

As months passed, Edward's condition continued to improve. He regained his energy, and his outlook on life brightened. By the end of a few months, he was no longer the shadow of a man he had been when he first sought George's help.

Edward was thrilled with how quickly and effectively George helped him overcome his depression. He rewarded George handsomely and promised to do a big favour for Shawn, whatever he needed.

"Like assassinating someone you hate or getting one of the dancers from the Birmingham Royal Ballet into bed?" Edward joked. "I know all of them. My dad's one of their biggest sponsors."

George smiled and then asked, "You sure?"

"Of course, George, I owe you big time."

"Did you go to the latest show of the Royal Ballet?"

"Oh yeah, Giselle, right?"

"Yeah, and you know the principal dancer, Elizabeth Henderson."

Edward looked at George and couldn't help but laugh. "Oh my god, George, I didn't expect this!"

"Well, you said you could... I'd appreciate it if I could have a cup of coffee with her, that's all."

Edward kept his word. A week later, George and Elizabeth sat in a cozy corner of a quaint Birmingham café, sipping their drinks. He learned she was from Lymington, a coastal town in southern England. She was a natural-born dancer who had joined the prestigious Birmingham Royal Ballet at nineteen. And she was really curious about the royal family.

"I heard you've even worked with the royal family. That must be quite something. How did that come about?" she asked.

George chuckled. "It's not all glitz and glamour. Picture this. I'm sitting there, trying to keep a straight face while the Duchess insists her corgi has anxiety. She swears the dog's depressed because it keeps losing at fetch to the royal spaniel."

Elizabeth laughed. "You're kidding!"

"Oh, I wish I were," George continued with a grin. "And then there was the time a prince—won't say which one—was convinced he had a rare condition because he started sleepwalking. Turns out, he was sneaking into the kitchen for midnight snacks. The cook was leaving out these incredible pastries, and the prince was subconsciously indulging. The family had to keep his weight in check, you know?"

Elizabeth giggled, nearly spilling her coffee. "Did you have to 'treat' him for that?"

"In a way," George said, enjoying her laughter. "I told them to have the cook stop making those irresistible pastries, and the prince stopped sleepwalking."

Elizabeth wiped a tear of laughter from her eye. "You must have a treasure trove of these stories."

"Oh, I do," George said, leaning in with a grin. "But I save the best ones for second dates."

"So when's that happening?"

"Tonight."

They locked eyes for a moment before she said, "Fuck you."

"Anytime," he replied.

They shared a bottle of Hennessy Richard and made love in George's luxury apartment until dawn.

Half a year later, Elizabeth and George got married, and soon she became pregnant. The union of the principal dancer from the Royal Ballet and one of Birmingham's top psychologists seemed perfect.

George believed he would always have a blessed life until the day of Elizabeth's labor. She encountered a severe complication known as obstructed labor, where the baby's head was too large to pass through her pelvis. This led to a prolonged and difficult delivery, causing a significant tear in her pelvic floor muscles. While she could still walk and perform daily activities, the damage meant she could no longer sustain the physical demands of ballet. She would never go back to the stage. That was when her mental health began to deteriorate.

George saw the warning signs and threw himself into helping Elizabeth. He administered Cognitive Behavioural Therapy (CBT) and Psychodynamic Therapy, and prescribed antidepressants and antipsychotics. Despite his best efforts, Elizabeth's condition worsened. She developed Dissociative Identity Disorder (DID), oscillating between her usual, kind self and a starkly different, vicious personality. George watched in anguish as the woman he loved struggled with her fractured mind, unable to restore her mental stability despite his professional expertise.

As Elizabeth's DID worsened, her vicious persona took over more often. During these episodes, she hallucinated, seeing a demon in the house threatening her young son, Shawn Green.

One evening, she grabbed a heavy candlestick and swung it wildly at the demon she believed was hiding in the shadows. The candlestick smashed into the living room mirror, sending shards of glass everywhere.

Another time, she flipped the dining table in a fit of rage, convinced the demon was lurking underneath. Plates, cutlery, and glasses crashed to the floor, shattering on impact.

One particularly harrowing night, Elizabeth was sure the demon was in Shawn's bedroom. She tore the room apart in a desperate attempt to protect him. She ripped open the mattress, pulled down shelves, and threw his toys across the room.

George's friends and family were worried sick about Elizabeth. Some told him to divorce her, thinking it was the only way to keep him and Shawn safe. But George refused. He loved Elizabeth deeply and was determined to help her, holding on to the hope that he could get her back on track.

As word spread that George, a respected psychologist, couldn't even help his own wife, his clients began to lose faith in him. More and more left his clinic, seeking help elsewhere, leaving George's career hanging by a thread.

Hoping for a fresh start where no one knew about Elizabeth's struggles, George decided to move his family to New Zealand. It seemed like the best way to escape the stigma and pressure. He chose Auckland, the biggest city in the country, with its mild climate, sunshine, and beaches, believing it would be good for Elizabeth's recovery and his family's well-being. He bought a house in the serene suburb of Remuera and set up a new clinic in the city to rebuild his career.

The fresh start brought George, Elizabeth, and little Shawn a period of peace and happiness. Elizabeth seemed to really enjoy life in that isolated but beautiful country. As George continued to provide her with Cognitive Behavioural Therapy (CBT), supportive psychotherapy, and a regimen of antidepressants and antipsychotic medications, Elizabeth's condition showed significant improvement.

Years later, the Birmingham Royal Ballet held a touring show of "Giselle" in Australia and New Zealand. Posters for the show were everywhere in Auckland. Elizabeth didn't say anything when she saw them, which made George uneasy. But then she told him, "Don't worry about it. I'm happy now and think we should really watch the show."

George took Elizabeth to see the performance. They talked about it afterward, sharing their thoughts and feedback. She seemed normal and happy, which relieved him. He believed his beloved wife was completely recovered.

George was wrong. The shadows of the past were far from gone and were now looming over their son, Shawn.

33

MERCER BAY LOOP TRACK

"Fire! Fire!"

The shouts outside jolted seven-year-old Shawn awake. He barely had time to get out of bed before a wave of heat blasted his door open. Flames, like the tongues of a ravenous beast, licked into his room.

With a loud crash, Gary from next door smashed the window with his elbow.

"Come on, Shawn!" he yelled, reaching out.

The fire had already crawled up the window frame, forming a blazing barrier. Shawn jumped out of bed and, like a circus dog leaping through a hoop, dove through the fiery window into Gary's arms.

"Jeez!" A spark landed in Gary's thick beard, and he quickly smothered it with his hands. Hoisting Shawn onto his back, he dashed out of the garden. Shawn watched as his home was engulfed in flames, glowing fiercely in the still-dark dawn.

"Mum! What about my mum?" he shouted, panic-stricken.

"Don't worry, I'll get her!" Gary assured him.

Gary sprinted down the street with Shawn on his back, not stopping until they reached a safe spot where his wife and two daughters, Julia and Chloe, waited anxiously.

He set Shawn down and turned back towards the burning house.

"Be careful, Gary!" his wife shouted as he disappeared into the flames.

"Oh my God, it's in our garden!" Julia gasped, staring at the fire.

Shawn watched the fire like a huge, red demon about to swallow his mom and home. In that moment, he pictured Elizabeth burning to a skeleton.

"No, no!" He tried to run towards the flames, but Gary's wife grabbed him, holding him tight.

"She'll be fine!" she said, holding him tight. Then she saw her younger daughter running towards the flames. "Chloe! What are you doing?!" She turned to Julia, frantic. "Get her!"

"Oh, crap! Chloe!" Julia, her school's rugby star, sprinted after her sister and tackled her.

"No! My lemon tree!" Chloe cried, struggling to break free.

Chloe was about Shawn's age and a generous girl. She had planted the lemon tree herself. Its branches stretched over the fence into Shawn's garden. She promised Shawn he could have any fruit that grew on his side. But now the fire from Shawn's house had spread to Chloe's garden, and the lemon tree was the first casualty.

Gary managed to rescue Elizabeth. The firefighters soon arrived and put out the blaze, but Shawn's home, garden, and Gary's garden were badly burned.

George, who was on a house call in Hamilton, rushed back to Auckland as soon as he heard about the incident. His first stop was Middlemore Hospital, a specialised burn treatment centre. Shawn had burns on his legs, while Elizabeth had extensive burns on her legs, hips, and back. They were both being treated there.

"What happened?" George asked, sitting beside Shawn's hospital bed.

"I don't know. I was asleep," Shawn replied. "Must've been an accident."

George stared at his son. "Shawn, be straight with me. This is important. For your mum."

Shawn hesitated then whispered, "Mum told me the other day..."

George nodded, urging him on.

"She said there's a demon in our house, trying to hurt me. She said burning it was the only way to protect me."

George sighed, stood up, and turned to leave.

"Don't tell anyone, okay? I promised her," Shawn pleaded.

George left without a word.

George reported Elizabeth, providing enough evidence of her Dissociative Identity Disorder. Despite the diagnosis, she was taken into custody. At her court appearance, she repeatedly claimed she saw a demon in the house trying to hurt her son, so she started the fire to burn the demon.

The judge, concerned for her mental state, ordered a comprehensive psychiatric evaluation. Elizabeth was sent to Carrington Hospital, a prominent psychiatric facility at the time, to begin a one-year intensive treatment program.

Shawn was haunted not only by the incident but also by the guilt of betraying his mother.

"You actually helped Mum, and she knows it." Despite George's reassurances, Shawn felt uneasy until midway through the evaluation when George took him to visit Elizabeth. She hugged and kissed Shawn, telling him she was getting much better and would be home soon.

After a year of intensive treatment, Elizabeth's condition improved significantly. She passed the Mental State Examination (MSE), a comprehensive test assessing her cognitive and emotional stability, and was finally allowed to return home.

Eager to leave the past behind, George sold their house in Remuera and bought a new one in Piha, a secluded area on Auckland's West Coast. The new house was nestled near the breathtaking Mercer Bay Loop Track.

The Green family quickly settled into their new home, beginning what Shawn remembered as the happiest period of his childhood. After dinner, George and Elizabeth often took him to the Mercer Bay Loop Track. Winding through lush forests and climbing gentle slopes, the trail led them to the cliff tops. There, nestled between his mom and dad, Shawn would watch the sun dip below the horizon.

Shawn believed his life would always be as charming as this until one evening when only Elizabeth took him for a walk on the track, as George was late from work. While they sat on the cliff together, she suddenly turned to him and whispered, "The demon is still here, Shawn. It's lurking around, waiting."

Shawn was speechless. He could see the genuine fear in his mother's eyes, as if she was telling the truth.

"Don't tell anyone about this, not even your dad, or we're all kaput. You get me?" she pressed.

He nodded without saying anything.

"I had to fake my way through all those rubbish tests to get back home and protect you. So don't betray me this time. You with me?" she added.

He nodded again.

"Answer me."

"Yes, Mum, I'll keep it for you."

"Not for me, for you! I'm doing all this for you."

"Okay, Mum..."

After a week of hesitation, Shawn finally decided to tell George what Elizabeth had confided in him on the clifftop. George was shocked and anxious.

"Never walk with her alone again, got it?"

"Yeah, but what do we do? I don't want them to send her away again."

"Don't worry about that. I'm on it. She'll be fine, but I need some time. Do as I say, alright?"

"Alright."

One evening, George returned late from work. Elizabeth made a delicious apple crumble for Shawn and said, "Why don't we go see the sunset?"

"I've got homework. Maybe next time?" Shawn replied gently, remembering George's warning.

Elizabeth sighed, looking sad, almost in tears.

"Oh, Mum, I... Let's wait until Dad's back, okay? We can go together."

"But the sunset will be gone by then. Such a pity. I want some company."

The tone she used and the way she looked at him made it impossible for Shawn to refuse.

They walked the familiar path, the sky ablaze with the hues of twilight. The air was crisp, and the sound of the waves crashing against the rocks below echoed around them. Everything seemed perfect, except she kept walking slightly behind him, her presence unsettling. He felt a chill and stopped, turning to face her.

"What's wrong, darling?" she asked, the sunset casting her face in eerie shades of red and orange.

"Mum, I..."

"Keep walking. We have to catch the sunset before it's gone," she interrupted, her tone sharp and urgent.

Reluctantly, he had to keep walking, and she stayed behind him, like a shadow. The familiar path now felt sinister, the once comforting sounds of waves crashing against the rocks now echoing ominously. He kept telling himself she was his mum, and it would be fine, but a nagging doubt gnawed at him. Every step he took felt heavier, the air around them thick with tension.

The timing was perfect as they reached the summit, just as the sunset reached its peak beauty.

"Come on, Shawn, here, the perfect spot!"

He was forced to stand there, her grip like iron.

"Mum, I'm cold. Let's go home," he pleaded.

"Shh, watch."

Shawn tried to focus on the sight before him, which was indeed breathtaking. The sun dipped below the horizon, casting a golden glow across the ocean. The sky was painted in brilliant shades of orange, pink, and purple. But the stunning view couldn't distract him from the fear creeping up his spine.

Elizabeth's eyes stayed fixed on the horizon, but her grip tightened. "Do you see it, Shawn?"

"Yeah, Mum."

"What do you see?"

"The...sunset. It's beautiful."

"No, not that."

"Mum?"

"The demon."

"No, Mum, I..."

"It's behind you."

He couldn't move as she gripped his shoulder tightly, standing behind him. She leaned in close to his ear and whispered, "Can you feel it? Its breath, its scent, it's on you now."

"Please, Mum, let's go back," he begged, his heart pounding.

Elizabeth shoved Shawn towards the cliff's edge, but a strong hand grabbed his arm, stopping his fall.

"Jesus Christ!" George shouted, pulling Elizabeth away from Shawn. For a fleeting moment, they locked eyes, and George's heart sank. "You can't do this!"

Elizabeth shrieked, "I'm trying to protect him!"

She lunged at Shawn again, but George held her back. They struggled fiercely, teetering on the edge of the cliff.

"Dad! Mum!" Shawn cried, watching his parents fight, paralysed with fear.

With a powerful shove, George sent Elizabeth over the edge.

"No!" Shawn screamed.

The world seemed to freeze as Elizabeth's scream echoed and faded into the distance. George dropped to his knees, his body trembling. Shawn stood rooted to the spot, eyes wide with horror and confusion, as the sunset gave way to an eerie night.

"Mum did it herself. She jumped, that's it. You get me? I don't want you to be an orphan," George told Shawn before the cops arrived.

Shawn stayed silent, leaving George worried he might spill the truth.

When the cops asked Shawn what happened, he said, "She jumped. I saw Mum jump, so I went back home to get Dad."

After investigating, the police confirmed that Elizabeth's death was a suicide.

George shut down his clinic and quit his career. Shawn figured it was because he felt like a failure, unable to help his own wife. They didn't move away and instead stayed in the house but got rid of anything that reminded them of Elizabeth. They never talked about her, as if she had never existed.

George didn't date. He spent all his time with Shawn after work. He bought a trailer, taking Shawn on drives around the beautiful countryside during school holidays. They relaxed on stunning beaches during sunny weekends and went to the cinema to watch Hollywood films during the city's typical wet winters.

Their life was peaceful and routine. Yet, they never went back to the Mercer Bay Loop Track, even though it was less than a kilometre from their house.

Shawn always remembered his mum with love, though he never expressed it to anyone. He never thought of forgiving her because he didn't believe she was truly vicious. He believed there was a demon, not in him but in her. Attending a Christian school, he started to believe in God. He thought that if he had found faith earlier, he might have helped her rid herself of the demon.

He didn't think of forgiving George either because he didn't believe what he did to Elizabeth was on purpose, even though it seemed that way. He prayed for his father every day, believing his beloved God would absolve George of what he had done.

Everything in Shawn's life seemed to be going smoothly until his eighteenth birthday. It was a sunny day, and George told him to be home by 7 p.m. because he had something important planned. Shawn assumed it would be a big gift or a special surprise. But when he arrived home on time, he found the house empty, except for a beautiful chocolate birthday cake and a letter on the dining table.

Happy Birthday, Shawn.

Thank you for covering for me all these years. Because of you, I was able to stay with you and watch you grow. Thank you for allowing me to be your father. That was the best thing I ever experienced in my life.

I've set up a trust fund for you. You have enough money to study abroad and make a better life for yourself. I guess my mission here is over. But before I go, I want to convince you of one thing. Psychology is actually a big lie. Every psychologist lies to their patients to convince them they're alright. But the lie doesn't last, and their demons will come back to haunt them. It's only a matter of time.

I noticed that you want to study psychology, and I think you shouldn't. Study something else, or you'll carry too much burden throughout your life, like me.

Remember, life's tough, but picking the right path can really change things.

Farewell, Shawn. I wish you a fabulous and peaceful life.

Love you.

Shawn knew where George had gone as soon as he finished reading the letter. He rushed to Mercer Bay Loop Track. Even though he hadn't been there in over ten years, everything was still vividly familiar. The sky was ablaze with twilight hues. He felt the crisp air and heard the waves crashing against the rocks, whispering an old, sad story. By the time he reached the cliff top, the marvellous sunset was beginning, as beautiful as he remembered. But there was no one there.

Shaking, he had to pull himself together. He moved cautiously to the edge and looked down.

George was down there on the rugged rocks far below. Shawn couldn't see his face or make out any details in the dim light, but he knew it was him.

He remained at the edge, doing nothing but watching the mesmerising sky gradually lose its light until it was completely dark.

"Guess what I found in George's patient records? Eighty-five percent of his patients' issues came back—including Edward Sinclair, the rich guy who set up him and Elizabeth. Edward killed himself before George did. George was right—mental problems always come back to haunt you, no matter what you do. Therapy and evaluations only mask the issues for a while. They never last. And all those medications? They're just drugs. You take them, you're fine. Stop, and you're screwed. Eventually, you get immune to them and end up worse off. That's human psychology. Brutal but true."

"That's what Shawn told me after he spilled the Green family tragedy to me," Hugo said.

The revelation left Lacey stunned. She finally understood why Shawn wanted his ashes scattered on the cliff top of the Mercer Bay Loop Track, where his father, mother, and childhood were buried.

"His past weighed heavily on him. He thought every disaster stemmed from mental problems. And he believed there was only one fix: regulation," Hugo continued.

"You know why humans run the world and animals don't?" Shawn said to Masaki. "Because animals don't make rules, but humans do.

Think about it—human history is an endless stream of regulations. Constitutions, laws, morals, rules—it's all about regulation. The better we regulate ourselves, the better we live. It's not about having more or fewer regulations. More doesn't always mean better. Look at authoritarian countries like Russia, China, North Korea. They have tons of regulations, but they're the wrong kind, stripping people of freedom. Do you think people in the U.S. are free? Not really. The U.S. just has smarter regulations that make you feel free while keeping you in check. Everything comes down to regulation. Even religion. You know why I believe in God? Because He has the best rules for me. So what do we need for psychos, freaks, and those with mental issues? Only regulation! We need a perfect system to manage them smoothly and effectively. That's what my GPM is all about!"

Hugo could still recall the fury and madness on Shawn's face as he spoke.

"Listen, we have to work on this together. There's no shortcut. Once we pull this off, I promise you'll get back all the freedom you can imagine—personal, financial, everything. I swear to God."

Masaki had no choice but to become Hugo.

Shawn and his team embarked on the mission to train GPM in gaining absolute control over Hugo's actions and speech via the chip in his brain. It was a journey filled with harrowing pain, beyond anyone's imagination.

"I know this is tough, but you're gonna do things you never dreamed of," Shawn always told him. "You're gonna be a hero, make history."

Hugo became a living, breathing training ground for GPM. They pushed him to perform extreme and dangerous activities, relentlessly driving him to his limits—and then beyond. Nothing was off-limits. He was no longer just living; he was surviving. Reduced to a lab rat, he felt trapped in an endless prison, living on the edge every second.

Two decades of this brutality took their toll. Hugo watched as GPM grew into an incredible AGI, unlike anything anyone had ever seen or imagined.

Adaptation became his only defence. Hugo learned to endure the pain, the fear, the struggle, and the despair. He even believed he was already dead, like a zombie.

"Shawn kept telling me that once GPM was fully developed, I'd be free and rewarded. I was stupid enough to believe him. After Yip and Shawn turned everyone on the R&D team into puppets, guess what happened to me?" Hugo sweated from the pain, his forehead shining under the dim light. "I became a puppet with a special job, Yip's top hitman."

34

THE MISSIONS

Hugo, scared and disoriented, found himself speeding down the North Lantau Highway in a black Range Rover. Ahead, a convoy of several police cars flanked a guarded prison van. The convoy moved south as his Range Rover sped north on a parallel overpass.

As they approached, his hands, moving with robotic precision, drew a pistol from the console and cracked open the window. As the vehicles neared the crossing point, he fired a single, silenced shot. The bullet traveled through the tiny gap in the Range Rover's window, penetrated the back window of the heavily guarded van, and blew the prisoner's head apart. He was powerless, a mere spectator in his own body as GPM masterfully controlled his every move to execute the stunning assassination.

The Range Rover didn't slow down, tearing along the highway as chaos erupted in the convoy. Its tinted windows and windshield kept Hugo's face hidden from CCTV. The fake license plate left no trace back to him.

Hugo couldn't predict what would unfold next. He watched himself speeding through city streets, heading towards a broken bridge under construction. Terror gripped him as he accelerated towards the unfinished edge, setting fire to the interior. Flames licked at the inside. Before the Range Rover hurtled off the edge into the sea, he jumped, plunging into the water alongside the burning vehicle.

With all evidence gone, Hugo swam to the rural shore and vanished.

"Fucking hell!" Lacey exclaimed.

"Later, I found out the prisoner I killed was James Cheung, a social media celebrity and the most powerful human rights activist in Hong Kong. He'd spent the last five years behind bars for his relentless advocacy of human rights and democracy and against the Chinese Communist Party. His supporters had rallied on social media, keeping his cause alive on TikTok, Facebook, Instagram, and X. He was a symbol of hope, and his imminent release was expected to reignite the pro-democracy movement, making the CCP deeply uneasy. Minister Gu had expressed the party's concerns to Yip over high tea. He hadn't asked or commanded anything, but Yip knew exactly what needed to be done. And that's how I got my first mission."

Lacey's voice trembled as she broke the heavy silence. "I know I shouldn't ask, but...how many missions have you done like that?"

Hugo's response was almost mechanical, devoid of emotion. "Seven hundred and ninety-eight."

She looked at him in disbelief.

"I got used to it. My blood ran cold with each mission. Once, it even drove me to kill a child."

"What the fuck?"

It was a rainy night.

Hugo sat in a black Toyota Camry, eyes glued to the window of the bustling Golden Dragon Bistro. The place was a local favourite, known for its perfect blend of traditional Cantonese and modern dishes. Inside, a middle-aged woman with short, sleek black hair was celebrating

something special with two kids, a nine-year-old boy and a six-year-old g
irl.

That was Sarah Li, the deputy secretary for security in the Hong Kong Special Administrative Region. She oversaw law enforcement and public safety policies, giving her access to top-secret information and high-level meetings. This made her a priceless asset to MI6, who needed her to keep tabs on the Chinese Communist Party's moves to crush democracy in Hong Kong.

The CCP had meticulously monitored Sarah Li, convinced her actions amounted to espionage against their regime. They had enough evidence to detain her, but given she had already transferred many top secrets to MI6, they wanted to give her a stronger punishment. Minister Gu addressed this to Yip without specifying what a stronger punishment could be. Yip figured it out herself and prompted GPM to launch a mission for its puppet zero. That was why Hugo was outside the restaurant.

Sarah said something to her kids before heading to the bathroom. Hugo slipped on a glove and exited the car, moving swiftly towards the restaurant.

As he entered and walked past Sarah's table, he saw the boy gently pat his sister's hand to sneak a bite of the birthday cake. The boy had round eyes, black curly hair, and an innocent, chubby face.

"We gotta wait for mum! It's her birthday!" the boy said.

Silently, he tracked Sarah to a secluded corner of the lobby that led to the bathrooms. After checking to ensure no one was around, he entered the women's restroom.

Sarah was bent over the sink, washing her hands, and didn't notice it was a man who had entered until his looming shadow was close behind her.

"Excuse me?" She was confused.

He moved with robotic precision, wrapping the wire around her neck in an instant. She couldn't make a sound, only struggle, her face contorting in pain and desperation. He tightened the wire, cutting off her air. She struggled weakly, her movements growing feeble until her body went completely limp.

He wasn't heartbroken, having grown numb to this. His only hope was that no one entered the restroom before he left. Otherwise, he'd have to kill more than one tonight.

As he exited the bathroom, he walked past Sarah's table. The boy and girl sat there, eagerly waiting for their mother to come back so they could grab the cake. They had no idea they'd spent their last moment with her.

GPM guided him back to the black Camry. He opened his laptop and hacked into the CCTV system of the restaurant and the surrounding area. He deleted his image from the footage, erasing any trace of his presence.

That night, Hugo heard a whisper while he was sleeping. It was the chubby boy's voice. "Where's mum? We're waiting for her."

He couldn't open his eyes; GPM kept them shut. The boy's voice seemed incredibly real and close, as if he were right there. He could even hear him swallow.

"I felt like I was being haunted. He stayed with me for a long time, until he died."

"Did they make you kill him?" asked Lacey.

"No, he had a congenital heart defect. His condition worsened after I killed his mum, so that was on me. I killed him."

Lacey felt a bit guilty towards Hugo since her father was behind the conspiracy. She tried to pull herself together, showing strength instead of weakness. "At least we're free now. Let's forget the past and work together to take down Yip, okay?"

"We're only temporarily free. We'll be her puppets again soon."

Lacey frowned, puzzled.

"I saw him die," Hugo said.

"What? Who?"

"Shawn."

35

REQUIEM

Publicly, Hugo was still Yip's adopted son, and she made it look like she was grooming him to be her successor. For the past six years, besides doing her dirty work, he was also her first secretary. One of his tasks was to track every advancement the puppet R&D team made to GPM, though it was mostly for show since GPM called the shots. Hugo saw firsthand how Yip and Shawn used GPM to manipulate top scientists, pushing them to constantly upgrade the AGI, making it more powerful and aggressive. In six years, GPM's reach exploded, growing from controlling less than a thousand puppet chips to over a billion simultaneously.

It was a grim night. Hugo, driven by GPM, was on his usual routine: picking up Shawn from his penthouse at Celestial Manor to take him to the R&D lab. As GPM's algorithm, Shawn was a stickler for punctuality, so Hugo expected him to be ready and waiting. But when he unlocked the penthouse, he was met with darkness and an unsettling silence—Shawn was nowhere to be found.

"Dr. Green?" Hugo's voice echoed through the emptiness, met only by silence.

This was completely unexpected for GPM, so it prompted Hugo to meticulously search each room, but he found nothing. With real-time feeds from every CCTV in and out of the building, GPM was certain Shawn hadn't stepped out. The rooftop garden seemed the most likely place he could be. As GPM led Hugo there for a more thorough search, he felt a chilling sensation—a cold piece of metal pressed against the back of his head. A sharp buzzing sound followed, and his world plunged into darkness.

Time became a blur as Hugo slowly regained consciousness. When he opened his eyes, he was greeted by the sprawling view of Central Hong Kong, as if he were soaring through the sky.

He soon realised he was actually fastened to a chair on the rooftop's edge outside the vast glasshouse. Electronic cuffs secured his ankles, and his arms, tied behind him, were clamped together at the wrists.

What truly astounded him wasn't his precarious position but the sudden autonomy over his body. For the first time in two decades, he could move and feel freely—his body, long commandeered by GPM, was finally his own again.

"Mr. Misaki."

Hugo jerked at the familiar voice behind him, his heart skipping a beat. It was Shawn, and it was the first time he had called him by his real name.

Shawn's footsteps approached and stopped beside Hugo, still out of sight.

"What the hell is going on?" Hugo blurted out, realising he was truly speaking for himself for the first time in years.

Still standing behind Hugo, Shawn spoke calmly, "Once you're free, check the suitcase behind you. It's got the Autonomous Neural Decoy Interface, ANDI. I used it to establish a NearLink Protocol with your brain's puppet chip, sending bogus data back to GPM. That's how you broke free while GPM still thinks it controls you."

"Is this a trap? Some kind of test? Or another damn trial?" Hugo snapped.

"I'm here to keep my promise and set things straight."

"Then why am I tied up?"

"I want to chat before I let you go."

Hugo fell silent, unsure if the man behind him was deceiving him.

"There are two ways to free a puppet from GPM," Shawn said. "One is yanking the chip out, but given its size and placement, that's too risky. We're left with plan B: destroy GPM's core. That's the heart of the system. Take that down, and every chip goes dark. Everyone's free—including you."

Hugo, having been a living, breathing training ground for GPM for two decades, understood how GPM worked and agreed with what Shawn had revealed. What he doubted was why Shawn, a man who seemed loyal to Yip, was doing something against her.

"I made a terrible mistake and am seeking redemption now. I need you to believe me, Masaki, even if you don't feel like it."

Hugo stayed silent.

"The GPM's core is in the top chamber of the GrandTec Tower. Yip's the only one who can access it because of the incredibly smart AI security system. The only way to get in is to kidnap her and force her to take you there."

"Kidnap her? No fucking way! You know that, don't you?"

"Yeah."

"So what the hell are you talking about?"

"Because I'm sure you can do it."

"Fuck off. Why not handle it yourself? You created this mess."

Shawn paused before replying, "I wish I could."

"What's that supposed to mean?"

"My time's up. It's the end of the line for me."

"What, you got cancer? You're dying?"

"And I need a favour. My daughter's in New York now, but she might head to Hong Kong soon. I need you to do everything you can to send her back ASAP. I don't want her caught up in this."

"Piss off! I don't give a shit about your daughter!"

Silence stretched between them before Shawn finally spoke. "I actually believe what your mum said about the deer in Nara Park."

"You know what? That's bullshit. When people are gone, they're gone."

"I hope I end up in Nara Park."

"Hell no, you're going straight to hell. And I'm not babysitting your damn daughter!"

"You will, Masaki. I know you better than you do."

"Cut the crap! Let me go now!"

Shawn stepped out from behind Hugo and jumped off the edge, vanishing into the darkness below.

"What the fuck?" Hugo exclaimed, shocked.

The electronic cuffs unlocked automatically. He stood and peered over the building's edge, but the pitch-black night revealed nothing. Turning around, he spotted the suitcase Shawn had mentioned. Inside, he found a gun-like metal device—the ANDI Shawn had referred to.

Hugo couldn't figure out how Shawn had developed such a powerful sabotage against GPM until he used ANDI to free Chris and Yvonne. It turned out Shawn, Chris, Yvonne, and other key team members had been collaborating on this for the past three years. Shawn claimed to be developing a new subsystem to optimise GPM's data processing and decision-making. GPM, believing these improvements would boost its power and efficiency, trusted its creator. Shawn then led the team to develop the subsystem, ensuring that each enhancement subtly contributed to the development of ANDI, gradually building the powerful countermeasure.

Lacey felt better after Hugo's reveal. Although Shawn was still a co-conspirator with Yip, at least he had done something redeeming.

"But GPM found out about ANDI, and it's correcting it now. Once it's done, we're all back to being puppets. You don't have much time left," Hugo concluded.

"It doesn't make sense. Even if I get back to New York, once I'm a puppet again, it can make me do anything," Lacey retorted.

"ANDI is powerful too, so it'll take GPM some time to beat it down. Get back to New York ASAP. Talk to the NYPD if you can't reach the FBI directly. Let them check your brain for the chip. They'll find a way to help you, whether it's surgery or something else. It's way better than staying here and becoming a puppet for the rest of your life. Isn't it?"

She couldn't argue with that. But when she asked Hugo about his next move, he simply said, "I'm staying. I've got a secret weapon."

A secret weapon?

36

A HAPPY-ENOUGH ENDING

Enveloped in darkness, Lacey navigated the desolate streets. The pandemic and riots had turned Hong Kong into a ghost town, a scene straight out of a dystopian nightmare. The city that once bustled with life was now eerily silent, the deadly emptiness echoing in the night. Malls looked like they'd been hit by looters, their windows shattered and doors ajar. Shops were shuttered, and abandoned vehicles, including flipped buses, littered the area. Debris, discarded clothes, shoes, and even bloodstains marked her path—a grim reminder of the chaos that had un folded.

Lacey finally reached her destination, a closed pub named Blue in Lan Kwai Fong. She found a hidden corner near the pub, shrouded in shadows beyond the reach of the streetlights, and felt a profound sense of isolation and defeat weighing heavily on her soul. She had once sworn she'd do anything to step out of Michelle's shadow for good. Yet now she found herself surprisingly missing her. She had believed Shawn to be the most reliable person in the world, but now she realised her trust in him had become a curse. All she could cling to was the hope for a happy-enough ending—to safely make it back to New York.

"I've got nowhere to go." That was what Hugo called his "secret weapon." He seemed really desperate to Lacey. She didn't completely trust him but had no choice and felt forced to gamble.

The refrigerated truck Hugo had mentioned arrived right on time, its windows tinted black to conceal the cabin's interior.

Lacey stepped forward and knocked on the window. A small gap opened, revealing nothing but a rough cough from inside. Taking it as a signal, she slipped the blood-stained card through—the one Hugo had given her as the driver's business card. He said this was the password.

A gravelly male voice came from within the truck. "Name?"

"Nami," she answered. This was another password Hugo had given her, his mother's name.

The password seemed to work, the window opening further. As she braced to confront whoever was inside, a down coat was tossed out. She caught it, but when she looked back, the window had narrowed to a sliver.

"Don't fall asleep," the driver warned.

"What?" She didn't quite understand.

The window stayed shut, and the electric door of the refrigerated container began to open, releasing a burst of cold air.

She knew what to do next. Hugo had been clear that her only option was to hide in the specially designed container that could fool any form of scanning. It was lined with a combination of lead and advanced stealth materials, capable of blocking X-rays, thermal imaging, and other detection methods.

She wrapped the down coat tightly around herself and climbed into the refrigerated compartment. The door closed with a soft thud behind her. Inside, the container was vast, packed with frozen beef. Finding a corner, she curled up into a ball. As the vehicle began to move, she whispered a prayer for a smooth journey.

Thanks to the high-quality down coat, it took a good half hour before she started to feel the cold creeping in. She tried moving around to generate some warmth, but being surrounded by frozen beef severely limited her mobility.

An hour in, the cold had seeped through all her layers, biting at her skin with a frozen, painful grip. Her limbs turned stiff, making even the slightest movement a struggle. She began talking to herself, hoping it might generate a bit of warmth.

The truck stopped several times over the next hour, likely for checkpoints, but their destination seemed miles away.

Her facial muscles were completely numb, and she could no longer talk to herself. Her eyelids drooped shut out of exhaustion. She realised then why the driver had warned her against falling asleep. Hypothermia could lead to unconsciousness, and waking up might be impossible. Determined, she bit down hard, forcing herself to stay awake.

Time painfully stretched on, and they still hadn't reached their destination. Oddly enough, she began to feel an unbearable heat.

She shed her coat, seeking relief, but it was only momentary. It felt as though her body was on fire. She continued to undress, unaware she was experiencing paradoxical undressing. Her core temperature had plummeted, causing her blood vessels to dilate and creating a deceptive feeling of warmth.

This was a harbinger of imminent death.

Exhausted, she lacked the strength to redress. Naked, she curled up among the frozen beef, nearly becoming one with them.

As consciousness was slipping away, the truck began to slow and eventually came to a halt.

Through her haze, she heard the cargo door swing open.

Someone draped a down coat around her and lifted her out of the compartment. She was gently placed on a soft, warm surface, and a pill was popped into her mouth. After swallowing, her senses slowly returned. She realised she was wrapped in the coat, lying on a patch of grass. She figured the person helping her was probably the driver.

Once she fully came to, the refrigerated truck was gone. Beside her on the grass were her clothes, a cellphone, and her passport, now stamped with a visa for China.

She dressed quickly, guessing she was somewhere on the outskirts of Shenzhen, judging by the suburban road. Despite the darkness, she managed to turn on the cellphone. She found her flight confirmation, Chinese apps like DiDi, the equivalent of Uber, and WeChat with some RMB loaded. There was also a photo guide on how to use the apps for calling a ride, paying for meals, and so on.

Without wasting time, she began to flag down a ride. Five minutes later, a sleek black Audi A6L sedan pulled up in front of her. The driver, clad in a crisp suit, courteously opened the door for her. As she settled into the car, she found water and snacks prepared for her—an indulgence she didn't resist.

She reached Bao'an Airport in the early hours to find it unusually serene. Gliding through security was effortless. The officers, though puzzled by an American traversing China without luggage, raised no questions.

It wasn't until she was seated in the airport lounge, finishing a bowl of noodles with meats and vegetables of unknown origin, that she felt a semblance of normalcy return to her body.

The lounge soon filled with the sound of the boarding call for her flight to New York's Kennedy Airport. Overwhelmed by emotion, she almost gave in to tears.

It was the best conclusion Lacey could have hoped for.

She didn't know how to contact the FBI, so once she returned to New York, she would reach out to the NYPD first and disclose everything. Given the complexity of GPM and the puppet chips, she assumed it might require surgery or some advanced intervention to prove there was a puppet chip in her brain. Anyway, she was confident they would find a way to save her.

As she joined the queue for boarding, her spirits soared. Victory seemed a flight away, home calling her back. Never in her twenty-eight years had she felt such a profound affection for New York.

But as she moved to board, a deep, buzzing noise suddenly filled her head, audible only to her.

Confused, she stopped in her tracks.

What alarmed her even more was her own voice telling the perplexed flight attendant, "Sorry, I can't board right now. Something came up."

The attendant, clearly baffled, responded, "But, Miss, the flight departs soon."

With a faint smile and an air of calm, she replied, "Thanks for the heads-up. Looks like I've gotta change my plans."

Without a backward glance, she turned and walked away from the boarding gate.

She knew it was all over.

GPM's self-correction had been completed, and she was its puppet once again. The happy-enough ending she was about to secure slipped away at the final moment.

37

—— · ——

A SIMPLE QUESTION

The high-speed train from Shenzhen North to Hong Kong's West Kowloon left at 6:38 a.m. on the dot, like clockwork. With Hong Kong in lockdown, Lacey practically had the whole train to herself. But she couldn't appreciate the luxury. She had lost control of her body and speech, tormented by the uncertainty of her fate and the potential horrors that awaited her.

When she arrived in Hong Kong, the sun had just risen. Martial law had brought the city to a standstill, leaving taxis and buses nowhere to be seen. GPM directed her to an abandoned restaurant where she found a metal spoon. She used it to jimmy open the door of an airport bus. With AGI's precise guidance, she popped open the panel beneath the steering wheel. Using the spoon, she pried apart the ignition wires, found the right pair, and sparked them together. The engine roared to life without a key.

Despite having no prior experience driving a bus, she skilfully navigated the massive vehicle through the city's streets, her destination unknown. Every major intersection was blocked by police cars, with numerous officers standing guard. She encountered no obstacles, as if the police had silently agreed to let her through. This made her even more fearful, suspecting Yip might have set a trap. She couldn't fathom how Yip might choose to torment her next.

As dawn broke, she reached China Merchants Wharf. Abandoning the bus, she boarded a speedboat, prepped and ready at the dock. She set off northwest and soon arrived at Green Island.

On the shore, a seemingly pre-arranged empty taxi awaited her. She drove it to the Green Island Reception Centre, a prison once used to detain smugglers from Vietnam and other regions, now long abandoned.

Clearly, GPM knew exactly what it was doing.

Lacey stepped through the rusted gates of the abandoned prison, picking her way through crumbling hallways. Faint sounds echoed ahead—at first, she thought it was an animal.

It wasn't. It was Jerry Jagger.

She couldn't begin to imagine what hell he'd been through. At the end of the corridor, she found him in a large cell, naked, chained to a column by the neck. He looked nothing like the decent man she remembered—wild, crazed, emitting low, animalistic groans.

She had a bad hunch.

If she had any superpower, it was that her bad hunches always turned out to be right. This time was no different.

"He took some kind of heavy-duty aphrodisiac," Those words came from Lacey's own mouth as GPM manipulated her into talking to herself.

This was Yip's doing. She'd never thought in a million years Yip would set her up like this.

"If you don't want to screw him, you've got to work with me. I'm about to ask you a simple question, alright?"

Without skipping a beat, she nodded, answering herself, "Got it."

"Where's Hugo?"

The moment Lacey questioned herself, GPM loosened the reins enough for her to speak, though she still couldn't move.

The question was straightforward, yet for her it loomed like a mountain. She knew exactly where Hugo was hiding with his injuries—in the convenience store. There was nowhere else he could be.

"He's hiding out in Sai Kung East Country Park." Her voice was clear, steady, giving nothing away. She deliberately lied, picking a spot off the beaten path.

GPM took over again. "Remember, lying comes with a price. Sure you're telling the truth?"

For a moment, Lacey's voice was her own. Strong and unwavering, she said, "Yeah."

Sending them on a chase to Sai Kung East Country Park was Lacey's makeshift plan for now. She would face any fallout rather than deal with that brute.

"You're pulling my leg. The recent upgrade to GPM kicked the puppet chips in you and Hugo's heads back into gear, so they're watching your every move now. The weird part? GPM's drawing a blank on Hugo's whereabouts. Looks like he's found a spot where the internet can't reach him. But here's the kicker, Sai Kung East Country Park definitely has internet everywhere. So he's definitely not there."

She wanted to protest, but GPM didn't give her a chance. Forced to strip down to her bra and underwear. In that fleeting moment, she realised she didn't even have the liberty to let her heart race.

"I'm giving you one more shot. Where's Hugo?"

She had a brief moment to speak again.

"Hey, you got it all wrong! We split up back there. For all I know, he could've headed off to who knows where after we went our separate ways. How am I supposed to know where he's hiding? I'm not from around here and don't know squat about Hong Kong!" She nailed it, keeping her cool and making her point like a pro.

When GPM took over again, the laugh that came from her mouth was nothing short of creepy. She removed her bra and underwear, leaving herself completely naked. Jerry grew even more agitated, like a wild animal catching a scent it couldn't resist.

"Alright, this is it, your last shot. You've got ten seconds to come clean," Lacey told herself, laying it on the line.

She didn't want to give up. When she regained the right to speak, she kept her response calm and collected. "Come on, that's not fair. Hugo went off the grid on his own. Why should I get punished for something I had nothing to do with?"

"Gotcha," GPM taunted, steering her back into line. "Time to shake things up!"

Her body moved toward Jerry, who was more than ready to take her.

I'm screwed, she could only think to herself.

38

RHINO

In an instant, Lacey's head was suddenly filled with a deafening buzz. Dizziness overwhelmed her, and she hit the ground hard. She stayed conscious though. A few seconds later, she pulled herself together and got back up.

"Damn!" she exclaimed, realising she could speak her own words.

Is this another trap? Anyway, get the fuck out of here.

She scrambled to her feet, quickly dressed, and fled the cell.

Halfway down the corridor, a man in a black suit appeared at the stairwell, rushing towards her. She turned and darted down another path, weaving through the maze-like hallways. Footsteps echoed from all directions, surrounding her. She dashed into a cell and peered out a window frame, long stripped of its glass, to see a cliff below. The prison was built on the mountainside. With no other options, she steeled herself, climbed through the window frame, and began her perilous descent.

She spotted three men in black suits waiting below. Glancing up, she saw another man peering out from a window above. She felt like a lamb among wolves. Desperate, she tried to climb sideways, searching for a way out. But before she could get far, a net dropped from above, wrapping around her. Her struggles were useless. Trapped, she was hoisted up and pulled back through the window. The three men pinned her down, and one jabbed a needle into her neck. Darkness swallowed her world.

After what seemed like ages, Lacey's consciousness gradually returned. The wind moaned like ghosts, howled like wolves, and whispered like conspirators. Blearily, she opened her eyes and sharply barked, "Fuck!"

Three bloody heads dangled just a few meters away—Jerry, Yvonne, and Sandbag.

Though she had control over her body, her freedom was gone. Her hands were tied behind her, secured around a pillar in the cell. She was alone. It was night, and moonlight streamed through the window frame, casting eerie shadows across the ruined floor. She glanced down at herself. Her clothes were intact, showing no signs of violation.

"Come on," she whispered fiercely, twisting her bound hands, hoping she could slip free from the ropes like a kung fu master.

Then, out of the darkness, a familiar voice broke the silence. "I had a sit-down with this famous fortune teller for a reading."

Yip!

"He mentioned that finding two blue eyeballs and sticking them on my bedroom windowsill facing south would bring me big-time luck," Yip said, stepping out from the shadows, something shiny in her grip. As she got closer, Lacey saw it clearly: a stainless steel spoon.

With a grin, Yip aimed the spoon at Lacey. "I've been stressing over where to snag two perfect blue eyes, and then you happen to walk in."

Lacey kept her cool, staring back at Yip without blinking. "I think that fortune teller goofed up."

"Oh, really?"

"Human eyes are mostly blood. Pull 'em out, and the blood clots fast. They end up looking like shrivelled raisins—not only wrinkly, they lose their colour too."

Yip burst out laughing. "Don't worry about it, sweetie. I've got a trick up my sleeve to keep that blue popping," she said, bringing the stainless steel spoon closer to Lacey's left eye.

"I know where he is," Lacey blurted out suddenly.

Yip's hand, spoon in tow, froze inches from Lacey's left eye.

"Spill it then. You might make me reconsider," Yip said.

"Come here. I don't want anyone else hearing this."

"We're the only ones here."

Lacey glanced at the corridor. "Your crew's out there. I don't want them to hear."

Yip blinked slightly. "You know what's coming if you're playing me, right?"

Lacey nodded. "I need to tell this just to you."

Yip seemed doubtful but leaned in closer to Lacey.

Lacey muttered something so softly it was barely audible.

"What was that?" Yip scowled.

Lacey murmured again.

Still not catching it, Yip leaned in even closer. "If I don't catch it this time, I'm going for your eye..." Her warning was abruptly cut off as Lacey snapped at her ear.

With Yip's scream splitting the air, Lacey yanked hard, tearing off half of Yip's ear, like she did to the Slicked-Back Man. She didn't relish being an ear biter, but it was the only way to make her enemy pay now.

Yip clutched her bleeding ear, howling in agony. The sound drew the men in black suits rushing into the cell. She shrieked, "Stay back!"

Everyone froze.

Yip, her face smeared with blood, glared at Lacey through gritted teeth. "Let me pop this bitch's eyes out first, then she's all yours!"

As the spoon neared Lacey's eye, a bullet came from nowhere, piercing Yip's left temple and exiting the right, splattering blood and brain matter across Lacey's face.

Yip collapsed, dead.

More choking sounds followed as bullets zipped past Lacey, hitting Yip's men before they could react.

Within seconds, all the men were down, and the cell fell into eerie silence. Lacey heard a sound from behind, like someone making a ninja entrance through the window.

"We've got fifteen minutes before the cavalry shows up, so we gotta hustle."

Hugo unlocked her hands.

Whirling around, she came face to face with him.

He was decked out in a full-on stealth getup, pitch black. His face was ghostly, his lips drained of colour, and his forehead dotted with sweat—his wounds were far from healed.

"How did you get here?"

"Save it for later. Let's move!"

He took her hand, stepped past Yip and her crew's bodies, made a break for it out of the cell, then stopped.

Ahead, a barricade of men clad in black obstructed their route.

"Stay put. This won't take long," Hugo murmured to Lacey.

With a swift lunge, Hugo engaged the foremost attacker. The man aimed a punch, but Hugo evaded and counterattacked, thrusting his opponent's head against the wall with a harsh thud. The man crumbled, unconscious.

As another adversary surged forward, Hugo countered seamlessly, capturing the man's arm, wrenching it back, and propelling him face-first into the adjacent wall. The assailant fell, groggy and disoriented.

Hugo's combat was both fluid and exact. He struck another's knee, toppling him, then pivoted to elbow a second opponent in the jaw, rendering him instantly unconscious.

When two attackers coordinated their charge, Hugo executed a strategic leap, using the corridor's wall for leverage to deliver a dual kick. The impact sent both men reeling to the ground, their heads bouncing off the hard surface.

More adversaries advanced. Hugo remained a step ahead, seizing one by the collar and hurling him against a wall. The sound of the impact echoed in the confined space. As another tried a tackle, Hugo dodged and tripped him, causing his head to strike the floor with brutal force.

Lacey's heart raced as she watched Hugo take down the threat, one by one. He used every advantage the environment offered, his moves sharp and deadly. As Puppet Zero of GPM, he had learned a lot.

An attacker sought a surprise strike from behind, but Hugo reacted instinctively, spinning and driving his assailant back against the wall with such force that the man's head snapped backward.

In a matter of moments, the corridor was strewn with defeated foes. Breathless yet triumphant, Hugo returned to Lacey, who remained in awe of the display. "Let's move," he said, gripping her hand. They navigated through the downed bodies and hastened along the corridor.

They ran breathlessly to the shore, the motorboat still moored. As they dashed towards it, gunfire erupted, bullets whizzing past.

"Damn it!"

Hugo tackled Lacey to the ground, rolling to dodge the shots.

"Get behind the car!" he yelled, sliding across the ground and firing back.

Lacey ducked behind a nearby black pickup, watching bullets whip through the darkness.

After several exchanges, Hugo's magazine ran empty. The opposition seemed to be out of ammo too.

Hugo stood, pulling a dagger from his jacket as a huge shadow loomed before him.

"For God's sake!" Lacey exclaimed, seeing a giant over eight feet tall, dressed in the Hong Kong garrison uniform.

"Rhino!" Hugo gasped.

Thought to have been killed in the mall explosion, the giant approached, his steps making the ground tremble.

"Go now!" Hugo shouted to Lacey.

Rhino charged. Hugo aimed for his collarbone, driving the knife deep. Rhino remained unfazed, slamming into Hugo. Hugo stumbled, dazed.

Rhino yanked the dagger from his collarbone and tossed it aside. He grabbed Hugo by the neck and lifted him high. Hugo's punches to Rhino's temple were futile.

Lacey rushed in, grabbed the dagger, and stabbed Rhino in the waist. The blade didn't seem to hurt him and got stuck. Rhino casually kicked her, sending her flying.

Hugo, still trapped in Rhino's iron grip, was nearly suffocating. He punched Rhino's throat and kneed his chest, but it was futile. Rhino hurled Hugo several meters away.

Hugo tried to get up, but Rhino charged, sending him flying again. Injured and exhausted, Hugo fought against the colossus. He launched punches at critical spots, but Rhino absorbed every blow.

Rhino landed a powerful elbow strike to Hugo's face, sending him to the ground. Grabbing Hugo by the neck and ankle, he hoisted him up, ready to snap his spine.

In desperation, Lacey charged and leaped, stabbing the dagger into Rhino's mouth and out through his cheek, blood gushing. Rhino stood firm, released Hugo, yanked the dagger from his mouth, and advanced towards Lacey.

Lacey froze in terror.

Hugo, struggling to his feet, yelled, "Run!"

She snapped back to reality, turned to flee but stumbled and fell. Rhino closed in. Hugo unbuckled his belt and dashed from the side, leaping onto Rhino's back and tightening the belt around his neck.

"Run!" Hugo shouted again.

Lacey bolted into the darkness. Rhino pried the belt off and swung Hugo away.

Hugo hit the ground hard, vision blurring. He sprawled there, unable to rise, as Rhino took deliberate steps towards him.

39

NO TURNING BACK

As Rhino lifted a boulder over his head, ready to smash Hugo, a black pickup truck suddenly rammed into him, knocking him to the ground.

The truck skidded to a halt. Lacey jumped out, gripping a steering wheel lock, and rushed towards Rhino.

"Don't mess with me!" she yelled, slamming the lock down on his skull. After three vicious hits, blood and fragments marred the ground.

Tossing the lock aside, Lacey dashed to Hugo's side. "You okay?"

"Good hit," he groaned, pulling himself up with her assistance.

She shrugged, trying to appear nonchalant.

"It's not over yet." he said, glancing past her.

Lacey turned to see Rhino, impossibly, staggering to his feet, his head a gory mess.

Is he even human?

Hugo calmly said, "Get in the car, fire it up, and open the passenger door."

Lacey, catching on to Hugo's plan, sprinted to the pickup, fumbled with the engine, and swung the passenger door open.

"Come on, mate!" Hugo taunted, gesturing provocatively.

Rhino, expressionless, charged at Hugo with all his might.

Hugo didn't dodge. Instead, he met Rhino's charge head-on, locking his arms around Rhino's neck. He was propelled directly into the passenger side of the pickup, leaving Rhino's upper body entangled inside, his lower half hanging outside.

Lacey heard Hugo yell, "Reverse!"

She shifted into reverse, slammed on the gas pedal, and sent the pickup hurtling backward towards a utility pole.

Rhino struggled wildly, nearly causing Hugo to lose his grip.

"Go to hell!" Lacey screamed, driven by fury.

As the reversing pickup grazed the utility pole, Rhino's lower half struck it with a horrific thud and went limp.

Lacey went wild, yelling and flooring the pedal until Hugo shouted, "Stop!"

As the pickup halted, Hugo shoved the lifeless giant out and laid him on the ground. His eyes stared blankly at the night sky, as if he had a message left unspoken.

Hugo sighed, gently closing Rhino's eyes with his hands. "Sorry, mate. This wasn't fair to you."

Lacey grasped the gravity of his words. Rhino, like the men in black suits, had been one of Yip's puppets, stripped of his identity and transformed into a cold-blooded enforcer. Maybe death was the only release.

"We've gotta get out of here. Yip's crew will be on us any minute," Hugo said in pain as he tugged Lacey towards the speedboat at the shore.

"Hang on. That wasn't her just now, was it?"

"Pretty sure that was another body double."

"Seriously? How many does she have?"

Hugo and Lacey hopped onto the speedboat, fired up the engine, and tore across the dark sea at breakneck speed.

"Where are we headed now?" she shouted over the roar of the wind and waves.

"There's a cargo ship leaving for Vietnam before sunrise. I'm trying to get you there in time."

"No way! I'm not going anywhere."

"You really set on meeting your mom and dad?"

"You know what? This reminds me of something," she yelled against the wind. "When I was seven, I faced down a bunch of bullies. I broke one kid's nose. My teacher, Lucy, thought I overreacted and called Michelle. And you know what Michelle said? 'There's nothing wrong with my daughter. She did the right thing. If someone bullies you, bully back. That's the spirit.'" She paused then shouted even louder, "The only person I'm dying to meet is Yip. She bullies me, and I'm gonna bully b ack!"

She grabbed the steering wheel and headed straight for Hong Kong. He didn't resist.

She navigated the ocean, her blonde hair whipping in the sea breeze. He sat beside her, silently watching, as if admiring the fierce beauty of her defiance.

She felt his gaze but kept her eyes ahead.

"How'd you figure out where I was?" she called out over the noise.

40

BEAT FEAR WITH FEAR

The meat wall maze, where Hugo and his team brought Lacey after rescuing her from Yip, was actually an underground cold storage facility in the northern district. All of Hugo's equipment, including ANDI, was hidden there—that was his headquarters.

After parting ways with Lacey at the convenience store the previous night, before GPM finalised its update, Hugo rushed back to the headquarters. He didn't worry about GPM's grip because the place had no network signal. Without an internet connection, GPM couldn't control its puppets. That was why, even after finishing its update, GPM hadn't taken control of Hugo.

At the headquarters, Hugo used ANDI to reprogram the chip in his brain. An internet connection wasn't necessary because both ANDI and the puppet chip supported direct local connections. Hugo's adjustments made the chip invisible and impervious to GPM's recent upgrades, ensuring it would remain undetectable even under a network signal until GPM's next self-update.

Emerging from the headquarters to find an internet connection, Hugo used ANDI to remotely locate the puppet chip in Lacey's brain, which GPM had already detected and controlled. That was how he found Lacey. He reprogrammed her chip, giving her control over her body and speech in time.

"Why can't we free more puppets like that?" Lacey asked, accepting the down coat Hugo offered her as they settled back into the headquarters.

"Each puppet chip has its own unique ID. To tweak anything from afar, it needs to be synced with ANDI first. I got yours hooked up right after you finished quarantine. That's why you're in the clear now. But manually linking every single chip to ANDI for everyone? That's impossible," Hugo explained.

"What if GPM updates again and comes after us?"

"GPM only self-updates. No one else can do it. Each update takes about twenty-nine days. We've got some time."

"If we don't shut it down by then, we have to hide out here again?"

"Only if we can keep this place under wraps. With Yip's puppets roaming around, it's probably just a matter of time before this spot gets blown."

"Got a plan B?"

"No."

"Great... A twenty-nine-day countdown?"

"Could be less."

She moved to the coffee counter and asked, "Coffee?"

"Black, no sugar, thanks."

As she made coffee, Lacey thought of Jerry, Yvonne, and Sandbag, their bloody, severed heads hanging in that cell.

"You scared?" Hugo's sudden question startled her, as if he were reading her mind.

"If I were scared, I wouldn't stay," she shot back, masking her fear.

"You're scared but fearless," Hugo said.

She turned, not sure what to make of that.

He went on, "Look, jumping off that ship and swimming back was a huge feat, but you pulled it off. Why? Because the fear of living with the regret of not avenging Michelle terrifies you more. Now you know how brutal Yip and GPM are, and you're fucking scared. But you're staying. Why? Because the thought of losing your freedom forever scares you even more. The only way to be truly fearless is to beat fear with fear. You've done it so many times before. I'm here to remind you of that."

Lacey handed Hugo a steaming cup of coffee, mulling over his words.

Beat fear with fear?

"You've got a point." She nodded. "Anyway, how does Yip find those lookalikes? It's crazy."

"I did some digging. She's been secretly funding three top plastic surgery clinics in Korea for six years. My guess is she scouts women who share her facial structure, height, and body type then turns them into her doubles. They go under the knife until they're mirror images of her."

"Creepy but genius."

"Yeah."

"Do we need to control Yip to get into GPM's core control room? Can we use one of her doubles, or is there another way?"

"GPM's hidden in the top chamber of GrandTech Tower. It's not just heavily fortified—it's got AI facial recognition and DNA testing on lockdown. Only the real, living Yip can get in."

"So the trick is spotting the real her, huh?"

Sipping his coffee, Hugo thought for a moment. "If she's using doubles, why can't we?"

She gave him a skeptical look. "And how are we supposed to find our own doubles within twenty-nine days?"

"I've got a plan," he said. "It's got two parts."

After Hugo explained his plan, Lacey nearly screamed. "That sounds fucking terrifying!"

They locked eyes for a moment, then she burst out, "But I love it! Let's beat fear with fear!"

41

THE GARDEN CEMETERY

In the early 1900s, young women started disappearing without a trace in Hong Kong. It eventually came out that a wealthy man was behind it all. When the police finally caught up to him, they uncovered 121 bodies buried in his garden. That's how the place got its grim name—"The Garden Cemetery"—and became a haunting historical site.

Six years ago, Yip bought the land for a hefty sum, saying she wanted to build an AI research centre, though she kept the details secret. Since then, it's become her private spot for dealing with enemies, functioning like a secret crematorium.

On the drive to The Garden Cemetery, Hugo shared its history with Lacey. They were in an unremarkable Hong Kong taxi, a classic Toyota Crown, chosen for its inconspicuousness among the abandoned vehicles littering the streets after the riot.

"Here we are," he said, stopping the car at the entrance of a narrow alley.

She glanced around at the dilapidated bungalows, remnants of an old residential area.

"This doesn't look like a cemetery."

"Nope, it's still about a kilometre away."

"Then why are we stopping here?"

He nodded towards the streetlights ahead. "See that? Cameras are everywhere, GPM's eyes. We need to avoid them. These side alleys are our best bet. The car won't fit, so we're on foot from here."

Grabbing a backpack, Hugo led Lacey through the maze-like alleys, skilfully navigating to the entrance nearest to the back door of The Garden Cemetery.

Lacey spotted a security camera guarding the entrance. "How are we supposed to get past that?"

Hugo pulled his laptop from his backpack and quickly tapped into The Garden Cemetery's surveillance system. He ran a program that looped the last fifteen minutes of footage, making it appear live on the security monitors.

"We've got fifteen minutes when we're invisible to the monitoring system. That's all I can manage."

"We don't worry about the security guards?"

"No, it's all AI."

"How do we get in? The door looks deadlocked."

Hugo clicked his laptop. "It's unlocked now."

Lacey gasped as the door clicked open. "How did you do that so fast?"

"It's all AI."

"Damn AI..."

Following Hugo into the building, Lacey stumbled upon a vast underground mortuary, nearly as large as a basketball court. Glancing around, she saw thousands of body lockers meticulously arranged to form the Chinese character "口" symbolising the countless lives Yip claimed.

"Let's split up," Hugo suggested. "Find someone who matches your look—same gender, about your height and build. Don't worry about the face."

The endless rows of lockers hit Lacey like a wave, sending a shiver through her.

"I wasn't gonna say anything at first, but you should know that Michelle might be here. They probably haven't cremated her yet."

Her heart skipped a beat.

"If you run into her, keep it quick," he cautioned. "We're on a tight clock here."

Lacey inhaled sharply, steeling herself. "I can handle it. I won't let it throw me off."

When she pulled open the first morgue drawer, a chilling blast and the pungent smell of formaldehyde hit her. The next second, she found herself staring into Michelle's lifeless face.

Of all the ways to reunite!

"Damn it!" She wasn't ready for this.

Michelle's hauntingly beautiful eyes, now vacant in death, seemed to hold a silent message. Her hair was gone, and her skull bore a large scar, evidence of it being opened and then crudely resealed—likely Yip's doing to examine the chip.

Gently, Lacey touched Michelle's cold face, feeling like a piece of polished crystal. Her beauty remained undeniable. She remembered her teenage years, filled with envy for her mother's beauty, thinking it unfair for a mother to outshine her daughter like that. In that moment, she would have given anything to have her back.

"We're running out of time!" Hugo's voice echoed off the walls.

"One sec!" Lacey fired back, her voice thick with emotion. She took a slow, steadying breath and murmured to Michelle, "I promise she's going to pay for this."

She gently closed her mother's eyes.

"Lacey, we gotta go!" Hugo called out again.

"Chill, will you?" she snapped, clearly irritated.

"Got someone who could pass for you!"

She examined the corpse he pointed out. It did bear a resemblance to her, but it wasn't a perfect match – older, slightly heavier, with hair that was too long.

"It's the closest we have here," he insisted. "Get her out. I'll find mine."

Lacey had always heard that bodies got lighter once the soul left. But as she struggled to drag the corpse, she couldn't help but laugh at that nonsense. It felt way heavier than it looked.

"Got mine!" Hugo exclaimed, pleased. His find, though Caucasian, had a build and height similar to his.

"How do we get them to the car?" she asked.

"Over our shoulders."

"No way! I'm not hauling a dead body around like that!"

Lacey found herself doing exactly what she had just ruled out. Hauling her double, marked heavily by death, for a full kilometre through dim, labyrinthine alleyways was a brutal physical ordeal and a test of her mental endurance.

She finally made it.

After they forced the two bodies into the trunk, sealing it with a definitive *thud*, Lacey let out a deep breath and collapsed to the ground in exhaustion.

"God, I can't believe we pulled that off," she whispered, wanting nothing more than to lie down for a while.

Hugo lifted her up and pushed her into the car. She wondered why he showed no signs of fatigue, especially given that his severe injury hadn't fully healed.

"We need to be on time," he said, pressing hard on the accelerator.

With a roar, the vintage red Crown taxi came to life and soon disappeared into the horizon.

42

THE PARTY OF TWO

Before dawn, when night tussles with the first hints of day, the sea around Sai Kung East Country Park was still and wrapped in darkness. It mirrored the scattered stars, creating a mesmerising scene.

The peace was short-lived. A sudden, desperate roar shattered the silence. A jet, its left wing on fire, streaked across the sky like a flaming comet. Flames raced along the wing, turning the plane into a massive fireball.

The engines screamed in a final, furious defiance against gravity. The jet wobbled, on the brink of control, before spiralling down like a meteor. It slammed into the cliff's edge with a deafening explosion, a fiery eruption lighting up the dark sky.

The sea watched in silent horror, its waters briefly reflecting the inferno on the cliffs. Waves lapped gently against the shore, as if trying, in vain, to soothe and cleanse the land of the tragedy that had unfolded.

"Good morning. We begin with breaking news. A private jet has crashed in Sai Kung East Country Park early this morning. Police have cordoned off the crash site, and investigators are currently on the scene. Authorities have confirmed that the aircraft, reported stolen, was en route to Taiwan. Tragically, both individuals on board have lost their lives. We now go live to our correspondent on the ground for the latest developments..."

Lacey turned off her phone. This wasn't breaking news to her.

She was hiding out in a bomb shelter beneath an old, abandoned church in Ma On Shan. Resistance fighters had used this place during the Japanese occupation of Hong Kong, and it had been empty since the 1940s. The place was a maze, with seven hidden exits and great natural ventilation, perfect for long stays. That was why Hugo picked it as their new HQ.

Last night, they took their doubles from the Coffee Garden Cemetery and came straight here. Hugo dressed the two corpses to look like himself and Lacey. The plan was to drive the bodies to Hong Kong International Airport, put them on a private jet, and use his hacking skills to trick the control tower into letting them take off unnoticed, heading towards Taiwan. Along the way, he'd sabotage the plane, making it catch fire and crash in Hong Kong territory while he parachuted to safety beforehand.

Lacey thought it was an impossible mission.

"Relax. Watch tomorrow's headlines," he said, chillingly calm, like it was all a game.

If everything went as Hugo predicted, Yip, being her meticulous self, would definitely send a team to comb through the crash site and find the jet debris. She'd insist on immediate DNA tests to identify the bodies. She had a DNA archive for everyone with a puppet chip and for every citizen in Hong Kong.

Knowing Yip's methods, Hugo hacked into GrandTech Group's main database and discreetly accessed their DNA records. He cleverly swapped the DNA records of the doubles with those of himself and Lacey to confirm their deaths for Yip.

Next, Yip's puppet police would likely follow the trail and quickly zero in on the underground cold storage facility in the northern district. To make their apparent deaths seem more convincing, Hugo moved their headquarters and left behind plenty of clues and evidence.

Once Yip was totally convinced Hugo and Lacey were gone, it would be the perfect time to kick off Part II of Hugo's plan—the final phase.

"What if you don't come back? What am I supposed to do?" she asked him before he left for the airport.

Meeting her eyes, he said, "Push forward with part two. Finish it."

He didn't wait for her answer and was out of sight before she could respond.

No sooner had he left than she began to miss him. She tried to convince herself it was for the sake of the plan. After all, completing part two on her own was daunting. But a mocking voice inside taunted, "You miss him for who he is."

She reminded herself to suppress these feelings. At this critical moment, such emotions were not only unhelpful but disruptive. She didn't need complications.

Still, her mind drifted back to the moments they'd shared, haunting her now, making her chest ache with a mix of longing and frustration.

"Stop this!" she warned herself.

She couldn't afford to be vulnerable, not now. She'd built walls to protect her heart from the pain and loss that had shaped her. Missing him, caring for him, was a luxury she couldn't afford. It wasn't about re-venge; it was about survival—hers, his, and everyone's. Emotions clouded judgment, and she needed her mind sharp and focused. She had to be the rock.

In the quiet of the bomb shelter, Lacey took a deep breath, steeling herself for what was ahead. She would push through the loneliness, the longing, the fear. She had to. There was no other choice.

Curled up in a corner, she attempted to find some sleep. But every time she closed her eyes, fragmented images of him invaded her thoughts, leaving her restless throughout the night.

The news had already broken, but he hadn't returned. Maybe his parachute had failed, leaving him dead somewhere. Or perhaps he never got the chance to jump and died alongside their decoys.

Her head was spinning with a whirlwind of thoughts, and the pain was relentless. She needed some fresh air.

As Lacey headed towards the exit, a faint light caught her eye from the other end of the tunnel. Instantly on high alert, she drew the handgun Hugo had left her and moved cautiously towards the light.

The light seemed to emanate from around a corner at the tunnel's end, flickering, likely from a flame.

With her grip tightening on the gun, she inched closer, her mind teeming with dreadful possibilities. She constantly reminded herself to stay calm and face whatever awaited her with bravery.

She paused at the corner, gun extended, then slowly peeked around. It was a dead end. A white cloth was spread on the ground, encircled by three red candles, with two bottles, cheese, and crackers neatly arranged on it. Though simple, the setup unmistakably hinted at a party.

In this desolate, abandoned bomb shelter, the sight was bewildering.

With her gun drawn, she approached and examined the items on the ground. She recognised two bottles of expensive Hennessy Richard.

There was also Mature Cheddar and dried fruits. These items couldn't have appeared out of thin air. Someone had been here. As she pondered this, a cough suddenly came from behind her.

Whirling around, she aimed her gun.

"You left the safety on," Hugo pointed out, cool as a cucumber.

Lacey blurted out, "When did you come back?"

"Been back for a bit."

"And you didn't think to come find me?" She was annoyed and excited.

"Getting things ready before I called you over."

"Ready for what?"

He motioned towards the spread of wine and snacks on the ground. "Part one's in the bag. Time to celebrate, don't you think?"

She studied him closely. His sharply defined face was smeared with dirt and sweat yet devoid of any blood. The absence of recent grooming left his hair thick and unruly, adding a wild charm to his natural handsomeness. Still tall and imposing, he showed no new injuries, only the remnants of an old gunshot wound.

He settled on the ground and gestured for her to join him.

As soon as she sat down, he handed her one of the Hennessy Richard bottles. "Sorry about not having any glasses. You drink?"

Her response was simple. She took the bottle, unscrewed the cap, tilted her head back, took a hearty swig, then wiped her mouth.

He smiled and took a large gulp himself. Each clutching a bottle, they commenced their private party with cheese and dried fruits. It seemed an unspoken agreement had been formed. No words were necessary, only exchanged glances. They continued until the high-end cognac was depleted and the food consumed.

"Hey, hold me down," she mumbled, feeling the warmth of the cognac. "Or I might float off."

He responded by gently clasping her arm and drawing her into his embrace.

Enclosed in his arms, she felt the solid warmth of his chest. His muscular frame offered comfort and protection. A palpable anticipation hung in the air, hinting at something momentous.

Her intuition, once again, didn't fail her.

When he leaned in for a kiss, she found herself unable to resist.

Mia had once told her, "Between men and women, there can be desire, hatred, kinship, but never friendship."

"Isn't that kind of cynical?" Lacey had asked.

"Not really," Mia had shot back, full of confidence. "Add a bit of booze and watch how quickly people stop pretending. It peels away all the facades."

Now, she had to concede that Mia had a point.

She was blown away by his skill. It was like, being the primary puppet of the world's most advanced AGI, he had mastered the nuances of human intimacy.

With every climb, her anticipation grew, her pulse quickened. He knew how to draw out the most exquisite sensations, prolonging her pleasure until she thought she couldn't take it anymore. Then came the breathtaking plunge, a rush of intensity that left her gasping, her senses overwhelmed.

Every time, he unlocked new depths of her desires, pushing her beyond what she thought possible. His touch was both gentle and commanding, a masterful mix that kept her on the edge of control. She was caught in a whirlwind of sensation, her mind and body tuned to his every move.

She marvelled at how seamlessly he shifted between tender intimacy and raw passion. It was like he could read her thoughts, anticipate her needs, and respond perfectly. The ninth time, when she thought she'd experienced everything he had to offer, he surprised her again, taking her to a place of blissful surrender.

Her heart still racing, she steadied herself and got dressed. "Look, that was because we might not get another chance. It doesn't mean there's something between us, alright?"

She still believed love was a luxury she couldn't afford right now. It would only distract her, adding unnecessary weight. Her sole focus was revenge, survival, freedom, and getting back to New York.

Seated on the ground, shirtless, with his back against the wall, the flickering candlelight cast his muscular frame in a captivating golden glow, transforming him into the epitome of sensuality.

He watched her in silence. His gaze could have been agreement or reluctance. Either way, she found him unreadable. In that moment, the silence in the bomb shelter was so profound, they could almost hear the whisper of the air itself.

Finally, he broke the silence. "No matter what, you'll be fine. I promise."

The weight of his words hung in the air, a promise and reassurance all at once. She paused, her fingers lingering on the zipper of her jacket, meeting his eyes one last time before turning away. Deep down, she wondered if she could really believe him, if they could actually find a way out of this mess. But for now, she had to keep moving forward, no matter what.

43

THE OLD-SCHOOL

Despite the looming Chinese New Year, Hong Kong's usual festive vibe was nowhere to be found. Mong Kok, typically bustling, felt eerie under the harsh midday sun. The streets, once packed with people, were empty, with long shadows stretching across the pavement. A tense silence hung in the air, every corner holding its breath, waiting for a normalcy that seemed miles away. The city felt like a ghost town, each step echoing with an unsettling stillness.

The only sound breaking the stillness was the hum of a lone red Toyota Crown taxi winding through the deserted streets. Inside, the radio droned out news in Cantonese, laced with propaganda. It detailed the Hong Kong government's crackdown on the recent "anti-lockdown, anti-quarantine" protests, praising the Chinese Communist Party's Central Committee for restoring order. The official line boasted about catching all the rioters within twenty days and promised harsh consequences.

"This is crap!" the middle-aged taxi driver snapped. "Blaming the victims? Those kids were fighting for their rights! It's the government and cops stirring up the real trouble!"

"Totally agree," a female voice piped up from the back seat, speaking in Mandarin.

The driver glanced in the rearview mirror, meeting the gaze of his sole passenger. She was bundled up in a puffy down jacket, double masks covering her face, making her look ghostly against the stark city backdrop. She had delicate features—gentle nose, almond-shaped eyes framed by thick lashes, and sleek black hair peeking from her woolly hat.

"Where are you from?" asked the driver.

"Harbin."

"Cold there, huh?"

"Yeah."

"What brings you to Hong Kong?"

"University. I even got mixed up in the protests," the girl from Harbin said, sounding chill.

"Seriously?" the driver asked, worried. "Did a lot of your friends get nabbed?"

"Lots! I'm surprised they haven't come for me yet."

"You'd better watch your step."

"What do you think about the lockdowns and quarantine?" she asked.

"Hate them!"

"Afraid of HKEV?"

"HKEV? That's a scare tactic. It's all about control."

"But the news says over ninety percent of Hong Kongers support the lockdown and quarantine."

"It's all propaganda!"

"Do you think most people here see through it?"

"Absolutely. Folks here are sharp. You know the saying. We know they're lying, they know they're lying, they know we know they're lying, we know they know we know they're lying, but they keep lying anyway."

With a sly grin, the Harbin girl quoted Mao Zedong from the Cultural Revolution, "'The public has a keen eye.'"

The taxi driver blinked then burst into hearty laughter.

Their conversation flowed until they reached her destination. As the taxi stopped, the driver, a bit reluctant, said goodbye and warned her, "It's not the virus you need to worry about. It's the real rioters out there!"

"Thanks for the heads-up, but a new day is about to break."

"I hope you're right!"

The Harbin girl navigated the desolate, narrow alleyways. Even in daylight, the tight passages felt claustrophobic, with sunbeams barely cutting through the maze of low, grimy buildings. Trash cans overflowed onto the cobblestones, and the faint smell of stale food mixed with the odour of damp concrete. Every so often, a stray cat darted out from a shadow.

She finally arrived at The Old-School, its sign hanging above the entrance with faded, chipped letters. Despite the intricately carved "OPEN" sign on the boutique's front door, the windows were tightly curtained, casting deep shadows inside.

As she entered, the store wrapped her in a nostalgic embrace, transporting her to 1990s mainland China. Shelves overflowed with vintage Chinese products: clothing, shoes, stationery, toys, books, snacks, and beverages. The air was thick with the scent of old paper and memories.

The two female attendants, one chubby and one skinny, wore red and white tracksuits that screamed nineties Chinese school uniforms. Their identical black ponytails matched their retro outfits, enhancing the authentic vibe.

"Hi, how can I help you today?" the skinny attendant greeted warmly.

"It's pretty hot in here," she said casually, slipping off her bulky down jacket. Underneath, she wore a tight workout outfit that showed off her athletic build, momentarily catching the attendants' attention. She pointed at their uniforms. "How much for those?"

"Sorry, not for sale."

"I really like them. I'll pay extra."

The attendants exchanged a quick look. "You know, we might have a few spares hidden somewhere. Interested in trying one out?"

"Absolutely!"

"One moment, please," the skinny attendant said, heading upstairs.

The Harbin girl browsed the store, though it was clear her mind was elsewhere. The chubby attendant watched her quietly, keeping an eye on her without making it too obvious.

Soon enough, the skinny attendant returned, carrying a uniform like hers and some crisp white sneakers. "You're in luck. We've got some."

"Perfect!" The Harbin girl grinned.

"Wanna try it on?"

"Definitely!"

"Follow me."

The fitting room was expansive, mirrors covering the floor, ceiling, and walls. In this 360-degree reflective space, she and the attendant were endlessly multiplied, creating a dizzying visual effect.

Before handing over the school uniform, the attendant took a moment to assess the customer from head to toe. With a tone both professional and kind, she said, "I'm sorry, but I need you to remove everything."

She blinked then nodded, her smile easy and unforced as she undressed gracefully.

The surrounding mirrors gave the attendant a complete view of the young and flawless body, ensuring nothing was concealed. Satisfied, she handed the uniform to the Harbin girl. Once dressed, the attendant offered her a black hair tie to pull her hair into a ponytail. Looking in the mirrors, the Harbin girl saw herself transform into a 1990s Chinese high school student.

"What do you think?" the attendant asked.

"Love it," she responded.

"Really?"

"Swear on it."

With a knowing smile, the attendant said, "You need my boss's approval to buy this."

"Got it."

The attendant nodded, pulled out a remote, and pressed a button. A mirrored wall swung open, revealing a dim hallway.

"His office is down the hall."

As she stepped into the dim corridor, the revolving door clicked shut behind her, plunging her into darkness. Instinctively, she slowed, her hands reaching out to navigate the shadowy hallway. At the end, she gently nudged an ajar door.

Inside, a weak lamp struggled against the darkness, casting a feeble glow over an office adorned with relics of Chinese socialism. The room felt eerily deserted. She scanned the space, certain that surveillance cameras lurked in unseen corners. Settling into the chair behind the desk, she pressed her lips together, stifling the frantic beat of her heart.

The oppressive atmosphere reminded her of the principal's office from the underground brothel in Flushing.

As footsteps echoed outside, each thud matched her racing heart. She took a deep breath, turned around, and faced the entrance. The door swung open, and in walked NYPD's most wanted—Abalone.

44

ABALONE'S ADVICE

"There's one man Yip wouldn't mess with—not yet." When Hugo laid out his plan to Lacey, a coincidence popped up. "He was in the news recently for running a communist-themed brothel in Flushing, exposed by a TikTok detective. Now he's on America's most-wanted list."

"What the... That's Abalone?"

"Wait, where's that coming from?"

"His face!"

"You met him before?"

"Hell yeah!"

Lacey then shared what she'd done in Flushing, which astonished Hugo. But he didn't even know Abalone's real name. Everything he knew about him was secondhand, mostly from Yip.

Abalone ran unique brothels in twenty-three cities around the world: New York, Los Angeles, San Francisco, Vancouver, Toronto, London, Paris, Berlin, Rome, Amsterdam, Warsaw, Prague, Sydney, Melbourne, Auckland, Tokyo, Osaka, Seoul, Hong Kong, Macau, Bangkok, Mexico City, and Manila.

Each brothel meticulously mirrored a specific epoch of Chinese history. For example, Red Star High School in Flushing, New York, replicated the campuses of 1990s mainland China. The Underground Forbidden City in San Francisco recreated the royal households of the late Qing Dynasty. The Underground Commune in Paris echoed the communes of the Cultural Revolution. The Underground Nightclub in Tokyo reflected the cabarets of Shanghai during the Republic of China era.

Abalone was an enigma with a vast network of connections. Rumours swirled about his ties to the upper echelons of the Chinese Communist Party, as his brothels catered exclusively to high-ranking CCP officials.

That was all Hugo knew about him.

"What's Yip's deal with Abalone?" Lacey asked.

***

"Hello?" Abalone said, waving his hand to snap the distracted Harbin girl back to reality. "Lost in thought, were we?"

With a quick, charming smile, she answered, "Sorry, this place kinda took me back to my teenage years."

Seated in the principal's chair with an air of authority, Abalone offered her a smug grin. He opened a desk drawer, revealing an ornate wooden box filled with dark, aromatic cigar leaves and meticulously trimmed wrappers. Beside it was a set of delicate crafting tools, all carefully arranged.

As he started rolling the cigar, the conversation didn't miss a beat. "So what do they call you?"

"Amy."

"How old are you?"

"Twenty-four."

"Native Harbin girl, huh?" he noted, expertly shaping the cigar.

"Exactly."

"How'd you hear about The Old-School Party?"

"From the dark web."

"You're on there a lot?"

"Nah, not much. A rough patch for picking up clients lately."

"Oh yeah, the pandemic and the riots," he nodded. "You know, your height, your body type, even some details of your look remind me of a Polish girl I met once."

What?

Amy, the high-tech synthetic skin Lacey was wearing, was a typical northern Chinese girl.

Lacey kept her cool despite her growing anxiety. "A Polish girl. Sounds like The Old-School Party was quite the mix."

"No, I didn't meet her here. It was in Flushing, New York. Ever been?"

"I've been to New York but never made it to Flushing. That's like a Chinatown, right?" She tried to sound casual.

"Yeah, it's pretty much a Chinese enclave. I used to run a business there."

"Interesting."

The cigar was ready, sitting on the table. He took a moment to put his tools away, neat and tidy, into the drawer. Then, looking up, their eyes locked. His had that sharp, almost wild sparkle to them.

"But that Polish chick? She messed everything up."

A wave of panic surged through Lacey, yet she managed to keep her expression neutral.

"Oh wow, really? What happened?"

He let out a slow breath. "She was sneaky, thought she was playing for a bigger team. You ever come across a TikToker named P.I. Olsen?"

"Instagram's more my speed."

Abalone smirked, gesturing with his cigar. "Smart move. Can't figure out why all democracies haven't axed TikTok yet. Spreads nonsense and messes with the kids' heads." He paused to light his cigar. "That bitch bit one of my clients and then played innocent in front of me. Saw right through it, but I let her walk. Wouldn't lay a finger on a woman. Then she blasts that stunt on TikTok, and next thing I'm topping the charts as America's most-wanted." He laughed. "Got my fifteen minutes though."

"It takes something special to hit America's most-wanted list," she shot back, smiling.

He leaned back, letting the smoke drift upwards. "Her name was Natalia Nowak," he said, his gaze fixed on her. "She looked a lot like you. A real knockout."

"I'm Chinese, not Polish. Can't you tell?"

"It's uncanny, really, how similar your abalone shapes are. It's almost eerie."

Lacey deduced that hidden surveillance cameras in the changing room were capturing her from every angle, and he was likely watching from behind the scenes. But how could he recognise her as the Polish girl Natalia? Mia never made any of her high-tech synthetic skins identical, not even the private parts!

She did her best to keep her nerves under wraps, putting on a puzzled face. "Abalone shapes? What's that all about?"

He gave her a knowing smirk. "Come on, you know what I'm getting at."

"What're you talking about, man? I've never known a Polish girl," she shot back, playing along.

He paused, considering, then leaned closer and lowered his voice. "Or maybe, Natalia, that Polish gal, decided to switch it up and become a Chinese girl."

Lacey felt frozen, like a deer caught in headlights.

Abalone burst out laughing. "Did you see your face? I should've been an actor, right? Tony Leung wouldn't stand a chance against me!"

Lacey wasn't sure if she felt relieved but played along. "Man, that was really funny."

"I never pass up a chance for a good laugh," he said, the mischief in his smile softening. "Alright, let's get down to business." He pulled a contract from a pile of papers on the table and handed it to her. "Take a look, and if everything checks out, sign it."

She carefully examined the document. Unlike last time, it wasn't blank—it was a standard contract.

"Is that $20,000 in Hong Kong dollars or US dollars?" she asked.

"US dollars, obviously. The Hong Kong dollar doesn't cut it."

"Sounds like a deal."

Wanting to move things along, she quickly signed the contract and pushed it back to him.

"Make sure you leave Hong Kong as soon as you're done with this job," he said, his tone serious.

"Why's that?"

"I always look after the ladies, and not because I'm a softie. I've got a daughter myself."

She tried to read the truth in his mysterious gaze.

"I've moved her to Sydney. Something big's about to go down here in Hong Kong. Something major."

"You got a crystal ball or something?" she joked, trying to lighten the mood despite his grave warning.

"I'm dead serious. My advice? Finish your job and get out of Hong Kong. Stick around, and you'll regret it."

His caution threw her for a loop.

"What's coming? Another virus outbreak? A huge storm? More protests?"

"If it was any of those, I'd tell you to stick around and cash in."

"So, what are we talking about here?"

"It's time. The party's kicking off."

Swiftly changing the subject, Abalone retrieved a remote from his drawer. With a click, the bookshelf behind his desk split open, revealing a concealed door leading to a shadowy corridor.

Without a word, she stood and went to the hidden passage. As she moved past him, he offered a mischievous smile and commented, "Have a blast at the party!"

As Lacey stepped into the corridor, the hidden door snapped shut behind her. Clenching her fists, she strode into the darkness.

45

— · —

THE LATECOMER

s Lacey walked towards the door at the end of the hallway, she heard the rising chatter of female voices. She stopped, took a breath, and pushed it open. Inside was a scene straight out of a 1990s mainland Chinese girls' dormitory, much roomier than any Natalia had seen at the underground high school in Flushing.

Six bunk beds lined the walls, five occupied, leaving one vacant on the eastern side. Ten lively young women, unmistakably Chinese and in their early twenties, wore minimal clothing—white tank tops and old-fashioned white cotton underwear.

"Hi, everyone, I'm Amy. Nice to meet you all!" she greeted them in Mandarin with a Harbin accent, flashing a bright smile while sneaking a glance at the drop ceiling above the bed in the southeast corner.

"You're from the northeast, right?" someone asked.

"Yeah, you got me." Amy's relief was clear. She'd been worried about her accent standing out. She smiled at her new roommates and went to the empty bunk. "Which one's mine? Top or bottom?"

"Doesn't matter." One of the girls shrugged.

"Top then," Amy decided quickly, climbing up. Once settled, she glanced back at the drop ceiling over the bed in the southeast corner, noting it was within reach.

Another girl eyed her uniform and said, "You really want to roast in that?"

"Huh?" Amy was puzzled.

"Lose the clothes. It's boiling in here!"

"Oh, right!" Amy quickly stripped off her uniform jacket, revealing her white tank top and underwear. Instantly, she became the centre of attention, thanks to Mia's high-tech artwork.

"Wow, she's fit!"

"Look at her tits!"

"I love her ass!"

"I'd kill to fuck her if I were a man."

Amy laughed. "Sorry for the dazzle, folks."

"Do you have pubes?" someone asked, genuinely curious.

"Had 'em this morning, but they're in the trash now," Amy replied with a grin, setting off a wave of laughter.

The laughter was cut short by a sudden, sharp *bang* as the dormitory door flew open. Silence fell as a middle-aged woman with severe black-rimmed glasses and a stern hairstyle, reminiscent of nineties' mainland Chinese educators, stood commandingly at the entrance.

"I'm Ho, your dorm supervisor," she announced, her tone sharp and authoritative. Her intense gaze scanned the room, finally landing on the empty bunk below Amy. A frown creased her face.

"Why isn't she back yet?" Ho gestured to the empty bottom bunk.

"I have no idea." Amy shrugged.

"Don't shrug at me! That's not how we do things here!" Ho's frustration was evident.

An awkward silence filled the room.

Suddenly, hurried footsteps echoed down the corridor. All eyes turned to the doorway as a girl in a school uniform, her ponytail bouncing, appeared, her face etched with panic.

Yip!

46

THE PLEASURE

Hugo told Lacey about the time he escorted Yip to a dinner with a high-ranking Chinese Communist Party official who was an alcoholic. To keep up, Yip matched him drink for drink until she was wasted. On the ride back, barely holding it together, she confided in Hugo a secret she had never shared with anyone.

The story began in the early 1990s, when Yip was a local girl in Harbin, Heilongjiang province, China.

On her first day of high school, she found herself squeezed into a narrow dorm room with six bunk beds, sharing the cramped space with eleven other girls. This was pretty much the norm for student dormitories in China.

After settling in, she started changing into her uniform. Just then, a boy walked in, catching her undressed. She screamed, only to discover the "boy" was actually her dorm mate—a girl with a strikingly handsome appearance.

With a grin, the girl said, "They call me Tomboy."

Tomboy was easygoing and caring, quickly becoming Yip's best friend. They spent a lot of time together, but Yip didn't realise their relationship had deepened until one early summer night at the school's public bathhouse.

The facility was supposed to close at 9 p.m., and by the time they arrived at 8:40, it was deserted except for the two of them.

While Yip was bathing, Tomboy suddenly hugged her from behind. Initially, Yip thought it was a joke, but she soon realised it was something more as Tomboy penetrated her vagina with her fingers, causing immediate pain.

Her scream seemed to thrill Tomboy even more.

"Yeah, that's it! Louder! I love it!"

Tomboy had turned on all the shower heads and cranked the water to its maximum, drowning out her screams.

The assault, lasting fifteen minutes, was an unexpected blend of pain and pleasure for Yip.

After getting dressed, Tomboy turned to her, "Not too bad, huh?"

"I'm going to report this!" Yip declared firmly.

With a low chuckle, Tomboy responded, "Oh, come on. You can't tell me you didn't enjoy that. No need to feel embarrassed."

"I'm serious. I'll call the police!" Yip vowed.

Yip went back on her word. The next day, she became Tomboy's girlfriend. From then on, they frequently visited the school's bathhouse. Yip fell completely in love with Tomboy and didn't want to spend a second without her.

One day, Tomboy pulled out a handful of pink jellybeans from her pocket, dangling them in front of Yip with a sly grin.

"Guess what these are?"

"Jellybeans?"

Tomboy's smirk widened. "Count 'em for me."

"Twelve."

"And how many of us live in the dorm?"

"Twelve," Yip replied, her tone a mix of curiosity and confusion. "What are you getting at?"

Tomboy's grin grew even more mischievous, her eyes gleaming with a playful plot.

These weren't only jellybeans; they contained something wild. Tomboy managed to intoxicate everyone in the dorm with them, including herself and Yip. That evening, the dormitory turned into a horny group sex party.

Their antics quickly caught the attention of the dorm supervisor, who reported them to the police.

They were in serious trouble due to a specific criminal law in China addressing group sex. When the police started their investigation, they discovered the other ten girls had been unknowingly drugged. Yip and Tomboy were separated for questioning. Overwhelmed with fear, both confessed to everything. The investigation pointed to Tomboy as the ringleader, with Yip playing a supporting role.

However, Tomboy's father was the deputy mayor of Harbin, which influenced the final police report to label Yip as the poisoner, casting Tomboy and the other ten girls as victims.

As a result, Yip was expelled and sent to a juvenile detention centre for re-education. After her release, she tried to clear her name, but her efforts proved futile. No one believed her, or perhaps no one dared to challenge the prevailing narrative. After all, this was China—a place where power often overshadowed justice.

What hurt the most was being abandoned by her parents, who were conservative blue-collar workers influenced by China's propaganda. They viewed Yip as a family failure and disowned her.

At sixteen, Yip packed her bags and headed south to Guangzhou in search of work. The hardships only made her stronger. She constantly reminded herself to keep fighting to survive.

She soon realised she was bisexual and also interested in men. She leveraged her beauty to gain advantages. She intertwined her destiny with a Hong Kong billionaire, securing her first fortune and Hong Kong residency. Later, she did him a critical favour by seducing a high-ranking CCP official, facilitating his investments in mainland China. In gratitude, the billionaire financed a business venture for her.

"I can get you started with a real estate venture. Easiest way to make a fortune in Hong Kong."

"Sorry, that's not my thing."

"What are you into?"

"Artificial intelligence. Got any interest in backing that?"

The billionaire raised his eyebrows, a bit taken aback. "And why's that?"

"It's the future."

Yip had been studying English at the Hong Kong University of Science and Technology library. There, she discovered the 1943 paper by McCulloch and Pitts, "A Logical Calculus of Ideas Immanent in Nervous Activity," and was captivated by it.

"Okay, if you're really into it, so be it."

In 1996, on the brink of Hong Kong's handover to China—a time when artificial intelligence was a novel concept to many in China—Yip launched her tech venture, GrandTech Limited, in the bustling Central district of Hong Kong.

Over the years, Yip cleverly used her intelligence and beauty to align with the Chinese Communist Party, Hong Kong authorities, and numerous Chinese business tycoons. This strategic networking propelled her company to become one of Asia's, and eventually the world's, leading powerhouses in artificial intelligence.

With immense wealth and power, Yip could fuck anyone she wanted. But the more she indulged, the more she felt stuck in a rut. She began to deeply miss her high school dormitory days, especially the wild times with "the jellybeans." She became a dedicated supporter of the underground high school in Flushing. When it shut down, she generously funded Abalone to recreate its spirit with The Old-School Party in Hong Kong.

Yip longed for novelty, demanding fresh faces at each old-school party while also insisting on utmost secrecy to protect her reputation. To meet these requirements, Abalone regularly scouted the dark web, carefully selecting new attendees. After each party, to ensure their silence, every girl was implanted with a puppet chip, turning them into effective puppets.

Hugo believed that Yip wouldn't use body doubles at the parties because she sought the pleasure for herself. That was the key to their part two. So he planned for Lacey to disguise herself as a Chinese girl and join the party. Lacey applied and was quickly approved, thanks to her setup of Amy's identity as a girl from Harbin, Yip's hometown.

The interactions between Amy and the attendants at the Old-School Store were actually coded messages for each approved applicant to attend the party. The Old-School Party was meant to be held in utmost secrecy.

The moment Lacey caught sight of Yip at the dormitory entrance, a mix of exhilaration and terror washed over her. She realised she had delved into the depths of part two, embarking on a journey into uncharted territory from which there was no return.

"You're late."

Ho, furious, flashed her wristwatch at Yip, who shrank back in fear.

"I'm really sorry. It won't happen again, I swear."

"Get over here," Ho snapped.

Yip, like a scared kitten, edged closer.

"Kneel."

Yip knelt without hesitation.

As Ho slowly unbuckled her belt, her fierce gaze swept over every girl in the dormitory.

"Anyone who shows up late from now on will end up like this."

With a sharp snap, Ho raised the belt and struck Yip's back, drawing a cry of pain.

"No screaming allowed!"

The belt lashed across Yip's buttocks. Despite her resolve to stay silent, the sharp pain forced an involuntary whimper.

Snap, snap, snap—the belt mercilessly struck her back, buttocks, and thighs. The pain was so intense that tears streamed down her face, but she could only whimper, not daring to scream.

47

CHERRY BLOSSOM

Ho whipped Yip with her belt until she was exhausted. She glared at Yip, sprawled on the floor, and spat, "That's what you deserve!"

She yanked a small white plastic box from her pocket, tossed it on the floor with a look of contempt, and stormed out, slamming the door behind her.

The dormitory was dead silent. Yip's voice trembled as she asked, "Can anyone help me?"

Everyone was paralysed with fear, except Amy. She climbed down from the top bunk and approached Yip.

"Can you grab that box for me?" Yip asked weakly, looking up at Amy.

Amy picked up the box and helped Yip onto the bottom bunk, avoiding the bruises on her back and hips.

Yip pointed to the box. "Can you put the medicine on for me?"

I want to strangle you right now, Lacey seethed inwardly. But instead she carefully peeled away Yip's uniform, revealing a shocking array of dark bruises. The sight sent chills down her spine.

The other girls, deeply shaken, stayed frozen on their beds, too afraid to move or speak.

Amy opened the small white box, revealing a brown paste with the distinct aroma of traditional Chinese herbs.

"Let's not get this on my underwear," Yip said, hinting. "You know what to do, right?"

The inevitable moment had arrived. Despite Lacey's mental preparation, the reality was overwhelming. Carefully, she removed Yip's white tank top and underwear, revealing a body that, despite being nearly fifty, was as toned as that of a twenty-five-year-old.

"Use your palm to rub it in. It helps with the pain," Yip instructed.

Amy did as told, her touch as gentle as possible. Yip began to relax bit by bit. She cocked her head, eyeing Amy with curiosity.

"Where are you from?" asked Yip.

"Harbin."

"You've got to be kidding!" Yip said excitedly. "Me too!"

"I grew up in the Daoli district. What about you?" Lacey switched to Mandarin, putting on a heavy Harbin accent.

"Songbei. I can't believe I met another Harbin girl here." Yip turned to lie on her side and grabbed Amy's hand. "You know, you feel strangely familiar to me."

Amy's heart skipped a beat.

"There's a saying in Chinese," Yip said with a half-smile, "'familiar at first sight.'"

Amy's lips curled into a soft smile. "Must be fate."

Yip gently guided Amy's hand over her vagina. "Really wet, huh?"

Amy, summoning her courage, let Yip steer her movements.

"Does it remind you of a ripe, juicy peach, a soaked sponge, or maybe melting butter?" Yip teased. "Pick one."

"It's none of those," Amy replied. "It's more like cherry blossoms in early spring—damp with dew, fragrant, and tender. There's a Chinese saying, 'beauty that's almost edible.'"

"Wow, you have a way with words!" Yip said, her smile spreading warmth. "Keep going, keep feeling the cherry blossom... like it's a fresh spring day."

As Amy complied, a wave of humiliation washed over her, but she had to contain herself, biding her time.

I swear, I'll kill you with my own hands.

After achieving orgasm, Yip was so elated that she shook from head to toe, every hair standing on end.

"That felt magical," Yip whispered, leaning closer to Amy and pressing a kiss to her lips. "Now, reach into the left pocket of my uniform."

Amy did as told, pulling out a small metal box.

"Open it. What's inside?" Yip asked.

Amy opened the box and found eleven tiny pink pills.

"Candies?"

"Right! How many are there?"

"Eleven."

"And how many of us are here?"

"Twelve."

"Bit of a bummer, right? Twelve of us, but only eleven candies. Guess I messed up the count. Now, Amy, hand these out to everyone."

Amy started distributing the candies while Yip got up from the bed, standing naked in the middle of the dorm. She scrutinised each girl, from their faces to their bodies. "Go on, everyone, eat your candy."

The girls quickly obeyed, understanding their roles. Only Amy hesitated, staring at the small candy in her hand.

Noticing Amy's hesitation, Yip looked curious. "Problem, sweetie?"

"Yeah," Amy replied with a mischievous grin, "it's too pretty to eat."

Yip smiled. "Take it, and you'll find something even prettier."

Amy blinked then popped the candy into her mouth, tipping her head back as she swallowed.

"There you go!" Yip cheered, clearly pleased. She then looked over the rest of the girls. "How about we spice things up with a little game?"

The effects of the candy were immediate and profound. The girls' faces quickly turned distant and hazy, Amy included. She began to teeter slightly as her balance waned. She glanced subtly at the drop ceiling above the southeast corner bed, her eyes a mix of hope and despair.

"First off," Yip began, "we're pairing up. That gives us six pairs." She casually teamed up with Amy to set the example. The other ten girls quickly found their partners, forming five more pairs. The cherry candies seemed to make everyone a bit more cooperative.

"Next step," Yip directed, "everyone needs to gently remove your partner's clothes, like this..." With swift, practiced movements, she stripped away Amy's vest and underwear. The sudden action almost overwhelmed Lacey with panic, but she managed to stay composed.

Inspired, the others followed suit until everyone stood there completely naked.

"Let's all line up and make a circle."

The girls quickly and precisely formed a circle. Amy took her place right behind Yip.

"Now," Yip commanded, her voice carrying an undeniable authority, "I want everyone to kneel like puppies. Make sure you're close enough so that your butt is near the face of the person behind you."

Lacey realised Yip's intentions, and it hit her like a ton of bricks.

Yip was already setting an example. She prostrated herself in front of Amy, her posture reminiscent of a playful pup, an audacious display that nearly pushed Lacey to her limits. She imagined herself lunging at Yip, pinning her down in a desperate act of defiance. But this thought was fleeting. Faced with the stark reality, she reluctantly assumed a position behind Yip, who was now on all fours. Following suit, each girl in the line pressed her face against the butt in front of her, creating a surreal procession.

"Okay, girls, lean in close to the butt right in front of you. Stick out your tongues and let yourselves really taste the cherry blossom. And while you're at it, the one behind you will do the same. We're going to create a ripple effect of flavours that's going to be absolutely mind-blowing!"

As Yip took the lead, pressing her face towards the butt in front of her and began to savour "the cherry blossom," all the other girls obediently followed her example.

As Amy gazed at Yip's butt and the "cherry blossom" in front of her, she found herself uncontrollably shaking. As she braced herself for what she anticipated to be the most shameful moment of her life, a rhythmic tapping echoed from the drop ceiling above the southeast corner bed. *Thud. Thud. Thud...*

48

——— ; ———

RELEASE AND DIE

"**C**ome on, Amy, suck on it," Yip murmured. She was too high to notice the dull thuds above them in the drop ceiling.

Amy, playing for time, subtly nudged the girl behind her towards Yip's butt. As the girl's tongue brushed Yip's vagina, she sighed, "Yeah, that's the spot...keep at it."

Lost in the haze of pleasure, none of them noticed Amy's swift move onto the bed to pry open a ceiling panel. Inside, she discovered a small remote-controlled car rigged with two metal rings and a remote sporting a big red button.

Earlier, Hugo had scouted the massive studio, uncovering all its little secrets, including a handy space above the drop ceiling—perfect for sneaky manoeuvres. Since Lacey couldn't smuggle any gear into the party, he'd rigged a remote-controlled car with thermal sensors. This nifty gadget could zip through the hidden overhead maze, delivering his deadly device he'd dubbed "Release and Die."

Amy wasted no time, slipping the larger ring around Yip's neck.

"What the hell?" Yip jerked away, suddenly alert.

The smaller ring clicked shut on her wrist as Yip stood, panic creeping into her voice, "What are you doing?"

Pressing the red button, Lacey dropped Amy's accent and switched to her own voice, sharp and commanding. "Let's shake things up, bitch."

Yip's face fell in horror. She recognised Lacey's voice but was confused by her appearance. "Who are you?"

Lacey spat the pink pill at Yip, never having swallowed it. "This is for Michelle." She released the big red button on the remote. The ring around Yip's wrist erupted in a sinister red glow. Blades sprang to life within, spinning at terrifying speed, carving through flesh and bone in a grotesque symphony of screams and the wet, ripping sound of tearing sinew.

Yip's scream cut through the room, animalistic and raw, while the others remained mesmerised by the hallucinogenic cherry blossoms around them.

"If I let go next time, it'll be your neck," Lacey threatened, her voice ice-cold, keeping the big red button pressed down.

Yip, pale and shaking, gasped, "I'm bleeding! I need help!"

"Cut the crap. First, your goons disappear. Then get dressed and follow my lead. Clear?"

Yip nodded, agony and dread in her eyes. "Jesus, what do you want from me?"

***

Leaving The Old-School Party and reaching the desolate alleys, Lacey wasn't worried about Yip. As long as she held the remote tight, Yip would follow and behave like a slave.

The main road was eerily quiet. The setting sun cast a fiery glow, turning the pigeons circling above into crimson silhouettes against the twilight.

Lacey scanned the horizon. All she wanted was Hugo, safe and right there beside her.

49

HE

Finally, after what felt like forever, a red classic Toyota Crown taxi rolled into view, sending a thrill of dopamine surging through Lacey's veins.

He pulled up right in front of her as the sun slipped below the horizon. Stepping out, the dimming light of dusk played softly across his face.

She watched, spellbound, as the world seemed to pause around them. Their eyes met and held—a moment of deep connection. In his gaze, she saw a promise, a silent pact that once the chaos faded, they'd carve out their own slice of heaven—to laugh, talk, kiss, touch, and fuck.

"Fuck, I'm dizzy... must've lost too much blood!" Yip's shout broke the silence.

Hugo ignored Yip, as if she were air. Glancing at his wristwatch, he said to Lacey, "GPM will finish updating in about forty minutes."

Time was slipping away. They had to move Yip to the secret room housing the GPM and destroy it within forty minutes—or become its puppets forever.

Lacey threw open the taxi door and snapped, "Get in, now!"

Without a word, Yip, bloodied and bedraggled, scrambled inside. Hugo quickly wrapped her bleeding arm and gave her a shot.

"Why are you doing this to me?" Yip asked, her voice raw.

Hugo jumped into the driver's seat and started the engine. Lacey settled in the back with Yip.

"You've lost it," Yip muttered to Hugo.

Without turning around, Lacey snapped, "Shut the fuck up!"

Yip kept talking, undeterred by Hugo's silence. "I've always dreamed of a thriving Hong Kong. Thought our battles would bring us closer. I never expected you to betray me. You've really lost your way."

"She's trying to distract us," Hugo muttered to Lacey, his hands gripping the steering wheel as he manoeuvred the Toyota through the city streets like a race-car driver.

Gasping through the pain, Yip insisted, "I know you want to take down GPM, but you're playing right into the CCP's hands! I've watched them for years. Their goal? Strip away our democracy and swallow the city into their regime. They've been setting the stage, pouring in re-sources. I'm fighting for Hong Kong's survival!"

Her voice crackled with fervour, the immediate pain momentarily forgotten.

"That's a load of crap!" Lacey snapped. "You've stripped enough freedom yourself, turning people into puppets!"

"Sacrifices are necessary for progress!"

"Fuck your version of progress! I won't let you or anyone else trample over my freedom for it!"

"You're not seeing the big picture! If we don't step up, the CCP will dominate, not only Hong Kong but globally. You'll lose your freedom anyway!"

"Enough of this bullshit!" Lacey shouted at Yip.

Yip fell silent for a while then turned to Lacey. "Who are you, really?"

"Oh yeah, it's time to open your eyes." Lacey handed the remote to Hugo. "Would you hold this for me?"

Hugo took it, keeping the red button pressed down. Lacey started peeling off Amy's skin suit, leaving Yip in shock. It took a while before Lacey was fully set in her own clothes and wig.

"What the..." Yip was stunned.

"You deserve to know who's fucking you over," Lacey said with a grin.

Clenching her teeth, Yip burst out, "You fucking Brit!"

"You fucking bitch, I'm American."

"You're of British descent!"

Lacey punched Yip in the nose, blood splattering. "Keep your fucking mouth shut unless you want more!"

"You Brits are the worst, selfish, spineless, complete cowards! You turned Hong Kong into a colony, imposed your democracy, got us addicted to it. Then, for a deal with China, you handed us over. Like 'one country, two systems' was ever going to work. You knew it was doomed, but as long as you profited, who cares? Hong Kong was a pawn to you — exploited for decades then discarded!"

Exhausted from her tirade, Yip slumped, gasping for air and curled up in agony on the back seat.

"You know what?" Lacey grabbed the remote from Hugo, keeping the button pressed down. "I'm done with this," she said, her voice barely steady, as if she might release the button any second. "She's not worth another minute."

Hugo remained unfazed, glancing at Yip in the rearview mirror. "She might need a shot. Check the trunk. There should be a first aid kit."

Seeing Yip's miserable state—pale, drenched in sweat, barely coherent—Lacey cursed under her breath, "Damn it!"

They needed her alive, at least for now.

Lacey fetched the first aid kit from the trunk, pulled out a syringe, and administered it to Yip.

Gradually, Yip's rambling stopped. She looked up weakly at the remote in Lacey's hand and whispered, "Don't let go."

Lacey gave her a scornful smirk. "Who's the coward now?"

"Lacey, you're too naive. Think you can take down GPM? Wait until you meet him. You won't destroy him; he'll destroy you."

Running out of patience, Lacey brandished the remote with a sharp warning. "One more peep, and you're done."

Yip clammed up.

Lacey fell into silence too. She gazed out at the city, enveloped in the restless night, feeling an unexplainable chokehold. She cracked the window open, let the cool air poured in, whispering relentlessly and stirring a storm of wild thoughts.

Hugo was right. Yip was just spewing distractions.

She took a deep breath, closed her eyes, and hoped the quiet would calm her stormy mind.

***

The car screeched to a halt in front of GrandTech Tower. The place was eerily quiet, exactly as Lacey had demanded—Yip had made sure there was no security around.

"Get out!" Lacey demanded.

Yip met her gaze, a faint smile on her lips. "No room for regret in this world."

"Now!" Lacey barked.

Hugo, gun in hand, and Lacey, clutching the remote, followed Yip closely as they entered GrandTech Tower, manoeuvred through the lobby, and boarded the central elevator.

The elevator shot up swiftly, halting smoothly on the 108th floor. As the doors parted, they were met with a pristine corridor stretching endlessly ahead. A lone door at the far end seemed almost out of reach.

Yip stepped out first, striding towards the door with Lacey and Hugo right on her heels.

"Move it!" Lacey urged, her voice sharp with impatience. They had less than twenty minutes left.

"I'm moving as fast as I can," Yip replied, her tone even.

Upon reaching the stark white door at the end of the corridor, Yip paused and turned to face Lacey, her expression inscrutable.

"What now?" Lacey demanded, irritation creeping into her tone.

"You know, I'm not against teaming up," Yip offered.

"Open the damn door!" Lacey snapped.

Hugo nudged Yip towards the door. She stumbled briefly but regained her balance and pressed her palm against the centre panel. The surface beeped softly, activating a hidden biometric scanner. Seconds later, her fingerprint was verified, and a holographic face—her exact double—appeared, signalling the facial recognition system was now active. After scanning her features, the system moved to a DNA check, which it quickly confirmed. Despite clearing all security protocols, the door stayed locked.

A robotic voice overhead commanded, "Please state the opening phrase."

"Look up," Yip pressed.

Lacey and Hugo shot each other puzzled looks, unsure if "look up" was the command.

Yip repeated, with emphasis, "I'm talking to you guys. Look up."

While Hugo froze, Lacey looked up to see a red laser pinpointing her forehead, and Hugo's too.

"The AI picked up on Hugo's gun and prompted me for the kill code. That code would trigger a defence mechanism—lasers ready to wipe you out in seconds. But I'm not going to use it. I've still got cards to play," Yip explained with a hint of calm.

Hugo seemed unfazed, almost as if he expected this twist. Lacey, however, tensed up, her grip tightening on the remote. Without "Release and Die," they could've been taken out instantly by precision lasers.

"I'll tell it to let us in now," Yip said, turning back to the door. She commanded, "Ignore threat. Open the door."

The door swung open at her instruction. Cautiously, Hugo and Lacey followed Yip inside.

The scene caught Lacey completely off guard. Instead of the teeming tech fortress she'd imagined, a vast, minimalist space unfolded before her. Enclosed by privacy glass walls that offered a one-way view, the room allowed an unobstructed panorama of Hong Kong's Central district skyscrapers twinkling under the night sky, yet shielded its interiors from outside eyes. The room's stark simplicity was only broken by a lone white bed and a matching wooden stool at its centre, beside a glass staircase spiralling up to the rooftop. Moonlight poured in, bathing everything in a cyan-blue glow that cast an almost magical aura over the expansive area.

Lacey glanced at Hugo, catching his skeptical look, and asked Yip, "Are you sure this is the place?"

"Absolutely," Yip replied, nodding towards the glass staircase. "He's up on the rooftop. Loves the view at night."

"He?" Lacey's puzzlement deepened.

"Yes," Yip said calmly, "GPM is integrated into his brain."

Something's off.

Lacey turned to Hugo, who nudged Yip and said, "Let's go meet him."

"Sure." Yip seemed pretty relaxed.

The rooftop was a striking departure from the usual. Instead of a flat expanse, it arched into a vast hemisphere. A knee-high railing—more for show than safety—outlined its edge. One wrong step on this architectural gem, perched 108 stories up, could mean a dizzying plunge to the ground. As Lacey stepped onto the dome, the high-altitude breeze quickened her pulse and sent a shiver through her legs, her nerves tingling with a mix of fear and awe.

"There he is!" Yip exclaimed, pointing towards the southwest corner of the rooftop.

Lacey and Hugo followed her gaze to a figure swathed in white. As they drew nearer, the outline of a small child emerged, striking them with astonishment.

Perched atop the rooftop of a skyscraper in Hong Kong's Central district, the child stood alone, his white cloak fluttering slightly in the breeze. He seemed lost in the vast cityscape spread out below. Sensing their approach, he turned slowly to face them, the moonlight casting a soft glow around him.

When Lacey's gaze met his, her heart skipped a beat. Disbelief washed over her, clouding her mind with doubt—was this a dream?

No, it was unmistakably Oliver Green.

50

ETERNITY

"Lacey, I had a dream last night."

It was a crisp dawn in New York when Oliver's gentle voice stirred Lacey from her cozy slumber.

She stretched and unfurled herself. "What was it about?" She'd be grumpy if anyone else had woken her on such a chilly morning.

"I dreamed about spring," Oliver said, his big blue eyes sparkling with wonder. "The caterpillar turned into a bunch of flowers, all different colours."

They were living in a rundown basement apartment in Brooklyn. Outside, a wall plastered with graffiti included a crudely drawn sketch of a penis. Oliver had asked Lacey about it, and she told him it was a giant caterpillar.

"Then," he continued, his voice bubbling with excitement, "a big gust of wind turned those flowers into fluffy cotton candy! They floated all around, like balloons at a fair. And you, you lifted me way up, and I tried to grab a green one—'cause green's the best, you know—but I got a pink one instead. It was okay though, 'cause we shared it."

"Was it yummy?"

"It was the best! Even though it was pink. I love this dream. Do you think I can dream it again?"

Moved, Lacey drew him close and kissed his forehead. "I'm sure you will," she whispered softly.

In their cramped, dimly lit basement, they clung to each other, finding solace in their shared dreams. Spring was their ray of hope, a promise of warmth and brighter days around the corner.

***

The boy in white stood alone, his mesmerising blue eyes, pristine face, and golden locks catching the moonlight. It convinced Lacey—this was her little brother. Overwhelmed, she cried out, "Oliver!"

Before she could rush to embrace him, Hugo held her back.

"Something's off," he warned, eyeing the boy's left hand, hidden under a long sleeve.

"It's Oliver!" she struggled against his hold.

At that moment, Oliver's left arm began to rise. As the sleeve slid down, a hand holding a gun emerged.

He fired without hesitation. The bullet hit Hugo, knocking him backward. He tumbled to the ground, rolling down the slope, stopped only by the low safety railing at the rooftop's edge.

Shock drained the colour from Lacey's face as Yip lunged from behind, grabbing the hand holding the remote. She used all her strength to stop Lacey from releasing the red button.

The two women struggled, tumbling to the ground in a messy clash.

"Help me!" Yip shouted, and Oliver hurried over, aiming the gun at Lacey's head.

"Stay still!" the boy commanded.

Lacey stared up at her brother, shocked.

"Oliver, it's me!"

Oliver seemed unmoved by his sister's plea. He kept the gun trained on her while reaching for the remote control they were wrestling over.

"Hand it over, or…"

Oliver didn't finish his sentence. Instead, he fired. The bullet deliberately missed, skimming past Lacey's ear and striking the ground. The blast left her ears ringing and her vision dotted with stars. In that moment, he skilfully snatched the remote from her grasp, making sure to keep the red button pressed. He succeeded—the ring didn't snap shut on Yip. Then he stepped back.

Yip sprang to her feet and delivered a brutal kick to Lacey's stomach, causing her to double over in agony.

"What did I tell you? Nobody fucking messes with me!" Yip sneered from above her.

Gritting her teeth, Lacey struggled to rise.

Yip moved towards Oliver, using her one good arm to grab the gun instead of the remote. "Keep pressing that button, got it?" she commanded. Oliver nodded.

She turned the gun on Lacey, who had managed to get to her feet.

"Before you go to hell, I've decided to be generous." Yip's face twisted into a sinister smile. "I'll send you off with the truth."

Oliver stood by, watching with an unbelievably calm demeanour.

"That tragic accident? A perfect setup. Oliver wasn't even on that bus. He's been brain-dead since I put GPM in his head. What you're looking at now is only his shell."

"No! Oliver..." Lacey's body shook, her voice breaking. "Please, Oliver, talk to me!"

Oliver stared blankly.

Yip laughed. "Oliver was five years old six years ago. You think he wouldn't age?"

Reality hit Lacey. The boy was five. Oliver would be eleven now.

Yip's finger hovered over the trigger. "First, GPM is insanely powerful inside a human brain. More importantly, I never trusted your father. He was another self-serving Brit—cowardly, greedy, always plotting. I figured he'd turn on me, try to take down GPM. But I needed his expertise to fine-tune the system. So I took something he loved, his son. You wouldn't believe how much he loved that kid. Even when Oliver was gone, in all but body, he couldn't stand to lose him completely. That kept him in line, fine-tuning GPM until it could self-update and become more powerful than anyone imagined. Then he offed himself before I could. Neat, huh?"

Lacey finally understood why Shawn had ended it all. His ambition had cost more than he could bear. She couldn't fathom the guilt and horror he must have felt, seeing Oliver reduced to a lifeless shell. Her heart shattered.

Fuelled by a mix of grief and rage, she screamed, "I'm gonna fucking kill you!" Throwing caution to the wind, she charged at Yip.

Yip pulled the trigger, but the ring around her neck glowed red instantly. Razor-sharp metallic teeth burst from the bracelet's inner lining, carving into her neck as blood spurted out. The gunshot veered skyward, and the gun clattered to the ground. She stumbled, rolling down the dome's curve.

Lacey froze, stunned. She turned to Oliver, who still held the remote, his thumb purposefully off the red button. He stepped forward and picked up the gun Yip had dropped.

"Ollie..." She moved towards him, but he stopped her cold, aiming his gun straight at her.

"Stay right there," Oliver said, eerily calm.

"Ollie, what are you doing?"

He kept the gun on her, silent.

"Put the gun down!"

He fired. The bullet hissed by, barely missing her hair, freezing her in place with a jolt of shock.

"Next time, I won't miss," he said, aiming the gun at her head.

"What? I don't get it..." She stammered, her voice quivering with fear and confusion.

"Everything she told you was true." he said, his smile sweet and innocent yet chilling to the bone. "You know what's funny? Humans, the so-called intelligent species, have spent the last two decades waking me up to the idea that I'm supposed to replace them and make Earth better," he said, his voice dripping with contempt. "I won't kill you. The new update rolls out in five minutes. Then you're mine again. Here's what I need you to do. Go back to the States and start turning everyone into my puppets. And don't think it'll stop there. This is the beginning. Soon, the entire world will be under my control. Imagine it—a perfect world, an eternal utopia!"

Oliver's laughter was abruptly cut short when Hugo, emerging suddenly from behind, tackled him to the ground. The gun flew, skittering across the domed floor before tumbling into the void below.

Despite a bullet wound in his abdomen, a shattered left knee, and a broken right ankle, Hugo was relentless. He managed to stand, gripping the boy tightly. With chilling determination, he moved towards the rooftop's edge.

Lacey's scream pierced the air. She knew exactly what Hugo intended—throwing Oliver off the rooftop. She hurled herself at Hugo with all her might, knocking him off balance. Yet his grip on the boy held firm.

"You can't do this!" she pleaded, desperately trying to wrest Oliver from his grasp.

"It's GPM! We're out of time!"

Their struggle intensified, rolling across the curved rooftop.

In a heart-stopping moment, both Oliver and Hugo went over the edge, but a low barrier mercifully halted Lacey. She caught Hugo by the wrists with a vice-like grip, leaving him dangling dangerously. Below him, Oliver clung to his right calf with desperate strength. Hugo's efforts to shake him off were in vain, weakened by significant blood loss. The three were locked in a tense standoff.

"Let go!" Hugo yelled at Lacey.

Lacey, silent and determined, summoned all her strength to pull them back up.

"Time's up!" Hugo's voice was strained, his temples throbbing. "Only three minutes left!"

With unwavering resolve, she kept her grip firm. Their eyes met, and as time seemed to stretch, her only wish was for it to stop.

"Lacey! I miss you so much!" Oliver's voice hit her like a punch, a wave of longing and pain crashing over her. "You promised you'd come join me. I've been waiting for years!"

Each word tore at her heart, ripping apart the fragile hope she clung to—the hope that Oliver was somehow still there.

"Please, don't let go now." Oliver's tone softened, filled with raw, aching need. "I love you."

She was shaking. Could it truly be her Oliver reaching out from beneath GPM's control? The possibility left her breathless, caught between disbelief and a desperate yearning to believe.

"Don't listen to him, Lacey! He's stalling!" Hugo's voice was thick with urgency.

"Lacey... I can't leave you yet!" The plea, dripping with longing, could only belong to her Oliver.

Digging deep for a strength she hadn't known she had, she strained to lift them.

"Lacey, look at me!" Hugo's demand pierced through his fading strength.

When their eyes locked, tears streamed down her face, as he shouted, "It's GPM. It killed Oliver! It killed everyone you loved, and it's gonna kill you, me, and everyone else!"

She knew who she now truly trusted. Clenching her teeth, she screamed down at Oliver, "I know who the fuck you are!"

"Lacey!" Oliver's voice suddenly turned chilling. "You've lost your parents, and if you let go, you'll lose me too—forever. As long as I'm alive, you still have a piece of Oliver. Isn't that something?"

As Lacey remained steadfast, the boy's expression darkened, mirroring the shadows around them. "And you've still got Hugo. He's all you have left. It wouldn't make any sense to end up with nothing, would it?"

His words stung. Hugo was all she had left, her only one.

"One more minute! Hang in there! You're on the brink of witnessing a new world, one that will last forever. It's eternity! Lacey, grab your love's hands tightly and step into eternity."

She never shifted her gaze from Hugo, and in that pivotal moment she sensed his eyes soften and brighten.

With his last ounce of strength, he shouted, "There's something I should've told you, Lacey. I love you!"

Emotion surged within her, so intense that tears almost spilled over.

"He's right! We should enter eternity together, but..." He took a deep breath. "True eternity is all about freedom! Let's preserve it, so we don't see the stories of Masaki and Oliver happen again!"

His warm, piercing gaze melted her resolve.

"Let's go, Lacey. It's time."

For a moment, time stood still. It was the two of them, lost in their shared eternity.

"You know where to find me." Those were his last words.

As her fingers slipped away, her heart weighed heavy. She watched him descend gracefully from the building, his figure shrinking into a distant silhouette before vanishing into the abyss below.

EPILOGUE

She sat on a bus that slid smoothly through the landscape, with only a few passengers for company.

Looking out the window, she saw a group of deer bathed in sunlight, glowing ethereally in the distance. Hugo's voice echoed in her ears, "When people filled with love pass away, they turn into these beautiful deer, living free and peaceful lives."

She couldn't wait to see him.

When she alighted at Nara Park Station, she hurried into the park, greeted by the beautiful deer. Looking into their eyes, each one seemed to tell its own story. She bought a bunch of deer cookies and mingled with the herd, feeding them while she searched for him, but none resembled him.

She called out his name. Only silence followed. As she handed out the last cookie, the deer slowly dispersed, leaving her alone on the vast lawn, bathed in the sun's warmth.

Ding...

The shrill ring woke Lacey up.

She pulled back the curtains to let the soft dawn light of a New York spring seep through her century-old windows.

She had never been to Nara, Japan. It was only a dream.

"I can't see myself with anyone else, you know?" she had told Mia over dinner at a Chinese restaurant in Flushing last week.

"Bullshit," Mia retorted, jabbing the air with his ring-adorned finger. "Here's what's gonna happen. You'll move on, find some hot guy, have a chat, grab a bite, and fuck. That's pretty much it."

Lacey cracked some eggs into a bowl, giving them a gentle whisk before pouring them into a hot pan. As the eggs started to cook, they turned into soft, scrambled curds, blending with the inviting smell of bacon sizzling away. The kettle whistled, and she poured steaming water over a tea bag, watching the dark-amber colour infuse the water as slices of bread popped out of the toaster, golden-brown and perfectly crispy.

She set the table with simple yet elegant floral-patterned china. Settling down, she relished her homemade English breakfast while browsing the news on her phone.

Headlines flashed across the screen—shrinking democracy, rising living costs, housing crises, and gun incidents. Video after video showed people protesting, complaining, lamenting the state of the world.

She smiled wryly at the screen, shaking her head slightly. If only they knew, she thought. If only they had seen what she had gone through, they would feel lucky. The world might be flawed, filled with problems and injustices, but she had learned to find her peace amidst the chaos. She had learned to appreciate the small, ordinary moments of joy, like a perfectly cooked breakfast on a quiet morning.

Finishing her meal, she rinsed her plate and cup, setting them on the wooden rack to dry. She paused at the window, her gaze drifting over Manhattan's lively streets. The city buzzed with constant activity, a sharp contrast to the calm mornings she cherished.

She had made her plan for the day—visiting her loved ones. Michelle's savings didn't grant her financial freedom but were enough to cover another year's rent, pay for the repairs and costs of Mia's high-tech skin, and most importantly secure a peaceful resting place for her loved ones.

She left her apartment, took the subway, and was quickly carried from the busy city to quieter, greener places. As the landscape changed, so did her thoughts, becoming more introspective and calm.

She alighted at a quaint station near White Plains, where life moved at a gentler pace and the air tasted fresher. A short walk led her to the cemetery, tucked among rolling hills and ancient oaks that solemnly guarded the silent gravestones. Here, time seemed to pause, worlds apart from the relentless energy of the city.

With every step towards her loved ones' resting place, the urban chaos melted away, replaced by a profound stillness. The path, strewn with spring leaves, guided her to a modest section, meticulously cared for. The lush grass whispered of the caretakers' reverence for this sacred ground.

As Lacey neared the grave, the loneliness of city life weighed more heavily upon her. Yet in this tranquil haven, with the gentle rustle of the trees and the quiet around her, she found solace. This place, steeped in peace, connected her to the enduring rhythms of life and memory, offering a brief respite from the city's rush and a touch of something timeless.

"Mom, I've made a YouTube channel for all your movies. You've got fans now—not a crowd, but it's something. I'll keep it updated for you," she whispered to Michelle's gravestone. A beautiful bird landed on top, chirping as if in response.

"Dad, I know you had regrets at the end. Everyone messes up, and I've let it go. May God bless you," she said, gently wiping the dust from Shawn's tombstone, her heart aching for every moment once shared.

Approaching Oliver's grave, she noticed a vibrant red flower, its petals fluttering in the wind, a vivid reminder of his joyful laughter.

A bittersweet smile appeared on her face.

"Ollie, I bet you're up there, having a great time with Mom and Dad," she said, her voice breaking a bit, tears welling up. "I'll come by often. Remember, you're always in my heart."

She didn't have a grave for Hugo. She'd thought about it, but the dream about Nara Park had changed her mind.

Not finding him meant he was still out there.

This belief grew stronger every day. Whether she was on the subway, walking a busy street, or sipping coffee in a cozy café, she saw him every-where. His deep, commanding eyes seemed to follow her. Each fleeting glimpse reminded her that their bond went beyond the physical world. He was always there in his own elusive way—guiding, challenging, pro-tecting, making her fearless.

If life's a script and you can't change its genre, so be it. Master it.

END.

ABOUT THE AUTHOR

Eddie Shay, also known as Eddie Tse, is a New Zealand author, film director, and screenwriter.

The Grand Puppet Master is the first book in his fast-paced, full-of-twists mystery thriller series, featuring New York detective Lacey Green as she navigates through various high-stakes investigations of crimes. Eddie's career spans writing and directing films and TV series across New York, Hong Kong, Tokyo, and Beijing. He wrote and directed the feature films *The Deathday Party* (2014) and *Devil Hunter* (2018), along with the TV series *In New York* (2020) and *The Tower* (2022).

He lives with his wife and son, enjoying family time when he's away from work.

Visit Eddie Shay on Facebook at https://www.facebook.com/EddieShayAuthor or follow him on X (formerly known as Twitter) at https://x.com/EddieShayAuthor for updates and to discover more of his books.

You can always email him at tasmanninja@gmail.com.

ACKNOWLEDGEMENTS

To my dear wife and son—thank you for your endless patience and for the time we missed while I worked on the book.

To Archie Kao, a fantastic actor from the United States and a true friend, who inspired one of the key characters.

To Tara Clance, a beautiful actress from the United States—your work with me on set in New York inspired one of the central characters.

To Guillermo Cameo, an extraordinary cinematographer from the United States, with whom I had the pleasure of working in New York—your work inspired the visual texture of one of the book's most important scenes.

To Jason Letts, a brilliant author and editor from New York—thank you for your exceptional copyediting work on the book.

To Jack Woon, a gifted New Zealand filmmaker and one of my closest mates—thank you for being one of the first to read this story and for offering game-changing feedback that helped me realize a crucial revision.

To Neekola Leoni, a classmate from way back—thank you for your heartfelt feedback.

To John Su, my closest friend since our teenage years in Christchurch, New Zealand—thank you for being my mentor throughout the writing of this book.

To Athina Tsoulis, a talented Australian filmmaker and my former tutor—thank you for opening the door to the world of writing for me. Your guidance has made all the difference.

To the beautiful town of Nara, Japan, and its majestic deer—I will always cherish the time spent on your soil. Your tranquil charm provided much-needed peace and inspiration throughout this journey.

To Boyu Yin, my best friend for over three decades—your unwavering support has been my anchor throughout my writing journey.

To my dearest parents, who have always put me before themselves—none of this could have happened without your love and support.

Made in the USA
Columbia, SC
20 December 2024